MW01130504

FOREVER, MR. BLACK

MR. BLACK DUET 2

SHANORA WILLIAMS

Published November 2016

Editing by Librum Artis Editorial Services

Cover Art and Design by Jersey Girl & Co. Designs

DEDICATION

I've dedicated one of my books to you before, but this one is for you too, brother.

I got through this book with your goofy smile on my mind and the vivid dreams you showed up in, which only proved to me that you're still here, in spirit.

I wrote for you, even through the teary eyes and the broken heart, because you would never let me give up. I pushed for you and I will continue to do so until the last breath leaves my body.

I miss you so, so much, brother. So much it hurts, but I will continue to live for you.

I love you, Montez.
Missing you like CRAZAYYY!

NOTE FROM THE AUTHOR

I'm always making notes for you guys in my books, I know, but this time I want to make sure that you all understand that before you go into reading this, realize that this book is **NOT TABOO** like the first. *Forever, Mr. Black* is a continuation of Chloe and Theo's love story, therefore those taboo themes that were in book one have pretty much faded. They are older and more mature.

My lovely readers asked for more and so I did my best to provide the best story possible. I was more than happy to see Theo and Chloe come together again and I hope that this book is just as entertaining for you as the first. :)

To read *Dear Mr. Black*, the start of Theo & Chloe's story, please visit www.shanorawilliams.com/the-tainted-duet

Much love,

Shanora

PROLOGUE

Theo

The sun beamed.

The curtains, white and clean, billowed with the Bristle Wave breeze. Music drifted up the stairs, playing loudly from the speaker. A song by Rihanna. One of her favorites.

My fatigue subsided for the time being, I felt refreshed. Pushing out of bed, I tugged on the jogging pants that were beside it, forgetting about the shirt. Walking to the bathroom, I gave my teeth a quick brush, washed up a bit, and then drifted out of the bedroom.

The coffee was rich in the air, a fresh brew. My stomach swirled at the thought of having that first grand cup, how it would taste running across my taste buds, officially waking me up. I met at the bottom of the staircase and rounded the corner.

Pans and pots clanked, and the music was louder now.

As I spotted the sunlight streaming in, thought of that hot coffee that would push me awake, and smelled the pancakes and warm syrup, none of it mattered because there she was, in the kitchen, humming while shaking those round, full hips.

She had a piece of melon between her fingers, the other hand occupied with the handle of a spatula. She sang a line from the song, still moving those hips, still singing, until I cleared my throat, folding my arms and leaning against the edge of the wall.

She gasped and whirled around without the pan, placing the now-empty hand across the heart of her chest. "Oh my God, Theo!"

"Scared you?" I asked, brow cocked.

She waltzed towards me, her arms wrapping around my waist, head craned to meet my lips.

I looked down at her, meeting soft hazel eyes. "Good morning, Knight."

"Good morning. Now kiss me," she begged, grinning adorably. "Stop stalling."

I looked up. "Are you cooking for me?"

"Theo."

"I mean, I love breakfast. The most important meal of the day and all, right?"

"Theo!" she giggled, slapping my chest playfully.

I busted out in a laugh, clutching her tight in my arms and lowering my head to press my lips to hers. Behind the kiss, I laughed, and she grinned, hugging me tight. Her body molded with mine, and my back pressed on the wall.

We remained this way for quite some time. I'm not sure how long. I didn't count. Several minutes passed, and a hunger took hold of her. I could tell she wanted me . . . again. Her body was hot now, loose. Open and vulnerable. She draped her arms around the back of my neck, bouncing on her toes and giving me a light boost to pick her up.

Those slender legs wrapped around my waist, my erection nestled on her lower belly. She moaned, and a deep groan slipped out of me as I twirled her around so that her back was to the wall. She still wore those short-shorts, the ones that I threatened to burn if she wore them in public again.

They were made of loose cotton, so access was easy . . . super easy for me. Her tongue slid between my lips and my cock strained, dying to be inside her now.

"Fuck, Chloe," I groaned, grasping her ass in my hands. Her teeth sank

into my bottom lip, catching it. I dropped my gaze to her mouth, our noses touching.

"I'm ready when you are," she breathed.

I focused on her mouth. I was born ready for this girl. My soulmate. My life. I pressed forward and crushed her lips, no warning. No hesitation. Something was burning now, the odor strong, but we were both too gone to care.

I slung her body around, marching for the table in the corner, dropping her down on it, and sliding out of my pants. Her shorts were pulled off in an instant, my cock settled between her thighs. I claimed every inch of her skin with my mouth.

God, I couldn't speak; I was so fucking eager. I couldn't think; my mind was so cloudy with thoughts of her.

My hands drifted across her silky skin, palms meeting at her hips—clutching, gripping—as her fingernails drug across my back. She was perched on her elbows, and gruffly I said, "Make sure you watch me, baby. All right?"

And she nodded, so eager, so ready. She licked those supple lips, eyes locked with mine. She'd grown accustomed to watching, to witnessing the magic my tongue could do.

Gently, I ate my girl, massaging her clit, slurping, licking, and sucking. I delved deep, the taste of her absolutely addicting; her moans sparking the fuel in me, causing me to pulse and throb like a motherfucker as I stroked myself.

She loved every bit of it, her body bucking as she held me just a little tighter.

"Oh, Theo," she breathed. I loved it when she said my name. It sounded so good coming from her mouth.

So sweet.

So innocent.

Though I'd tainted her innocence over and over again, there was no going back. She loved being the bad girl for me. She loved giving me full control. She knew my need to dominate, to own her. It'd been this way for months.

Even though she'd lost my daughter as her friend. Even though I was married to Sheila. Even though she was engaged to Sterling. None of it mattered, because we were us. We loved one another, and fucked like we hated each other.

If that wasn't perfection, then I don't know what is.

I took my Knight. I fucked her on top of the table, thrusting, slamming, and causing the legs to wobble. Her head fell back, her neck exposed, and I took advantage, sucking on the tender skin right above her collarbone, grinding harder, and swelling up deep inside her sweet pussy.

The burning smell was thick in the air now, almost suffocating. But I couldn't stop. I had to keep going. It was too good. So tight. So wet. I didn't want to stop . . . but she already had.

"Theo," she gasped. "Theo. Stop. Fire. There's fire."

"I know," I growled. "We're on fucking fire, baby. We always have been."

"No, Theo," she said, moving closer, hugging me tight as if she were afraid.

I frowned down at her. I was fucking confused now.

"Theo, there's fire. This is hell for us. Don't you see?" she whispered, voice cracking. "We don't belong here. We can't keep doing this. We'll die going through the smoke and flames if we do."

I clasped her face in my hands, hating the tears that stole her happiness. I kissed them away as they skidded down her cheeks. I smoothed the remains away with the pads of my thumbs. Then I kissed her, so deeply, so passionately, and she returned the same ferocious passion, arms tight around me.

Pulling away, I said, "If I have to die just to be with you, then so be it. I can't fucking live without you, Chloe." I said this, but I don't think she heard me.

No.

I know she didn't, because she was no longer in front of me. She wasn't half-naked anymore. And I was fully dressed. She was now standing by the door. Her exit. Her escape.

She swallowed hard and waved at me, eyes full of remorse, just like the day she made love to me on Dirty Black for the last time. With sorrow and desolation, I called her name, begging—literally crawling my way to her through blistering heat, smoke, and flames.

"Chloe, please," I begged. "Don't do this to me again. I fucking need you. I —I can't let you go. I fucking can't. Not again."

She looked down at me, tears lining her cheeks.

"I have to go, Theo." She reached down and stroked my face. "But maybe in another lifetime."

I'd said that for months now, repeating the mantra to myself, as if it would restore hope, but another lifetime would never compare to this one. The one we shared. The love we built. It was too much. Too deep. So perfect. It could never be topped.

She opened the door, and walked out. I don't know how she got out of my hold, my vice-like grip, but she did, and I watched her walk away, each step forming a crack on my black heart.

And, soon, her silhouette was gone.

The smoke and flames vanished, but I still felt too hot.

I was still holding something.

It was cold. Hard. Flat. I lifted my head, staring right at my own reflection. It caught me off guard, and I startled a bit, gasping. I didn't get it. I hated my face—the one in the same mirror I had shattered after taking Chloe's virginity.

How is it repaired? Why the fuck is it here?

It was here; like that night never fucking happened. It shimmered and transitioned into a photo of my daughter. My Izzy Bear. Her and Chloe . . . together. Smiling. So young and carefree. So happy together. Nothing could break their sisterly bond . . . no one but me.

I broke them apart. I fucking ruined them.

The area that surrounded me was pitch black, but light shined down on the mirror, leaving me no choice but to see myself as it transitioned again. I stared at myself—the hurt in my eyes. The damage dominating my well-being. The pain . . . so unbearable.

The guilt swallowed me whole, and I sank.

I dropped.

I plummeted right into a black hole and wept for days. Months on fucking end.

I'd become even more damaged than I ever had been before, begging for Chloe to come back to me. Calling, and getting nothing but her voicemail. Emails with no replies. Text messages with no responses at all. Nothing was what I got in return for my everything. It was almost like she never even loved me to begin with, and maybe that was the point of it all. She was never supposed to love a man like me. Ever.

I called, emailed, and text her, begging for this girl to bring me joy again —to take care of me again . . .

But then, I woke up, panting, sweating.

And then I realized one thing.

All that shit—all of it was a dream.

A façade.

I'd lived with nightmares for years—dealt with death, deceit, and battles. My time with Chloe was a glimpse of my own little fairytale— things that wouldn't happen in real life, or at least the way they should have. My own little story, full of never-ending happiness, a river of peace.

It was a beautiful, fragmented mess.

And in this bed, as I stared ahead and thought about it all, I came to know one thing.

I was alone.

I was forgotten.

I was . . . still heartbroken.

And, yet, I was still so madly in love with Chloe Knight.

CHAPTER 1

THEO

This should have been one of those perfect mornings. You know, like how they run in the movies.

The sun is bright; the sheets white and crisp. It's beaming down on our skin through the curtain slits.

It's peaceful and quiet, and soon some orchestrated music begins to play. The wife rolls over, and as the husband you are supposed to stare at her. You're supposed to wonder how the woman you married is so damn beautiful.

You can't keep your hands off of her.

And then you put your hands on her—anywhere. You pull her closer. You kiss the tip of her nose and she rustles about in her sleep. It's adorable to you. She groans, and begs you to "stop it" with her morning voice, but you can't help yourself, especially when she speaks, because she has the voice of an angel.

You flip her onto her back, slide between her legs, and kiss her from head to toe.

You tell her how much you love her as you eat her pussy, sweet and fresh from the shower she took the night before.

And when you're done eating her, you *take* her. You make love to her. You make her yours all over again, all while murmuring you will *never* let her go.

Do you see it?

Do you get it?

Well, I don't.

I didn't feel this way today. I hadn't felt this way in years. My wife wasn't in bed. She was in the shower, because she was too tired to take one last night.

I didn't want her to come out. I know that's bad to say, but it was true. I wanted her to disappear.

It was a mistake. *Us* . . . we were never supposed to do this. But she was so ignorant to it all.

She thought we truly were in love. She told her sister and her mother something silly about us every single day. I swear to God I was tired of overhearing those fucking phone calls.

She exaggerated most of the shit.

Well, more like *all of it*.

I wished I was in love with her, I really did. Being in love with her would have made this whole remarrying thing a hell of a lot easier.

But I wasn't.

And I don't think I was ever going be.

I rolled flat on my back, staring up at the white ceiling. The shower shut off, and I clutched the sheets.

She stepped out of the bathroom moments later, her hair damp, and her face clear of all makeup.

She wasn't ugly.

She was beautiful. Gorgeous, really. She reminded me of the Barbie dolls Izzy used to play with. Tall and slender, but not taller than me. Blonde hair and wide, glass-blue eyes.

She spotted me looking, but she didn't say anything. She just smiled, and walked to the closet to take down her outfit for the day, all while swinging her hips.

I couldn't tell you how long it took for her to get dressed. When she was away, I didn't count the seconds or the minutes, waiting for her to return to me. I enjoyed my time alone. It gave me time to think.

She came back out, and her lips were on my cheek, and then my mouth. "I'll see you later," she said, and she flashed another pearly smile at me before walking out of the bedroom.

I didn't watch her go.

I didn't care.

When I heard the garage door open and then close, I rolled over and picked up my cell phone off the nightstand.

I signed on, and then I hit the search engine on *Facebook*. I searched for *her* name, like I did often.

The only name I wanted to see.

Chloe Knight.

Her profile picture was beautiful. It was simple.

She was smiling. It was a candid photo. It could have been taken by a photographer, but I was certain it was by *him*.

The fucker that not only stole my deceased wife from me, but my Knight too. Frustrated, I closed the app and sat up straight.

I couldn't fucking do this shit anymore. I couldn't handle knowing she was out there, away from me. I couldn't accept that the mother-fucker was putting his hands all over her.

I needed her, more than I fucking thought.

I swore I could let go, make things easier for both of us, but I was so wrong.

I never should have left Bristle Wave the last day I saw her. I should have stayed right there and dropped to my knees.

I should have tossed my ring in the ocean and never looked back.

I should have made her mine again, because if I had, I wouldn't be feeling this.

Heartache.

Abandonment.

Lonely, even while married.

I would have had her. I would have been complete.

CHAPTER 2

THEO

One Week Later

This day marked three years and six days since the last time I saw her.

It was hard not to count. The smallest things circled my mind back to her, not to mention the tribal tattoo I had inked on my body.

That dream I had was way too fucking vivid for me to ignore. It meant something. And I was ready to find out.

I couldn't keep taking this pain—knowing the woman I was wholeheartedly in love with was out there with the fucker that caused my first wife to cheat on me.

The more I thought about it, the angrier I became. I couldn't control Janet's actions back then because I didn't even know it was happening. And the kid had no idea who the hell I was, but he knew now, and he stole Chloe right away from me.

Another person I loved.

Fuck that.

I knew where she lived now. I knew how to get her back, but I kept my distance out of respect.

I missed her. I *needed* to see her again. I knew she still thought about me. She had to. She may have denied it for that piece-of-shit, but I fucking knew. A love like the one we had doesn't just fade. It can't disappear.

A love like the one we shared lingers in your heart—sweeps through your soul. It robs you of your sleep, and gives you nightmares when you dream about losing them.

It ignites, and with each day that passes without that person, you slowly wither away—deteriorate and crumble—until you realize you need to get your shit together and make it work.

There would be consequences in going back for her, but I was okay with that. I was getting my Knight back. I didn't give a fuck if I had to fight to do it. I was going to make her remember all we had— all that we'd gone through—and I wasn't going to leave Bristle Wave until the job was done.

With that in mind, I stared down at the thick packet of papers in my hand. A mistake? Perhaps. But *she* was worth the gamble.

Picking up my car keys and duffle bag, I walked towards the kitchen counter and placed the divorce papers down on the center of it. It was pretty self-explanatory, what had to be done.

Sheila was going to flip her shit. I already knew that, but there was no doubt she hadn't seen this coming. No matter how badly she wanted to deny it, it was a reality.

I had no regrets about moving forward. I was gone in a matter of seconds, on my way to Bristle Wave.

I didn't look back once.

CHAPTER 3

CHLOE

2 Days Later

The grandfather clock on the wall finally struck twelve. He still wasn't home.

It chimed loudly, and I glanced at it, rubbing my left temple lightly before focusing on the papers below me. My red pen was running out of ink and I was losing steam.

I couldn't keep waiting up this late for Sterling to get home. I was trying, but having to wake up at four every morning prevented that. I sat back in my chair, looking towards the front door.

Normally he strolled in around this time, but not tonight. I glanced at my cell phone. Not a single ring or beep. Sighing, I finished up the paper I was grading and then stacked them all, collecting them in a folder.

I gave my cell phone one last glance. Why hadn't he called? What was keeping him?

I understood being a college professor made him busy, but I was certain none of the students were staying after school every night just to improve their musical skills. He was doing something else, and I wasn't sure if I wanted to know what it was.

He'd been coming home with barely two words to rub together. He always looked tired . . .and bored. I would cook, but he wouldn't eat. He'd just say he was tired and then crash on the red recliner.

Janet's old red recliner. He didn't know it was hers, but it's like he sensed it.

I picked up my phone and walked up the stairs. After starting the shower, I sat on the toilet seat for a brief moment. My phone was clutched in hand, my leg bouncing. I did this every night since Sterling had been acting weird.

It was every other-other night when things were okay between us, and I felt guilty for doing so, but not so much anymore.

I unlocked my phone and went to the *Facebook* app. I started to spell *his* name out in the search engine, but it popped up first . . . because I had searched for it many, many times before.

He had a *Facebook* account now and I was surprised. He only logged in if he had something important to announce. Like the car shows he attended, or how he upgraded the shop and his workers with new tools. He shared inspirational videos and pictures, which really didn't seem like him at all.

Most of them said things like *"Pick your head up and keep going"* or *"Fight as hard as you can. Never give up."* His profile picture was a photo of him sitting on Ol' Charlie. His face was solid, no trace of a smile, and those brown eyes of his were heavy.

I smiled as I studied the bike, remembering those freeing rides.

There was one picture he had as his cover photo. It was of him and his wife. Seeing her with him made my heart plummet every time.

She was stunning. Her blonde hair and thin frame. She had bright blue eyes and wore the biggest grin. He held her around the middle from behind, smiling down at her. His eyelashes touched his cheekbones, a smile faint on his luscious lips.

It was a picture from their wedding day. He wore a black tux with a green tie and she had on a beautiful white gown.

My heart squeezed in my chest and then my hands shook. It was out of pure envy. I wondered what it would have been like if it were *me* in that dress instead of her. I should have done something. I never should have let him walk away.

I was happy for him—glad he found someone he could be with. Someone he could love after me. But I would kill just to see him one more time.

I held the phone tighter in my hand, blinking my tears away as I logged out and shut the screen off.

I heard a thunk outside the bedroom. Sterling was finally home. I got undressed and decided to shower up instead of going out to see him right away. I made it a quick one. I had way too many questions to ask him.

It'd been four weeks in a row of this.

After putting on my robe, I walked out of the bathroom and found him sitting on the edge of the bed. His head was ducked down, his hands rubbing across his face. His hair had grown out a lot more and the stubble on his chin and around his mouth proved just how little he had been home to take care of himself.

"Sterling?" I called, stepping closer.

His picked up his head a bit, but didn't look at me.

My eyebrows pulled together with concern. "Are you okay?"

"No," he mumbled. "Far from it."

I hurried his way, sitting beside him. "What's wrong?"

His throat worked up and down, and then he picked his head up to look me in the eye. "I have to go to Orange County. My mom is sick."

"Margie? What? Why didn't you tell me?"

"I just found out."

"When?"

"A couple days ago." He shrugged, like it didn't matter.

I frowned. "And you waited a couple days to tell me?"

He ignored my question completely, as well as the attitude laced in my voice. "The doctors think it's pneumonia. I told them I would be there as soon as I can."

"Oh . . ." I paused. "Well, do you want me to go with you?"

"No," he said rapidly, and his eyes grew wider, his jaw flexing. He said it so fast that I cringed.

"Sterling, what the hell is your problem lately?" I stood, glaring down at him. My voice was louder than intended, but I'd had it with him and this mood. "You've been coming home late. You haven't been answering my phone calls or responding to my text messages. Have I done something to piss you off?"

"No." He dropped his head again. "That's the thing, Chloe. You haven't done anything to cause this. You are fine, but I am just . . . I'm losing it. I'm not okay with this."

My throat thickened as he clasped his fingers. "What do you mean? Okay with what?"

He stood up straight, and his eyes were glistening as he focused on me. "I need some space, Chloe. Some time to myself. I think going to see my mom alone will be best for me."

"Space?" I lowered my gaze. "Okay . . . if space is what you need, take it. I understand." But really I didn't. What had I done?

He bobbed his head lightly and then went to the closet. He took down some clothes and stuffed them in a suitcase. He didn't put much in them and I was relieved. That meant he would come back to talk about this . . . at least I'd hoped so.

He came in my direction and pressed his lips to my cheek when he was close. Not on my lips or even the forehead. But the cheek. Too distant. Something was definitely wrong.

He hadn't touched me in weeks, and it may have been because he sensed that I was pretending he was Theo. I wasn't even sure if I'd ever let something slip, but either way I felt guilty.

"Are you sure you don't want me to go?" I asked again, asserting myself.

He turned, jaw ticking. "I said no, Chloe. What part of that do you not understand?"

I frowned, searching for words, but I had none. He'd been crabby for months now. Irritable and so short-tempered.

"I'll be back soon," he muttered, then walked to the door, but I called after him once more.

He turned halfway, but didn't meet my eyes. "Are you doing this because of her?" I asked.

And after I did, his eyes immediately darted up to mine. His jaw locked, but he said nothing. And I knew that was the exact reason why.

It was Janet.

He missed Janet. He couldn't get over her, not even after all these years.

He stormed towards me, pointing a stern finger at my face. "Stop asking me about her, all right? Not everything is fucking about her, Chloe! Maybe, just once, I don't want to come home to you nagging and asking me a million fucking questions about a dead woman! A woman that was the wife of a man you can't even get over! A man that you still want to *fuck!*"

His nostrils flared and my throat went bone dry, my heart pounding in my chest. I couldn't believe he'd said that to me. I wanted to lash out at him, but I was so damn speechless . . . and only because it was true, and it was Sterling's first time ever throwing that in my face.

He pulled his finger away and held his hand up in the air, backing off with wide eyes. Before I could pull out of my wordless state, he was rushing down the stairs. I flinched when the door slammed behind him.

I slouched down on the cushioned bench in front of the bed, focused on the carpet. I sat there for a moment, knowing Sterling wouldn't return. Knowing now how he really felt. An ache formed in my chest, tears swamping my eyes.

Guilt.

And then there was rage. Full-blown rage.

I pushed off the bench and went back to snatch my cellphone off the bathroom counter. I logged back into Facebook and searched for his name again.

Theodore Benjamin Black.

I clicked his name, and there was one new update that caught me by total surprise. I must have missed it before, probably because I was too busy staring at their wedding photo.

My eyes stretched at the update. There was no sort of explanation. Just this:

*Theodore Benjamin Black changed his relationship status to **SEPARATED***

Wait...

Was this serious?

For a second I thought I was on the wrong profile, but I knew I wasn't. This was Theo.

I clicked one of the updates and saw a few comments. Some were asking him if he was okay. Others asked what happened. Some just left shocked emojis beneath the thread.

I wanted to put one myself, but we weren't friends on Facebook. He didn't know I was silently stalking him, but if he had, I'm sure he would have told me to fuck off. I ruined him for this woman.

From the moment I saw him again in my new house—his old house—I could tell he was settling, just as I had. He wasn't elated or over the moon about her. Like I said, he was *just okay.*

But *okay* obviously wasn't enough for one of them.

I shut the screen off before I could do anything stupid. I wanted to add him, message him, and play catch-up, but he was dealing with separation and I was . . . well, I don't know what I was. I was still engaged to Sterling, but we weren't on the same page.

Was I angry Sterling left like that? Yes.

But if he needed space, I had to be willing to give him that.

I climbed into bed, staring up at the spinning ceiling fan. Theo came to mind, along with all of the beautiful memories we'd shared. So much happened, living across the street from that man.

But thinking about him always led me to thinking about Izzy. I thought about her every day. I wondered what she was up to—what she was doing. I might have been crazy for trying to search for her on

Facebook recently, only to come up with nothing, but that's how much I missed her.

I felt awful for how things left off. She didn't have social media for a reason. Probably so she could avoid women like me—women that wanted to make love to her father.

I huffed a dry laugh. Make that, women who *loved* her father.

This was my life now. I'd finally accepted it. It might have been a little fucked-up at the moment, but I guess this was the bill I had to pay for being so selfish—not only by leaving my sweet Theo behind, but by betraying my first and only best friend.

This was the sacrifice.

It was time to accept it and move on.

CHAPTER 4

Chloe

The alarm blared on the nightstand.

Groaning, I shifted beneath the sheets, pushing them off of my face and sluggishly sitting up. I looked to the right and disappointment settled in.

I don't know why I thought he'd come back. I guess when he said he needed space, he meant it. Orange County was only a city away. I figured he would have called me when he got there, but I waited up until 2:00 a.m. and never heard from him.

And now it was 6:30 a.m.

Wait—what? 6:30!

Shit!

I pushed out of bed, stumbling towards the closet to take down the outfit hanging in the closet. For God's sake, I needed another damn shower with all the sweating I did while tossing and turning last night, but I didn't have the time. I was already running late.

"Fucking Sterling," I bit out, clasping my bra and then tugging my pink short-sleeved button-down shirt on. I slid into my black skirt and ballet shoes, zipping into the bathroom to grab my toothbrush.

My cellphone rung on the stand as I started brushing my teeth and for a split- second I thought it was Sterling. I rushed for it, snatching it up, only to see Kim's name. Sighing, I answered—well, more like spit a few droplets of toothpaste on the edge of the bed with exasperation. I put the phone on speaker as I made my way back to the bathroom.

"Hey Kim!" I garbled out.

"Are you late *again*, girl?"

I rinsed my mouth out and then looked into the mirror, picking up my eyeliner. "Yeah. I know, I know. I was up a little too late grading papers last night."

"You used that excuse two days ago, Chloe. School starts in less than thirty minutes and you aren't even here. Are you okay? Do I need to make a trip over there?" she asked.

"I'm fine, Kim. It was just a long night."

She released a heavy breath. "Okay . . . well, if you're running late, you might as well bring coffee. I'll cover for you while I can."

"Ah, thank you so much, Kim. I owe you one."

"Two," she laughed.

"Two," I laughed with her. "I should be on time unless traffic is bad. White chocolate mocha with extra espresso, right?"

"You know it."

"Okay. See you there." I hung up and applied my eyeliner quickly. After putting on mascara, I picked up my cellphone and rushed back for my tote bag.

I bustled downstairs, picking up my folders, stuffing them into my tote, and then snatched up my keys.

I was out of the door in a flash.

I scurried down the third grade hallway, folders tucked beneath one arm, two cups of coffee in hand, my key ring hanging around my pinky finger, and a cheese Danish wrapped in plastic trapped between my teeth. The bell hadn't rung yet and I was so relieved.

I met in front of my classroom just as Kim was coming out of hers. She had a kinky, full afro and loved hippy fashion. In fact, one of her headbands was how we worked up our very first chat—not to mention her classroom was right next to mine and I was a nervous shit my first day.

She welcomed me right in with open arms.

She made a tisking noise when she saw me coming, but didn't hesitate on swiping her mocha out of my hand.

"You got lucky, girl. Forty-five seconds and that bell rings." She studied the Danish. "Is that for me too?"

I grabbed it and shook my head, smirking. "Definitely not. Didn't eat breakfast. Need it!" I wiggled my eyebrows at her before marching into my classroom.

"Hi, Miss Knight!" the entire class said in unison.

I grinned. "Oh my goodness! What a wonderful way to start my morning! Hi, my lovely, beautiful students."

"Why are you late again?" Johnny, one of the smartest (and nosiest) asked.

I placed my coffee down on the podium up front and walked around it to stand in front of the dry erase board. "Well, last night I was up grading that little quiz we took yesterday. Do you remember?"

"Yes," Jessica said enthusiastically. "It was about Dr. Seuss."

"Yes! And not only that, but this class did so well on it that we get to watch a Dr. Seuss movie today!" They all cheered and I laughed as they turned red with excitement. "It is Friday, after all." I grabbed the remote and turned on the TV. "Now, make sure that you actually watch the movie, okay? Watch and listen because I will be asking you all a few questions afterwards."

"I've watched all of the Dr. Seuss movies, Miss Knight," Johnny, the know-it-all, stated.

I planted a hand on my hip, smirking at him. "I'm not talking about the new ones with all of the big visual effects."

"What other ones are there?" he asked, and he was truly confused.

His face scrunched up in the most adorable way. This was why I loved third grade. They were still innocent, but they weren't too wild. They knew better, but they still loved to learn at this age. Yes, I'd had a few duds here and there, but it had truly been worthwhile.

Becoming a teacher was one of the best things to ever happen to me. I didn't regret my choice of career. It was hard work, but there was nothing like seeing the kids succeed and knowing you took part in that.

"You'll see." I winked at him as I popped the DVD in. Good thing I had this all figured out before leaving yesterday. While they were watching the movie, I was going to play catch up on next week's assignments. "Now I don't want any talking, okay? Not until it's over. Is that understood, guys?"

"Yes, Miss Knight." They all said it in unison and I nodded appreciatively at them before pressing play, shutting the lights off, and then walking to my desk. When I sat down, so much relief washed over me.

I just needed a quick breather. I couldn't keep putting myself in this position because of Sterling. He had his issues and I wanted to help, but I also had a life and a pretty demanding career.

I needed to stay on top of my agenda, not fall backwards. I did that once—when I first started here.

I thought about Theo all summer long. Not even Sterling could cheer me up. He would always ask me what was wrong, but I would lie and say it was cramps, or a headache, or that I was just tired.

But the truth was, I missed Theo. Every single fucking day, I missed him. I wanted him back. I didn't know what he was doing with his new wife. I wanted to call him—actually, I tried once. He'd changed his number. Of course he did. He was moving forward, and for a while I was backtracking.

I turned in my seat, peering out the window. I was grateful to have a classroom with an ocean view.

It was nice to come to work every day and hear the waves, and the kids loved it so much. But when school started, I damned myself. I could see the ocean, and every time I was on lunch break or had a minute to myself, I looked out and all I could think about was *him*.

I grabbed my keys and unlocked the top drawer of my desk. I glanced around the classroom, but they were all glued to the screen. I rolled back in my chair and read the sticky note that was taped to the bottom of the drawer. I'd had it there since my first day.

"Told you I would get it. I guess being a Black has its perks."

I laughed quietly.

It was probably silly, but I read it everyday. For some reason it motivated me—the sticky note Theo left for me on the last day I saw him.

Someone knocked on the door, pulling me out of my state, and I shut the drawer quickly, spotting Principal Lint.

Oh, shit.

He waved a hand, and I nodded, pushing out of my chair and hurrying for the door. I stepped out and cracked it halfway behind me.

"Good morning, Miss Knight." He had that usual light smile on display.

"Good morning, Mr. Lint. How are you?"

"I'm great." He stepped back and folded his fingers in front of him. "I didn't mean to pry, but I saw you coming in really close to the bell. I heard about you doing the same thing a few days ago. I just stopped by to make sure everything is okay?"

"Oh—psshh. Please. Everything is fine! Yeah, I'm so sorry about that. I've just been working really hard at night, so much so that I forget I actually need sleep like a normal human being."

He chortled. "That is true. We do need our rest." He looked me over briefly before peering over my shoulder and looking at the class. "Listen, I know there isn't much time left, but if you need a substitute or anything to fill in for you, just let us know. You have never missed a day here since you've started and we are so grateful for that, but don't let yourself get worn down. I don't say this often, and I know it's the end of the school year so it doesn't seem very helpful of me, but we all need a little time off to take a breather here and there when things get overwhelming. I wouldn't mind if you asked me, just as long as you kept that statement between us. Can't have all of my teachers bailing on me."

I nodded, pressing my lips to smile. "I understand, Mr. Lint. But no worries, really. I'm fine. I think I can hang in there until summer starts."

He looked down at my shoes and his face scrunched up a bit. I looked with him, and *holy mother of all saints.*

"Are you sure?" he asked again, this time with a small smirk.

My face turned beet red as I studied my flats. One was brown with a gold piece and the other solid black. "Oh my goodness. I am so embarrassed." I deserved the face palm I gave myself. I had never had this happen before. And how in the hell didn't I notice? "I have another pair of shoes in the classroom—not my nicest, but at least they match."

"You may want to change those before the kids get a crack at it," he said, laughing. "But don't be embarrassed. It happens to the best of us sometimes."

"Thank you," I huffed.

He capped my shoulder. "Have a great day, Miss Knight." I watched him walk away until he disappeared around the corner. When he did, I hurried next door to tap on Kim's window.

She was standing in the middle of the classroom, using her hands to make crazy gestures. She was a great teacher. Wonderful with kids. She was vibrant and energetic, just what they needed.

She heard my knock and looked over. I waved a quick hand and she said something to the class before coming to the door.

When she stepped out, she asked, "What's wrong?"

"Why in the hell didn't you tell me I had two different shoes on, Kim? Principal Lint saw them, and I made a complete ass of myself!"

She looked down, and unable to help herself, she burst out laughing. "Oh, wow. I wish I would have seen that before I grabbed the coffee! It would have made my whole day!"

"This is not funny. He's questioning me . . . watching me. He heard that I was late twice this week."

"So what?" She frowned a little. "Did he make a big deal about it?"

I stepped back, glancing down the hallway. "No . . . but I hate that he's watching me at all, you know?" I wrapped my arms around myself.

She grabbed my shoulders, sighing. "Get back to class and change your shoes. Take a deep breath and try to relax. Everything will be fine. During recess, we'll talk more."

I nodded. "Okay. Right." She released me, and then turned to walk back into her classroom. I headed back to mine and sank into my leather chair, kicking my mismatch flats off and sliding into a pair of Crocs.

I normally wore them after school, when all of the kids were gone and I wanted to be comfortable, but I guess today I'd just give up early.

I was absolutely drained when I got home. I stayed a little later to make up for the lost time I could have had in the morning to get my assignments together. We were a week away from summer break and I could not have been happier.

I needed to relax. I needed some *me* time. I was tired of waking up early and staying up late for the sake of another person. I wanted to sleep in for a change. This year had been bumpy and rough—with Sterling acting out of sorts and me trying to make sense of it all.

Ugh.

It just wasn't the same.

I walked to the patio door and pushed it open. The breeze was light. A soft gust blew through my hair as I kicked my Crocs off.

Walking toward the beach, I stared out at the ocean, wrapping my hands around myself—not because I was cold, but because for the first time in years, I was alone.

This wasn't normal. I wasn't used to this kind of loneliness at all.

I lifted my cellphone and scrolled to Sterling's name in my call log. My finger hovered over the call button. I chewed on the inside of my cheek, knowing that if I called, I would probably make matters worse. He asked for his space.

But maybe if he could hear my voice, he'd realize he actually needed me there in Orange County with him. I loved my job, but I also had a personal life that I wanted to take care of.

So I called.

And I was glad he picked up.

"Chloe?" he answered.

"Hi, Sterling."

"What is it?"

"Nothing," I murmured. "I was just calling to check in. Haven't heard from you since last night."

"Oh . . . yeah. Got caught up." He said nothing more, and the silence was both deafening and awkward.

"Is Margie okay?"

"No." He groaned, and I knew he was doing his frustrated thing. Rubbing his face so hard—like it would rid him of his troubles. "Things aren't really looking up. I don't know what to do for her. I've been sitting here in the hospital all day. She can barely even talk."

"I'm so sorry, Sterling."

He didn't respond. Another awkward silence.

"Are you feeling okay?" I asked lightly.

And he didn't say anything to that either—at least, not right away.

"Chloe . . . listen."

His voice had changed dramatically. It became deeper. Heavier. The sound of it made my heart shrivel up in my chest. I stepped forward, tucking a lock of hair behind my ear as I focused on the sand.

"I . . . can't do this right now. I can't be with you like this," he mumbled.

"Like what?"

"I love you . . . but I'm not sure if I'm *in* love with you . . . and I know you aren't in love with me either. Your heart has never belonged to me."

I swallowed the large lump that had formed in my throat. "I do love you, Sterling."

"But you aren't *in* love," he stated rapidly. "Look, I get it. I get it because I feel the same way. You and Theo? I saw what you had. I was there. I witnessed that shit firsthand." Tears collected in my eyes when he said his name. "And, fuck . . . there's Janet. You were right. It is her sometimes. I'm still not over her. I know she's gone—I fucking know that it's been years—but . . .fuck. I don't know. I'm trying to accept that shit and move on, but I can't move on, you know? I can't because I still feel guilty—like it was my fault she died. Look," he sighed, "I want to make this work with you. I want to do what I can to make you happy, but how the hell can I make you happy when I'm not even happy with my damn self?"

"Sterling—"

"No, Chloe. Don't argue with me about this. You know I'm right."

He was right. So fucking right. "So . . . what are you saying?" My voice wavered.

He was silent for a long time. I would have assumed he'd hung up, but I could hear a machine beeping in the background. Margie was on machines. Everything around us was going awry.

"I think we should call off the engagement. My head isn't clear enough for marriage, and I refuse to put you through that."

My eyes dropped to the ring on my finger. "Sterling, don't you think we should talk about this in person?"

"We can . . . but what's the point, Chloe?" He paused and then cleared his throat. "I check your phone at night sometimes. Your Face-book. You search for him."

My heart plummeted.

Shit.

"I don't blame you. I look at old pictures of her in the lock box I tell you to never go through. We shouldn't do this to each other— force something that we both know won't last. We were great friends before we attempted this love thing. Let's just go back to being friends for now. Okay? Maybe we can see what happens later?"

I lowered to my knees. The sand was cool to the touch. My heart wasn't cracking, but it damn sure was aching. After spending so much time with him, Sterling was the companion I relied on.

I mean, of course we had our differences, but I really tried to put him first.

"I understand," I whispered.

"Don't take this harshly. Okay?"

"I won't."

"Thank you, Haze." My tears fell when he said that. A nickname of his. My hazel eyes. He adored them, or so he claimed.

The wind grew stronger, and the waves became bigger, crashing as they hit the shoreline.

"I'll be home next week to get some stuff. I'll stay at my mom's place until I figure this all out."

"Kay."

He released what sounded like a huge breath of relief. "I do love you, Chloe. You should know that."

"I know," I choked out. "Listen, just keep me updated on Margie. She was good to my dad and I feel like I should be there for her since she was there for him, but . . . well, you know. School and all."

"Right." I could hear him laughing. It was very faint. "I'll be sure to keep you updated. Hopefully I can get her out of here soon."

"Hopefully."

"Well, goodnight, Chloe."

"Night, Sterling."

I hung up and dropped the phone in the sand. My tears had dried up from the wind, but the stronger it grew, the more I felt the storm brewing inside me. It was coming, and I hated it.

I wanted to be strong, but I was irrefutably weak. The crazy thing was that it wasn't losing Sterling or calling off the engagement that hurt me most. It was the fact that I was alone again.

It was because Theo was still out there, and he could pick and choose whomever he wanted. He didn't even know what the hell I was up to. He didn't need me back in his life. Not while I was this unstable.

Plus . . . Izzy. Fucking Izzy. I still had respect for my ex-best friend. I loved her to death. I saw pictures of her at the wedding and she was so happy for her father. There were pictures of just her and Theo, and I could tell she'd completely forgiven him.

What kind of person would I have been to drive a wedge between them again?

I couldn't.

I pushed up to a stand and picked up my phone, heading back to the house. Yanking the freezer open and taking out a tub of chocolate ice cream, I placed it on the countertop and then walked to the wine pantry to take down a bottle.

I placed a wide glass down, popped the cork of the wine bottle, and then poured. Nearly to the rim. I had to take a sip before picking it up, but trust me, that first sip was everything I needed plus more . . .

But it still wasn't enough.

I sat at the counter and removed the lid from the ice cream. But when I picked up my spoon, I caught sight of the damn tattoo. The tribal tattoo I got—the one I lied to Sterling about. It was a boat. It was Dirty Black, but only I knew it.

Why the fuck did I get this thing?

Why would I do this to myself—torture myself with memories of a man that I let go?

What the fuck was I thinking?

I stared at it until my vision became blurry. I could no longer see it and it made me furious.

And then I broke down.

Into a complete sob I just . . . *let go*. Because as I sat in that empty house, wondering what the hell I'd gotten myself into, I only wanted one person there to comfort me.

The man that showed me *true love* for the very first time.

The man that made me his everything, and more, while he was in this town.

I wanted Theo, but instead I had *no one*.

CHAPTER 5

CHLOE

My phone was buzzing on the stand.

I looked towards the window. The sun was just coming up, splashes of it on the creamy walls. My phone continued buzzing and I let out a tired groan, twisting over to pick it up.

It was Kim.

Of course it was. We didn't exactly talk about my issues during recess. One of her students puked all over the hallway floor and she had to take care of that. She was curious though . . . and truthfully, I needed someone to vent to right now.

I hardly slept last night. I climbed into bed around 3 a.m. and it was 7 a.m. now.

"Hey, Kim," I sighed into the phone.

"Wow. I'm surprised you answered," she said, her voice full of life.

"Yeah, well, I didn't really get much sleep last night." I swiped a hand over my face.

"Again? Why not?"

"Wait." I frowned as I sat up. "It's a Saturday morning. Why are *you* calling me this early?"

She laughed. "I had to drop something off for my mom. She's renewing her driver's license. Lord help her."

I laughed.

"Trust me," she continued. "You know I wouldn't be up this early or calling you if I didn't have a reason to be awake."

"Well, I appreciate you calling me."

"We didn't get to talk yesterday. Should I come over?"

"That would be great. Maybe we can go to the beach. I could really use some sun today."

"Okay, but I hope you don't mean right out to your backyard. I need a new setting, woman."

"What's wrong with my backyard?" I laughed as I leaned on one elbow.

"Nothing at all, honey. I just want to see some half-naked men this time. You know the drill."

I shook with amusement. "Okay then. I know the perfect spot. See you at eleven? I'm gonna shower, freshen up—all that good stuff."

"Yes. And make sure you wear matching flip-flops too." She busted out laughing.

I fought my laugh, but it was useless. Her guffaw was infectious. "Yeah, yeah. Whatever," I laughed. "That was one time and I will never embarrass myself like that again."

"Mm-hmm. I'll be there at eleven. I have a few errands to run but as soon as I'm done with them I will be on my way to your house. Try to catch a nap or something. You sound exhausted."

I am.

"I'll try."

I ended the call and then looked towards the window. The sun had risen a little more, the rays now smothering my ivory bedspread. I flopped backwards and tossed a pillow over my face, knowing damn well that if I didn't get at least an hour more of sleep, I would be in the worst of moods.

Kim sounded chipper and like her morning was off to a great start. I needed to carry the same attitude . . . and that all was going to start with a nap.

CHAPTER 6

Theo

"Dad, pass the sunscreen, will you?" Izzy stuck out her hand and I looked towards the blue bottle on my lap that she was demanding me to hand over. I picked it up and handed it to her, and she gratefully accepted it. "I've really missed this place," she sighed, squeezing a dab into the palms of her hands as she gazed around.

I pressed my palms into the hot, white sand behind me, leaning back and looking towards the ocean. The water rippled, bright and blue. The sun was blazing today, and it felt good on my damp skin.

We were at Bristle Wave Beach. In the perfect spot. I'd only come here once, a few years back. Back when Chloe and I were . . . whatever we were.

It was the same spot. I remember because there was a purple and white beach rental shack that wasn't too far away. It wasn't a busy place, since there was a larger competitor by the harbor, but ever since Izzy and I placed our towels down, we'd given them more business than they probably expected today.

Especially her. Asking for everything, from sunscreen, to an extra towel, a bottle of water, and even a shaved ice with cherry flavoring.

She finished off the shaved ice before we returned to our spots. I figured while all of that sugar was flowing in her bloodstream and a smile lingered on her face, right now would be the best time to tell her how I was feeling.

She'd called me three days ago to let me know she had a shoot in Orange County for a commercial. Since I was already in Bristle Wave, she decided to fly in here and hang out at my hotel until it was time for her to go. I didn't mind. I had a lot to tell her—not only about Sheila, but other stuff she probably didn't want to hear.

I sat up and looked over at her.

She rubbed the cream around her elbows and when she noticed my stare, she asked, "What?" with a slight laugh.

"There's something I want to tell you, Isabelle. About me and Sheila."

She looked down, focusing on the bottle. "You're separating, aren't you?"

My eyebrows dipped as I met her eyes. "How'd you know?"

"Well, she's not here with you. You said it was a vacation for you but knowing Sheila, she would have tagged along. I know she doesn't work much on weekends, and when I'm in town or coming around she's always trying to see me and 'build a bond.'" She rolled her eyes at that. "I guess it just seems obvious something's wrong."

I looked away when she attempted to meet my gaze. "You aren't upset about it?"

She shrugged. "The only thing that is upsetting is that you can't keep a woman." She was teasing, but she winced when she said that. "Except . . . Mom. That was different."

"And Chloe?" I mused, meeting her eyes and arching a brow.

She stared at me, but said nothing at all. Instead, she stood up, dusted the sand off her bottom, and then made her way towards the ocean.

Chloe was still a tough subject for her. I wasn't sure if she was

34

holding grudges about it, or if it was so hard for her to talk about because of the way they left off.

There wasn't a day that went by where I didn't remember what she'd said to Chloe when I had that condo—how she bashed her because she'd fallen in love with me, her father.

I constantly took full blame for it. I came onto Chloe. I made her mine and in my mind, nothing was going to interfere with that.

Not Trixie.

Not Sterling.

Not even my daughter—my own flesh and blood.

I watched the water run around her ankles when she met at the shore. She tucked a lock of curly brown hair behind her ear. I knew what that gesture meant. She was thinking. And she was upset.

I guess right now would have been a bad time to tell her that after our father-daughter time, I was going to try and find Chloe while I was here. I knew where she lived. I didn't know her schedule, but I would wait, if it came down to it.

I looked around the beach. There weren't many people around—then again this part of the beach wasn't the attraction area.

This area was much more serene, but slightly bumpy. Lots of shells, but that wasn't a bad thing.

I peered to the left, towards the shack, when I heard someone laughing—a woman's laughter, and it sounded familiar.

Too fucking familiar.

Brows dipping, I sat up straight and continued looking in that direction, watching the shadows grow taller on the sand.

Two women rounded the shack several seconds later. One was heavyset, with a beach umbrella strapped around her, a red bathing suit on, and a red headband. She was talking while moving her hands in an animated manner.

And then there was another woman.

She was taller. Thinner, with curvy hips. A Coke-bottle shape. Her skin was tan and flawless, her legs shiny and silky. Her full, pink lips curved upwards, and her cat-like eyes were as memorable as ever.

Her hazel irises were bold beneath the eyeliner she wore. Her hair swam around her face. It seemed messier than usual, but like she had it that way on purpose. She tucked a lock of hair behind her ear, lifted her head, and pointed where she didn't know I was sitting.

But then she saw me.

And she stopped dead in her tracks.

Her jaw fell, her chin practically hitting the ground.

Her body froze.

Her eyes stretched wide and she dropped her arm in a flash, blinking quickly, as if blinking that fast would get rid of the person that sat only a few steps away from her.

But it wasn't going to happen.

Because I was there.

I was real.

Slowly, I stood, staring right at her, my heart thundering in my chest. I was absolutely fucking speechless.

My Little Chloe Knight—though she wasn't very little anymore.

She'd grown even more, her body settling into her curves, those assets on full display. Her slim belly barely hid beneath the cover up, and neither could those perfect, creamy thighs, or her full, perfectly sized tits. She looked fucking stunning, and seeing her standing there made my cock pump with nothing but desire.

I didn't even know what the fuck to say.

Where to begin . . .

This didn't seem real. What the hell was she doing here? On the same beach we walked once before? On the very same day as me? What kind of fucking coincidence was this?

Everything I had planned to say to her had flown right away with the beach breeze. All words lodged in my throat. I wasn't prepared.

Her friend stopped walking when she realized Chloe was in a frozen state of mind. She looked from Chloe to me, and then her mouth gaped. She didn't know who I was, but she obviously liked what she saw in me.

I took a step forward, focusing on my Knight. "Chloe?" I called.

She stepped away and I paused on the step I was about to take.

"Dad, I was thinking we should go to Dane's for some drinks tonight, too," Izzy called out behind me.

I glanced over my shoulder and back to Chloe as Izzy came closer. She spotted Chloe when she met up to my side, her smile evaporating almost instantly. Her jaw dropped, her body static.

Chloe looked over at Izzy, and then she did something I didn't see coming.

Instead of confronting her past—instead of facing us and striking up a conversation—she turned on her heels and ran away.

CHAPTER 7

CHLOE

Shitshitshitshit!

This couldn't be real.

This couldn't be happening.

My insomnia must have been getting to my head now.

I didn't care what or who I hit as I stormed away. I didn't care that my feet were moving so fast I might have tripped over anything that was in my way and fell face first into hot sand.

To my luck, I didn't, and I made it into the Tiki shack, dashing down the aisle and towards the coolers. My heart was pounding so hard that my head was spinning as I gripped the handle of the cooler.

I needed to control myself.

I needed to breathe.

But I couldn't regulate it.

I was panting so hard, clutching the handle tighter and tighter, hoping to gain some control and stability. There were dark spots swirling in my vision.

Calm down, Chloe. Just calm down.

I straightened my back, staring up at the honey buns on the shelf above. There was a tiny bumblebee on one of them and I immediately reached up to grab it.

I didn't care that it had three days' worth of carbs, or that there was so much icing on it that it would probably make me puke later on. I just needed to distract myself, and get as far away from *them* as I could.

What the hell were they doing here anyway? And especially Izzy? I thought she would never come back to this town after what I'd done.

"Are you okay?" The woman behind the counter put on a friendly smile when I turned in her direction.

"Yes," I breathed, my lips stretching to smile. I held up the treat and walked towards the counter. "I just want to buy this."

"Good choice," she chimed, picking it up and punching it into the cash register. As she was doing that, I looked towards the door. No one was coming. Not even Kim.

Wait . . . actually, I was wrong.

Someone was coming, and I was hoping it was Kim so we could bail . . . but it wasn't her.

It was *him*.

His strides were casual, and I could see him looking through the window, right at me. He was shirtless—still with the body of a god. Those tattoos of his glistened on his skin, the sunlight reflecting off his nipple ring, and as he got closer, his tongue traced his bottom lip.

My stomach formed into knots at the sight of his tongue, and it was not in a bad way.

I glanced at the woman again and she was still punching numbers in. I drummed my fingers on the counter, hoping she'd catch the signal that she needed to hurry—that I needed to get out of here ASAP.

She finally placed the treat down on the counter and I tossed her some cash. "You know what? Keep the change. It's okay," I said hurriedly, and then I rushed towards the back door.

The bell above the front door chimed, but I didn't look back to see him come in.

I heard the back door slam behind me and then I scurried ahead, pulling out my cellphone to call Kim. I didn't get very far before I heard the deep, familiar voice call my name and the door slam again.

I froze, but I shouldn't have.

I couldn't help it.

His voice sent a chill down my spine, even though it was slightly above eighty degrees outside. I heard him coming closer.

And closer.

Until finally he was right behind me.

Breath bated, I lowered my phone and stared at the sand between my toes.

"Chloe," he murmured. His voice was both demanding and desperate. Was he angry? Did I care?

Hell, of course I did.

I turned a fraction of the way and that's when I looked at him. Up close. In full.

He was still so damn beautiful, and I wanted to hate him for it, but I couldn't. His beauty was rare.

He was flawless. Slight wrinkles around his deep brown eyes. That was something different, but if anything this natural change made him . . . *sexier*.

His dark brown hair wasn't just brown anymore. There were light streaks of silver throughout, mostly at his temples, which revealed his age. But with a body like his, a smile that wicked, and a face that handsome, he could have still been judged to be in his late thirties.

He was twenty years older than me, which made him forty-six now.

Our eyes instantly locked as I turned to face him. His mouth twitched when he finally got my attention, and his shoulders sagged a bit as he stepped closer.

"You've got to stop running away from me," he said, almost too empathetically. He probably thought I was a fool now. An idiot, sprinting off like I was in some kind of Olympic race.

"I—I wasn't running," I stammered.

His cheek tilted upwards, and one of his breathless smirks was put on display. "Yes, you were. And if I'm recalling the past correctly, this is the third time this has happened between us. These random encounters where you run off. First at the park years ago, and then the grocery store when you came back from college that summer, and now here. I guess I shouldn't be so surprised. You've never liked facing conflict."

I swallowed hard, rubbing my elbow nervously. I glanced down at his hand—focusing mainly on his ring finger. The ring was gone, but there was a tan line there. I did my best to hide my hand behind the honey bun.

"Theo," I said lightly, and he perked up, giving me all of his attention—not that he wasn't supplying it before. "What are you doing here? There—in that spot?"

"You mean *our* spot?" He tilted a brow, smirking.

I pursed my lips.

"Just visiting," he said.

"Why?" I couldn't help but narrow my eyes at him. Why was he back?

He thought on it before he spoke. "Izzy has a commercial shoot in Orange County next week. She wanted to spend some time here with me before she went to work."

"Oh." I stepped aside. He was watching me too closely—not that I minded. It was just a tiny bit awkward now.

This whole encounter had taken me by total surprise. I wasn't expecting to see him sitting there—almost like he was waiting for me to show up. If destiny was pulling cards, they'd better be correct when dealing them this time. I didn't have the energy for these heart games again.

My battered heart couldn't take anymore than it already had.

He sighed and took another step closer. "Could you stop treating me like a stranger?" he asked with a light chuckle.

"I'm not. But you're here . . . with Izzy . . . who just so happens to hate my fucking guts. I can't really just *hug* you, you know?"

He half-shrugged. "I'm sure she wouldn't mind."

I started to speak again, but my mouth clamped shut. "How would you know?"

"She's changed," he stated. "She's not what she was before. I know it. She knows it, though she never talks about it."

I snatched my gaze away, staring down at my feet again. The icing of my honey bun was melting now, and it wasn't from the blazing sun. It was due to my sweaty hands.

So what if she'd changed? That didn't mean she was going to welcome me back into her life with open arms. I knew Izzy well enough to know she didn't just let shit go, even if she had matured a little.

She used to be the queen of grudges.

"I heard you're separated now," I acknowledged.

"You heard or you *saw?*" I whipped my head up as soon as he said that, and he flashed a crooked smile, looking me up and down.

What?! "I heard," I fibbed.

"You saw, most likely on my Facebook." My heart stuttered in my chest. " But that's a discussion for another time. Come on. Say hey to her." He started to step away, but I caught him, gripping his wrist and tugging on it.

"Theo . . . I—" I struggled for words when his warm brown gaze met mine. "I can't go back there. To Izzy."

"Your friend—Kim, right?—is setting up a spot for you two as we speak."

"Well, tell her to pack up and meet me here. I've had a shitty week and I'm just not ready to face Izzy yet."

He looked down at the hand I had wrapped around his wrist. His face changed. His features softened a touch, and his lips parted. "Look, I know it's been a while, but can you trust me?" He grabbed my hand and hauled me closer. His large body hovered above me, his head tilted as he looked right into my eyes.

He smelled delicious, and his skin was hot. I could feel the heat radiating off of it. For a split second, fear consumed me. This man— Theodore Black. He was standing right in front of me—treating me like some prized possession. Almost like he'd forgotten all about our disastrous past.

About his wife.

About how I'd disappeared on him.

Why had he forgiven me in the first place?

Memories of when he appeared at that house after a year broke through. His smile. It was so sweet, but his words. They were heartbreaking.

He was broken. I was broken.

I never should have let him go that day.

We never should have let go at all.

"I want to trust you. I have no reason not to trust you," I murmured. "But I can't, Theo. I'm not ready for that."

He released a ragged breath. "Okay. I get it." He pushed a hand through his hair. "You don't have to come back with me, but I want to talk to you, soon. Preferably tomorrow. I'll still be in Bristle Wave."

"What is there to talk about?"

"Us." He said this so clearly—so simply—that I knew he wasn't joking around. "Do you want to know why I'm really here, Chloe? In that exact spot?" He leaned forward.

"For Izzy."

He chuckled, and then he stepped back several steps, pulling his hand away from mine.

"No." He continued his deep, sexy laugh. "I'm here for you, Little Knight. But I think you knew that from the start."

CHAPTER 8

Theo

She looked at me as if I'd lost my mind.

"Why would you be here for *me?*" she asked, voice low, like someone would overhear.

"You already know why."

"But I don't get it. Your wife? *Izzy?*" She asserted Izzy's name is if it were a damn drug.

I sighed, picking my head up and looking towards the ocean. "Izzy is a grown woman. My world doesn't revolve around her as much as it used to. She's independent now, figuring life out as she grows. I love her but she knows about me."

"Knows *what* about you?"

"That I'm not over you." Her mouth gaped a fraction. I stepped close again, pulling out my cell phone. "What's your number?"

"Why do you need it?"

I inclined a brow. "Chloe."

She realized the seriousness in my tone and straightened her back, swallowing hard. Looking at me warily, she tucked the honey bun beneath her arm and then took my phone from me.

As she grabbed it, I caught sight of that fucking ring. She plugged her number in, but I couldn't stop staring at the damn diamond. When she handed it back, I was slow to receive it. She noticed and jerked her hand away. I turned the screen of my phone off and slid it into my pocket.

"I'll be in touch then," I murmured.

"Okay," she said quietly.

She wanted to say more—*I* wanted to say more. But I couldn't rush this. She was hesitant. Guarded. She knew I was "technically" still with Sheila.

She'd been watching. I knew it. She accidentally liked one of my posts before. I saw it one night when I was drunk. I thought I had imagined it, but no. It was her. I'm sure she'd been watching my profile for a while.

It made me feel like I wasn't tripping out about this—that she wanted me back just as badly as I wanted her back in my life.

We lingered for way too long. I had the urge to pick her up in my arms and run off with her. It didn't matter where, as long as she was in my arms. As long as she was touching and kissing me. As long as she allowed me to love her.

I couldn't push this. I didn't know what she was thinking right now. It took me some time to wiggle my way back in the first time she left for college. But this time it was different.

She'd matured even more. She was on her own, and something about her had changed.

She seemed dull in the places she used to carry brightness. Like someone had come in and stolen the light right away from her.

For a second, I thought of that motherfucker Sterling. He better not have ruined her. I would kill him if he did and I put that on my own life.

"Do you want me to go and get your friend?" I finally asked when she shifted and stared down at her feet.

Her head picked back up. "Sure. Tell her I'm waiting here."

I exhaled, studying her face. Admiring it. I didn't give much thought to what I did next.

I caressed the right side of her face with the pad of my thumb and she released a quiet breath, her hazel eyes locking on mine. I wanted to kiss her so fucking badly.

"I'll go get her," I said, leaning in. Our lips were close, and I don't think she realized, but she pressed her chest forward and her breasts brushed my arm. Her lips even puckered, her neck stretching so she could get closer.

I smirked, dropping my head and placing a light kiss on the apple of her cheek. "I'll call you," I murmured in her ear, and I could have sworn I heard a defeated moan slip out of her as I backed away.

Releasing her, I stepped back, watched her briefly, and then turned to walk back to where Izzy was. I glanced back once and she was still standing in the same spot, watching me go.

I winked over my shoulder and she jerked her gaze away with a blush. She was twenty-six now, still so fucking young and innocent. That woman had no idea what kind of things I wanted to do to her. Walking away was fucking killing me—each step making my legs feel like a block of lead had been placed inside them.

I wanted to stay. I wanted to run away with her. But I had to face reality.

I wasn't divorced yet.

She was still engaged, from what I saw of that damn ring on her finger.

I was on vacation with the very daughter I hurt years ago because I'd wanted Chloe so much.

We had a lot of shit to deal with, and knowing how Chloe was, I knew her guilt would eat her up and swallow her whole before she even attempted to give us another chance.

I both loved and despised that about her. I wished she didn't give a fuck—that she'd just be mine again and not think twice about the repercussions.

So much bullshit already.

"Where'd she go?" Izzy asked sullenly as I sat down on my towel.

She was running her fingers through her hair. I couldn't read her full expression because of the bug-eyed sunglasses she was wearing.

"Home, I guess."

"Humph."

"What's that for?" I pressed.

"Nothing," she sighed, drawing her knees to her chest. "I just can't believe how fast you ran after her. Not even a full week of being separated and you're chasing her again."

I laughed, pointing my line of vision at the ocean. "I was going to talk to you about it."

"What's there to talk about?" I looked over and she shrugged. "You aren't over her. You want her back. That's why you want to leave Sheila, right? Because you were never happy with her and because you were most likely comparing her to Chloe the entire marriage." She swallowed hard. "You settled . . . and I can't help but feel like it was because of me."

I turned fully to look at her. "That's bullshit. Don't speak like that. It wasn't because of you."

"She's probably afraid of me after all the shit I said to her that day."

I hesitated when she said that. "Well . . . maybe you should talk to her."

She snatched her sunglasses off. "Are you insane?" she screeched. "You know how I am, Dad. I'd probably end up swallowing my tongue before apologizing to her in person."

"You're not like that anymore." I nudged her arm with my elbow and she fell sideways a little. "You've changed, though you won't admit it. But I can tell. I can read you like a book, Isabelle."

She groaned and planted her hands on the towel, resting back on her palms. "What if she's changed? She used to take so much shit from me. She might not anymore. She's probably all badass and serious now. I'm sure I burned her so much it left an imprint."

"I doubt that. Not with the way she just ran off."

47

She was quiet for a whole minute before speaking again. "Are you going to see her while we're here?"

I didn't respond right away. I would have loved to see my Knight. I would have loved to catch her alone just to talk and catch up, but the thing was I wasn't sure she would have wanted the same thing. She was still wearing that fucking ring on her finger.

"I don't know," I sighed.

"Oh." She looked away.

I stood, dusting my ass off before taking a step her way. "I think that's enough talk about that. Come on. Out to the water with me. Gotta enjoy ourselves while we can, right?"

She nodded, placing the sunglasses on the bridge of her nose.

So maybe Izzy hadn't made a dramatic change. She was still somewhat self-centered, but she didn't expect the world to revolve around her like she did when she was younger. She damn sure didn't feel like she was entitled to shit anymore.

She was actually working hard for the things she wanted, like the filming she had coming up within the next few days. I was proud of my daughter—damn proud.

But knowing that she knew I really wanted Chloe was strange. It was painful watching her eyes. It was almost like I had stolen Chloe from her—like I'd robbed her of their friendship by replacing it with a love so fierce that neither of us was prepared when it ended.

I didn't give a damn if Chloe was still with that fucker.

He didn't know her like I did.

He couldn't please her like I could.

He wished he could own her heart, but she knew damn well it still belonged to me. I saw the way she looked at me—how hard it was for her to breathe when I came closer.

I was becoming impatient now. I knew as soon as Izzy and I got back to the hotel, I was going to make a plan. See her, or wait.

But waiting felt pointless.

Why wait when we both felt the same thing?

Why waste time?

Why worry about what the fuck anyone else had to say?

That's the shit I didn't have time for. Caring about other people's opinions. My happiness was important, and so was Chloe's. She was happiest with me.

She belonged to me.

Fuck the bullshit.

I was getting her back.

CHAPTER 9

CHLOE

"So you know I have to ask, Chlo." Kim turned in the passenger seat to look at me. I gripped the wheel tighter, turning on my signal and starting up the freeway. "Who in the hell was that gorgeous man? And furthermore, why in the hell did you run off like your ass was caught on fire?!"

I avoided her eyes. I was sure she had more questions than that. My actions back there, she'd never seen before. She never saw me run away like that, or panic to the point that I wanted to hide.

I'd never told Kim about Theo. Ever.

Not because I didn't want to, but because he was too hard to talk about. Letting him go. Breaking my sisterly bond with Izzy, his daughter *and* my former best friend. I didn't want to come off as some slut, or for her to think I was going to make a play on her father next.

I swear that wasn't me.

Theo was just . . . different.

"It's a lot to explain," I finally sighed when I felt her staring a hole into the side of my head.

"Yeah? Well, we have all damn day. I'm not going anywhere. Spill it." She crossed her arms, and I glanced her way. Her lips were pressed and one of her eyebrows inclined.

I couldn't help but laugh. "He used to be my neighbor. And the girl —his daughter—she *was* my best friend before she found out about us and everything became a shitstorm."

Kim's arms dropped slowly, and for a moment she didn't speak. "Wait . . . hold on. You mean to tell me, you used to sleep with your best friend's *father?*"

I nodded, hardly looking at her. Hearing it out loud was embarrassing enough.

"Shit." She huffed a laugh. "Now I see why you ran. I would have done the same thing, but knowing my chubby ass, I would have taken several tumbles before I had actually gotten away."

I busted out laughing, taking a right turn into my neighborhood. When I parked in the garage, I unclipped my seatbelt and then slouched in the seat. The amusement seemed to fade, realizing I was going to be home. Alone. Again.

"Are you okay, Chlo?"

I waved a hand. "I'm fine. I'm just shocked I guess. I wasn't expecting to ever see him again." I looked over at her, chewing my bottom lip. "I gave him my number before I told him to tell you to meet me."

Her eyes expanded. "Seriously? But what about Sterling?"

I frowned. "Fuck Sterling." Annoyed by his name alone, I pushed out of the car and walked to the door, jamming the key into the lock. "He called the engagement off on Friday night." I dropped my bag on the kitchen counter as she came inside, shutting the door behind her. Her eyes never left me.

"He did WHAT?!"

"Yep." I blew a thick puff of breath. "He's been acting weird for weeks, and he finally admitted he's not over someone from his past. And she just so happens to be Theo's deceased wife and Izzy's mom."

"What the fuck? Chloe, what kind of shit were you involved in?! This sounds like some Jerry Springer shit!" She held her hands out, completely flabbergasted. "You're telling me Sterling was with Theo's dead wife before you?"

"Yes, but at the time, we didn't know. Not until he told me. Sterling knew she was married when they were together, but who would have known he would actually meet the husband one day, which just so happened to be through me." I opened the fridge and pulled out a Diet Coke. "It's all one big mess, which is why seeing him today shocked the hell out of me." I side-eyed her. "He said he would never come back here. To Bristle Wave."

"So why did he?"

"Supposedly for me."

"Ohhh." She grinned like a child in front of a pile of candy. "And are you going to give him the chance to slide back in?"

I shook my head and cracked open my soda. "He's married now, Kim. Hell no."

"From what I heard the daughter say, he's free to run after you—that he's getting a divorce anyway," she mused.

Fucking Izzy. I couldn't believe she'd said that.

I ignored that comment for the most part.

"Yes, but I'm sure it's not final. I don't want to get into the middle of whatever he has going on with her."

"You're such a terrible liar," she laughed, resting her elbows on the countertop. "The way I see it, what do you have to lose? You guys talked before, during worse circumstances, honestly. His marriage is on the rocks. He wants you back. Why not do it again? Sterling is being a straight-up asshole and this silver fox wants your goods. What the hell is holding you back?"

"Izzy," I stated, and then I looked away, focusing on the tan marble. "I can't do that to her again. I mean, even though we aren't technically friends anymore, I still have respect for her. It would be wrong of me. Of us. It would tear her and Theo apart all over again."

"That thought doesn't seem to be stopping him. And I'm sure he cares more about his daughter than himself."

"Just like any other guy, he's thinking with his dick, not his brain," I laughed. "Theo has always been known for doing that."

"Well, maybe she doesn't have to know?" She squinted her eyes, giving me an obvious look.

"No—Kim, don't you get it? We snuck around before and it hurt us more than it helped us. It hurt her a lot. She trusted me, and I betrayed her. I don't want to do this again and behave as if the loss of our friendship didn't matter."

"Ugh. That's bullshit." She stood up straight, gluing her hands to her hips. "Did you love him?"

I blinked at her, unable to form words. She looked me all over, watching as my cheeks flamed red and my eyes became watery.

"By that look alone, I'm taking that as a yes? And that you still do?"

I swallowed hard, snatching up my soda and taking a sip.

"Chlo," she murmured, "meet that man soon. I saw how he looked at you, and I damn sure saw how you looked at him. The way he chased after you proved to me and her that he still feels something for you, and if she's that blind to it, she needs to take a seat and get over herself. She should want him to be happy too, no matter what he wants." Kim walked around the counter and gripped my shoulders. "Make yourself happy for once. Stop punishing yourself for what you did in the past. You deserve some fun, and I'm sure that sexy silver fox can deliver it."

She winked and I snorted, swiping the collected tears away. "I . . . I don't know. I can't, Kim. I can't do that with him again. What I did almost made me fail college. I couldn't stop thinking about it. Imagine how it would be now, with my students. My *career*!"

She blew an agitated breath and pulled way. "I don't want to hear that shit. Summer break is in a week. They aren't getting any real work right now anyway. Look, if you don't, I will," she teased.

I walked around her to get to the living room. I sat down on the loveseat and she took the spot beside me.

"What if Sterling comes back?" I asked. "What if he wants to try again?"

She rolled her eyes. "Would he even be worth taking back?"

"Would Theo?" She seemed confused when I asked that. "With Theo, there isn't just Izzy. There's his wife. Our past. And then *us*. He's twenty years older than I am. He's way more mature. He knows a lot more than I do. What if what we had was only supposed to be a summer fling and nothing more?"

Kim sat back, craned her head backwards, and stared up at the ceiling. "I guess you won't know the answers to any of those questions if you don't try, now will you?"

I stared at her, unsure of what to say.

She was right.

So right.

But I was so damn afraid.

I loved Theo, yes. I loved him more than words could explain. When I thought of him, my heart always skipped two beats. When I saw photos of him, I felt heat rise in my belly and my heart would ache, knowing I couldn't touch him.

When I wanted to be near him, I felt like crying. Because all I wanted was him, even after all this time. I . . . *needed* him. But so much stood in the way.

So many obstacles that I wasn't sure we could tackle and conquer.

I knew Kim was right. I wanted to give it another chance. I had nothing at all to lose. Sterling didn't want me anymore. Theo's divorce wasn't final, but he was still separated. Izzy and I weren't friends anymore.

There was a possibility the wife could come running back to him and he could dump me right on my ass for her.

There was a possibility that Izzy would spit in my face if she saw me near her father again.

Theo was right about me running away from conflict. I always did, but only with people I cared about.

I was being weak, but I knew all I needed was a chance to talk to him.

A chance to fall for him . . . all over again . . . just like last time.

———

Kim and I sat in lounge chairs in the back yard, grading papers, soaking up the sun, and sipping on cranberry wine spritzers. This felt much more freeing than if we'd have been sitting beside Theo and Izzy. Talk about awkward.

"You keep checking your phone," Kim mused, tilting her sunglasses down to look at me when I picked it up.

I playfully rolled my eyes at her, setting it on my lap. "Oh, hush."

"You're waiting on a call or a text from him, aren't you?"

"I am not." I was lying. I *was* waiting on a text or a call—preferably a call.

Kim snickered and stood up. "Well, I'm going to start cooking the dinner I promised. You just keep on waiting for that phone call."

I nodded and she walked off. When I heard the door close behind her, I picked my cellphone up and went straight to Facebook.

I searched for Theo's account again. He'd added a photo. It was of him and Izzy on the beach. A selfie that Izzy obviously took, because his hands were planted behind him. They looked similar, but she favored Janet a lot more.

I smiled at the two of them. They were happy. And then I thought . . .

What kind of person would I be to destroy their bond again? I was confused, though. He chased after me, and she saw it happen. She didn't stop him. She spoke to Kim very briefly about the divorce. (And yes, I made Kim spill every detail but it didn't explain much.)

He said she'd changed, but people don't often change the very essence of who they are. She forgave me in that letter, but that didn't mean she had to tolerate me.

I sighed, placing my phone on my lap again, and pointing my face up towards the sky. He needed to hurry up and contact me. Now, I was desperate. And eager. And my only wish was that I had asked for his number in return.

After Kim finished cooking dinner, and we chowed down on her amazing shrimp scampi, I cleaned the dining room and kitchen while she worked on papers a little more.

"Still nothing?" she called from the living room.

I scrubbed the pan, glancing over my shoulder. "Nothing."

"Think he'll actually call?"

He'd better. "I don't know," I said instead.

"Crazy fox."

Around 10:00 p.m., as Kim was packing her things and collecting her keys, I finally got the call I had been waiting for all day.

I wasn't familiar with the number, but it came with a San Francisco area code. Kim paused on everything she was doing, straightening up as I literally jumped out of my seat with my phone clutched in hand.

"Is that him?"

"I don't know," I said hoarsely. "I hope so."

"Oh shit. Well, let me go, but make sure you call and tell me everything!"

"I will!"

She walked towards the door and wriggled her eyebrows at me before shutting it behind her. I stepped back and hurried up the stairs, entering the bedroom.

It continued ringing as I sat on the bed's bench, staring at the number. I had already memorized it, just in case.

My heart was hammering down on my ribcage now. With shaking fingers, I pressed the answer button and then lifted the receiver up to my ear.

I swallowed the thick emotion in my throat before speaking.

"Theo?"

"How'd you know?" he asked, and his voice was smooth and deep, and so fucking sexy.

"The number says San Francisco under it. You told me before you left Bristle Wave that you were moving there . . . with her."

He was quiet for a moment. "Yeah, I remember." I remained just as quiet and then he grunted. "Do me a favor?" he said after it sounded like a car door had shut.

"What?"

"Look out of your window."

My eyebrows drew together. *"What?"* I looked towards the window, confused now.

"Look out of your window," he repeated, and I stood slowly, tiptoeing across the carpet. I pushed the sheer white curtain aside and peered out. I didn't see anything at first, but then I saw the black Chrysler parked across the street.

I'd never seen anyone next door or across the street with that car. And it was black. All black. Black rims. Black paint. Tinted windows.

He was here.

I looked towards the sidewalk where my mailbox was, and he was standing right by the curb, one hand in his front pocket, the other used to hold the phone to his ear.

"Oh my God, Theo, what are you doing here?" I hissed, as if someone would overhear me. But there was no one here. No one but me.

"I'm here for my Knight."

"But—Izzy," I stammered. "Aren't you supposed to be with her?"

"She's rehearsing a script. She told me she would be at it all night, so I told her I'll be at Dane's. I guess fate wanted me to come here instead."

I cleared my throat, my heart beating a mile a minute.

"Are you going to let me in?" he asked, and his head tilted. "Or is that fiancé of yours lingering around?"

I stepped away from the window, staring down at the ring on my finger.

"Chloe?" he called.

His voice sent a swirl deep in my belly. I was all wound up—not thinking clearly. My stomach was in one big knot, and I knew the only person that could unravel it was him.

"Give me a second," I murmured. I ended the call and tossed my phone on the mattress. I stared down at my ring, not blinking. Contemplating.

If I took this off, it meant I was giving up on Sterling. It meant I was done with what we had, and I wasn't turning back, no matter what happened between me and Theo.

I wanted to help him.

I wanted to be there for him . . .

But Kim was right.

I needed to stop punishing myself. Sterling wasn't over Janet. And I wasn't over Theo. And Theo . . . he wasn't over *me*.

So I chose to do the wiser thing . . . *I think.*

I snatched off the ring and walked towards the jewelry box, tossing it in one of the slots where my old jewelry was, and then turning for the door. I rushed down the stairs like a kid on Christmas morning, dashing for the front door and yanking it open.

Perhaps I was being reckless—stupid even—but I didn't care. He was here. *He was here.*

When I looked out, he had his back facing me but he turned around when he heard the creak of the door, his hands in his front pockets.

I walked out slowly, my heart beating harder now. I was barefoot, so the cement was cool on the bottoms of my feet.

I stopped about halfway.

He stood there, looking me up and down in my jean shorts and black tank top. My hair was still frizzy, but I'd tossed it into a messy bun to keep it off of my neck.

Our eyes held for a long time.

It was so quiet between us that all I could hear was my chaotic heartbeat. I didn't know what I was doing. I wasn't thinking straight, and neither was he.

He ran his eyes up and down my body several times before locking onto my face. My lips.

And then he walked forward, towards me.

He moved quickly, his thick boots crunching on the pavement, his jaw locked, his broad chest upright.

When he met up to me, he stopped, and he studied my face—every single detail. Everything. It was like he wanted to memorize every feature all over again, though I was sure he'd never forgotten them.

His eyes traveled down to my lips.

I almost stopped breathing as I did the same.

And then . . . he did exactly what I wanted.

He cupped a hand around the back of my neck, and his lips came crashing down on mine. He took a sharp inhale, like his breath had become constricted—like my presence stole the air from his lungs He kissed me so wholly that I melted in his grasp. His possessive grip on me made the knot unravel in my belly, just as I knew it would.

He worked his velvety tongue through my parted lips and then he picked me up in his strong arms, storming inside the house.

The house I'd been sharing with Sterling for years.

CHAPTER 10

CHLOE

I don't know how the door ended up shut behind us. Maybe he'd kicked it. I don't know.

I don't know why I was letting him lay me down on the couch, or why I was allowing him to have his hands all over me, with all the shit we had going on in our lives, but I refused to stop him.

He groaned as he continued the kiss, and I threaded my fingers through his thick hair, wrapping my legs around his waist, and hauling him closer with my thighs.

"Goddamn, Chloe," he rasped when our mouths momentarily parted. But it didn't last long because he came back down with my face locked in his hands.

He didn't hold back.

I *refused* to hold back.

All day I had waited for him. Hell, let's be honest. For years, I had waited for him. This was wrong all over again, but this . . . this moment was fucking *bliss*.

I didn't care that he had remarried. I didn't care that Izzy was in town and probably less than ten miles away. I didn't care that Sterling could walk right through that door and catch us.

I honestly didn't give a single, flying fuck.

My Theodore was back, and being light and easy was not an option. I was greedy for every single part of him. So greedy that I ended up reaching down to unbutton his jeans.

He groaned behind our kiss and pulled his hands away, planting an elbow outside my head.

"How long's it been?" he murmured, voice thick and raspy.

I shook my head, catching his bottom lip with my teeth. "Too long."

A beautiful smirk played on his lips, and he sat up, locking my wrists in his hands and pinning them to the couch.

"Where is he?" he questioned.

I exhaled raggedly. "Not here."

He looked at my fingers, noticing the ring was gone. "Are you still marrying him?"

I shrugged. I could have told him he had called off the engagement, but it was better this way, for him to not know anything. I wanted to know how far he would go if it meant I still belonged to Sterling.

He frowned, nostrils flaring. "Don't fucking marry him."

"You married *her*," I scowled.

"You left me no choice."

I narrowed my brows and snatched my hands away from him. "I didn't do a damn thing, Theo! I didn't tell you to run off and marry another woman!"

"Yeah, but you left. It was either try to move on, or dwell on a woman that didn't want me anywhere near her."

"I never said I didn't want you near me."

"That's what it seemed like. Lost all contact with me." He raked a rough hand through his hair.

"Well, if you feel that way, why are you back?" I sat up, frustrated, tucking my hair behind my ears. *There goes our moment.*

He looked at me with hard, serious brown eyes. "Because I fucking miss you, Chloe. I'm forty-fucking-six, and I should be fucking happy and going after whatever the fuck I want before it's too late." He held my face in his hands again, bringing me closer, our lips a sliver away. "I don't want her. You know it. I know it. I never did."

"And I don't want him—not more than you . . . but we can't."

"Why the fuck can't we? I'm tired of denying what I feel for you. I don't give a fuck if other people think it's wrong. It felt right and I want it back."

I tried to pull away, but he held my arm. "Theo . . ."

"No—Chloe, don't say my name like that." He pulled one hand away to lower the strap of my tank top. I wasn't wearing a bra, and when he realized, his eyes dilated. "Every single day since you left, I have been miserable without you. I couldn't sleep for months, and if I did end up catching some sleep, I would dream about you. I know you're scared," he murmured against my lips. "I know you think we shouldn't be together again after what happened last time, but just like I said before we started the last time: Don't think about it. Don't *worry* about it. Let's just be us, Little Knight. Let's focus on *us*."

He watched my face carefully. I could only stare at him. I didn't know what to say, so I decided not to say anything at all. There were no words right now. He'd stolen them right off my tongue and put them out for both of us to hear.

Instead of speaking, I threw my arms around his neck and yanked him forward. He fell on top of me, our lips locked, and he unbuttoned and yanked my shorts down. Our lips fell apart when he snatched off my tank top.

All that was left was my panties, and he carefully slid them down, exposing me. All of me.

I was breathing so hard.

He was panting so deep.

He was so hungry for me.

"Look at this body," he whispered, sliding his palms between my thighs. "So perfect," he mumbled, lowering his face to my sex. "So sweet." He kissed the outside of my pussy and I bucked. He pressed a hand on my pelvis, shaking his head. "So fucking beautiful. *Fuck*, I've missed you."

With no hesitation at all, he slid his tongue between the slit and then sucked gently. I cried out, clutching the edge of the suede sofa, my back arching and my mind numb. I ached below as he teased and toyed with me, crying out even more when he slid his damp tongue inside me, drawing out my pleasure. This was happening so fast—too fast, all over again.

I glanced down, and his eyes were right on mine. He sucked on my clit, and my legs quaked around his head. He cupped my ass in his hands when my hips tilted up in the air, and he sank his face even deeper, eating me like he hadn't been fed in years.

"Oh my God, Theo," I sighed, sliding my fingers through his hair. I didn't mean to, but I hauled him even closer, and he groaned, causing a vibrating sensation between my thighs that shot me over the fucking moon.

I came. Hard. Harder than I had in years. That fast. *Goodness.*

He was the only one that could do this to me. He knew my body, and he knew it well. It was like he'd never forgotten how to please me, not even after all this time.

He pulled away, placing a kiss on the area right above my aching nub. "You've always been mine, Little Knight. You know it." He sat up and I did as well, panting raggedly. "I know it."

I yanked his jeans down when they were loose and his boxers next. His thick cock sprung free, and my core clenched with need. I looked up, running my hands over his thighs and wrapping them around his hips.

"Can I show you that I missed *you?*" I begged a little, and his eyes lit up like they were on fire.

He stroked my hair. "Yeah," he rasped. "Show me I'm not the only one feeling this way."

I nodded and then spread my lips, working them around his thick tip. He tensed, squeezing his hand in my hair, holding tight with each savory inch I slid into my mouth.

I looked up again, and his eyes were trained on me. He was breathing so fast and his cock was so hard, I swear he was about to come in my mouth already. But I knew he wouldn't.

He was a patient man.

That was one of the things I loved most about him.

I took his entire member into my mouth, and he palmed the back of my head, keeping me there for a moment before releasing me. I pulled back, inhaling before giving him the blowjob of a lifetime.

I wanted him to know I missed him.

I wanted him to know that he wasn't the only one feeling this way.

So I sucked. Faster. I pumped the base of his cock with one hand and he groaned loudly, pulling my hairband off and combing his fingers through my frizzy hair while cupping one side of my face. He thrust his hips forward and backwards, working up a light stroke. He was growing harder and harder, solid and heavy in my mouth, the pleasure dripping from his tip.

And then he jerked out, picked me up, and brought me down on the couch again. He was on top of me in an instant and then, before I knew it, he was *inside of me.*

He plunged so deep that my nails dug into his back and dragged all the way down to his hips.

He watched my face, absorbing every single sign of my pleasure.

"Take me back," he said, panting roughly. "Tell me you're mine, Little Knight. Tell me you want this again."

"I want it again," I whimpered. "I do."

"Say you still love me."

"I still love you."

"Say you still need me," he groaned, "'cause, shit, Chloe, *I fucking need you.*"

There was something about his words. Something about the way he said *need*. He needed me. He'd needed me for years now.

My walls clenched around him, and he felt it. He sighed, bringing his head down to suck on the tender skin at the crook of my neck. Our bodies were so close to each other's that I could feel his heartbeat.

"Shit, I'm about to come," he groaned. "It's been so long. Too fucking long."

And when he said that, I locked my legs around his waist. He had my wrists in his hands again, and he thrust faster. Harder. He was releasing all of the stress from the past.

This was make-up sex at its finest, and the best damn make-up sex I'd ever had.

We were making up for all the time we'd lost.

All the tears we had shed.

All the loneliness we felt without one another.

My head fell back and he feasted on the bend of my neck. His body tensed above me and then he stilled.

He let out another groan, deep and loud, with his mouth on my neck. His body shuddered repeatedly, and he thrust his hips forward three more times before he finally collapsed.

He panted wildly, still stuck in the moment, his forehead glued to my cheek. Sweat was everywhere, along with the smell of liberating ecstasy.

I turned my head when he lifted his, and when our eyes met, I couldn't believe what'd just happened.

After so many years . . .

It was still the same—we were the same. Honestly, it was even better than before.

"Why did I let you go?" I whispered, stroking the right half of his face. Tears rimmed my eyes as well as his.

"You didn't let me go. I've been here. I never fucking left you, babe."

My throat thickened with emotion as I dropped my hand and looked away. I had no choice but to unleash the tears.

He swiped each droplet away, then he said, "Chloe, look at me." I looked up and a smile graced his lips. "We were never done. You hear me?" His mouth came closer. "Look at what we just did—how fucking *powerful* that was. I haven't felt like this in years. Not since I was with you."

I nodded, just enough for him to see. I sat up to get a better look of his eyes. "Please don't tell me you want to divorce your wife because of me."

His lips pressed. He was ashamed to confirm it, but obviously it was true.

"Why? What if I would have rejected you? What if I would have said no?"

"You wouldn't have. I didn't come here to be turned down. Failure wasn't an option." He chuckled and I couldn't help but laugh. "I don't need to be with her anyway."

"We shouldn't sneak around behind Izzy again, Theo."

"We won't. I'll tell her."

"When?"

"As soon as I know you're actually *mine* again and not thinking about that fucker that stole you from me."

"He didn't steal me." I pulled my legs away and stood. "We just . . . got to know one another better. Same way you and your wife did."

"Stop calling her that," he muttered.

"What?" I threw my hands in the air. "She *is* your wife, Theo. You're still married and the divorce probably won't be final for months." Knowing that made my heart squeeze in my chest. Months seemed ridiculous. All of this felt like a damn dream.

He stood up when I turned away and stepped into my shorts. "You're upset," he noted.

I turned quickly to face him. "Of course I am. I was happy for you before, but now I'm just . . . envious of her, I guess." I waved a hand.

"Why, when I already told you I don't want her, but I want you?" He was utterly confused now.

"I don't know, okay?" I shrugged. "But I guess this is what I deserve after leaving the way I did."

He studied me as I slouched back down on the sofa. "Is that why you've been checking my *Facebook*?"

I jerked my head up, shocked. "How do you know that?"

He sat back down and turned my way, giving me his undivided attention.

"How did you know that?" I asked again, and he smirked.

"You liked one of my posts by accident. A picture of Izzy and me. It was a few months ago. It was also a public post. I made it my cover photo."

Embarrassment swallowed me whole. "Theo—I—"

"No need to explain." He folded his fingers. "I was doing the same thing."

Well that was a relief. "You were?"

He bobbed his head. "That's why I made an account. To look for you."

"Well, at least I don't seem like too much of a stalker now, but it's still pretty embarrassing."

He laughed. "I think I would be a little more upset if you *weren't* checking up on me." He watched my eyes carefully and then he sat back, pulling me closer. I rested my ear on his chest, and he kissed me on the top of the head.

"I want you back, Chloe." His voice was firm.

"And I want you, Theo. But wanting each other doesn't come easy. People will get hurt."

"Yeah, but we'll get through it. It's okay to be selfish sometimes, you know?" He tipped my chin so I could look at him. "Just don't run away this time." He grinned and I playfully smacked his chest.

"I can't make any promises on that one."

CHAPTER 11

THEO

It was nearing 3:00 a.m.

I was still in Chloe's house, but we were in bed now. I wrapped my arm around her middle, pulling her closer. I needed her close. I wanted the warmth only she could provide.

I craved another taste of her sweet, young pussy, but I knew it was best to wait it out. I didn't want to add too much pressure to the situation. I could tell she was thinking about what we'd just done. I hoped she wasn't regretting it.

She had to have been thinking about it. I was, lying in the same bed this fucker slept in with her. I hated the thought of it, but stuck it out for Chloe. It was late, and she was still awake. Something deep down made me wonder if staying up this late was a normal thing for her.

"This seems . . . strange," she said quietly as she rolled over to look at me.

"How so?"

"I don't know . . . us getting back together. It was way too easy, don't you think?"

I pushed up on my elbow and she rolled over so I could look down at her. "Should I have made it harder?"

"No," she blurted out.

"Good. 'Cause I don't believe in playing games. I know what I want. Why fight it?"

She shrugged, bashful now.

"You're too used to him playing games with your heart. That's all. He's a bullshitter. I'm not, and you know it. Real men don't do shit like what he does."

She scowled up at me, but said nothing. Her lips twisted as if she were thinking about it. She knew I was right.

"What?" I asked.

"He left because he's not over Janet."

That, I must admit, caught me by total surprise.

She sat up on one elbow with me, tossing her hair over her shoulder. "He called off the engagement because he still thinks about her."

I looked away, towards the streetlights that were filtering in through the window. "So do I, but I know I can't dwell on it. Nothing will bring her back."

"She was his first love."

"And she was mine too," I snapped. "Probably before he was even born."

She looked me straight in the eyes, unflinching. "I didn't mean it that way, Theo."

"I know you didn't." Turning over, I sat on the edge of the bed, exhaling deeply. "It's not that he's not over her. He's just a fucking coward. Same as I was. He's not ready to let go of the memories or the idea of her." I swiped a finger across my nose. "What he doesn't realize is that he doesn't have to. It's okay to keep the memories. What wouldn't be right is if he acts like she never even existed. At least I told you when I was thinking about her. I could talk to you because you understood."

"I know," she murmured.

I looked over my shoulder at her. Her hair was smoother now from the shower she took. I could smell her vanilla scent from where I sat. She smelled good—sweet enough to eat again.

"Should I go?" I asked.

Her head shook. "No. You don't have to. You can stay if you want."

Reaching over, I stroked the apple of her cheek and then tucked a lock of her hair behind her ear. Her smile was soft, but tired. "I think I should go. Give you some time to think about all of this." I stood, walking to her side of the bed. My lips pressed on her forehead and I sighed.

Her skin was so soft, and her hair smelled so damn good. I missed this girl. I missed her so damn much. She honestly had no fucking clue how much.

"I'll text you in a few hours. We can go for lunch later," I said.

She bobbed her head with a smile. "I'd like that."

"Wish I could pick you up on Ol' Charlie." I smirked.

She giggled. "Ahh, the memories."

Her laugh tickled every fiber in my body. Grabbing her hands, I picked her up and reeled her in, cupping her full ass in my hands as she fought her amusement.

"Theo," she giggled with warning.

I grinned, looking down at her. "What? Can't help myself." I draped my arms around her waist instead.

"I missed your laugh." I kissed the tip of her nose. "I missed every-thing about you. See how fucking cheesy you make me?" When she picked up her head, I caught her lips. Her arms fastened around the back my neck, chest pressing on mine. I could feel her pebbled nipples through the fabric of our shirts.

She moaned lightly, and that moan alone was enough to make me want to take her again. I was a little rough earlier, but I couldn't help myself or hold back.

It'd been so long.

I'd wanted her pussy for years, pretending Sheila was Chloe just to temporarily satisfy myself. Chloe's pussy was remarkable in every way—impossible to forget.

Wet.

Soft.

Snug.

She fit around me perfectly.

Next time I was going to take it slow.

I would make it last a little longer.

I would be gentler.

"You'd better go," she teased, running a finger across my bottom lip. "I wouldn't want you to end up not making it back to Izzy."

She licked her bottom lip, only fueling the raging fire in my jeans.

"I'll be back tomorrow."

"I know you will." She placed one last kiss on my lips and then pulled her arms away.

"Go back to bed. I can walk myself out. I know you're exhausted."

She slid beneath the sheets again, rolling onto her side, still looking up at me. "Drive safely, Theo."

I bent down, placing a kiss on the apple of her cheek. "I will. Sleep tight, Little Knight."

It was too late for Isabelle to be awake . . . or should I say too early?

I unlocked the door to my suite and walked in, peering towards the bedroom. The light was off. She was most likely sleeping.

Dropping my keys on the counter, I let out a deep sigh of both relief and euphoria, walking towards the mini-fridge to get a bottle of water.

As I cracked the bottle open, I heard a door squeak on the hinges and looked back. Izzy was walking out of the bathroom, rubbing her eyes. Her hair was a mess, and she wore a knee length shirt that said "Mornings Suck".

I took a quick sip and turned to look her.

I'm sure she wouldn't have noticed me if I was sitting, but I was standing right by the window, the moon shining right down on me.

"Dad?" she called.

"Yeah, sweetie?"

"What are you doing up? It's almost four in the freakin' morning."

"Just got here, Iz."

She stepped closer. "You were at Dane's for that long?" Her eyes stretched a little bit. She was scrutinizing me now.

"We had a lot of catching up to do," I told her. *Fuck. Why lie? Just tell the fucking truth. I promised Chloe . . .*

"Oh. I guess that makes sense. It's been, like, five years or something, right?" She yawned. "I hope you aren't hung over in the morning because I am not taking care of you. Drink some water."

I chuckled. "I won't be. I'll be fine. Go get some rest."

She bobbed her head, her messy ponytail bouncing up and down. She turned off the bathroom light switch, and then turned around, shuffling back into the bedroom and shutting the door behind her.

I pulled my shirt off and set up the sleeper sofa next. As I crashed in my boxers, I couldn't help thinking about Chloe.

It was a risk—me showing up there and not knowing if he was around—but it didn't matter.

A real man takes what he wants.

A real man *knows* what he wants.

And a real man will never give up on what he knows he needs.

I wished shit with us was simpler. I wished that I'd never given Sheila that ring. I never should have acted out of spite. Deep down, it was payback for Chloe. For leaving me. For abandoning me.

I thought, *well if she doesn't want me, someone else will.* And I was right, but it was a big fucking mistake.

Now, I didn't know what Sheila was going to do. I didn't exactly wait to hear what she had to say. I saw no point, and was kind of glad I didn't stick around when I received the hundred voicemails about how she "hated" me and wasn't going to settle with the negotiations.

She needed to cool down. She said she was going to fly to Florida and be with her sister because she couldn't stand to be in the house. But I knew even if she signed, she wasn't going to do so until she took everything I owned.

I owned a business. I made a better income than her. I hoped she would be a decent adult and treat the situation respectfully.

Being in Bristle Wave brought back so many memories, so many things that I tried to forget. Chloe wasn't too far away. My Little Knight wanted me back just as much as I wanted her, and this time I wasn't letting her walk away, no matter the circumstances we were in.

CHAPTER 12

THEO

Pans clanked. Water turned on and off. Music was blasting from speakers.

I groaned, rolling over. Izzy was in the small kitchen, tampering with the stovetop. She had a red bowl in her hand, her hair piled on top of her head. From this view, she looked just like her mother.

I sat up, rubbing the sleep out of my eyes. "Iz, what time is it?" I asked, voice dry and raspy.

"8:30," she responded with a grin. A grin because she knew how much I hated mornings.

"What the hell are you doing anyway?" I countered, pushing off the couch and stretching.

She was about to answer, but then her eyes dropped down to the area between my legs and they grew wide. Her eyebrows shot up as her face turned cherry red and she yelled, "*Eww!* Oh my God, Dad! What the hell! Put it away!"

She turned her back to me just as quickly as she yelled. I looked down, immediately cupping my morning wood. *Shit!*

Izzy was facing the stove, doing her best to laugh it off, but I'm sure she was shuddering with disgust more than anything. I picked up a pair of sweatpants and covered up, marching towards the bathroom. My eyes were still wide when I met at the door and tugged the pants on. "You weren't supposed to see that," I stated, voice hesitant.

Izzy took a side-glance but then snatched her eyes away as if she would catch sight of it again. She tried not to laugh—she really did. I was so fucking embarrassed. Too embarrassed to even speak on it, better yet tell her to stop fucking laughing at me.

"I knew I should have gotten my own room," she choked out, holding the bowl of pancake batter close. She still wasn't looking at me, and I couldn't even blame her.

She started up a nervous giggle—not an *oh-my-gosh-this-is-so-funny* giggle but an *oh-my-fucking-God-I-just-saw-my-dad's-boner-and-am-so-fucking-grossed-out* kind of giggle. I hoped she wouldn't go around thinking about that shit all day. Fuck.

"Yeah, yeah," I mumbled, opening the bathroom door. "Just . . . pretend you didn't see that. Shit—Iz, I can't even talk about it with you! Just don't look at me for the rest of the day. All right? Good."

She shook her head, her face still flamed red. "You don't even have to worry about that, Dad. I'm not sure there's much I can say to justify the awkward as hell situation we're in right now anyway." She looked sideways again, but not fully at me. I could tell. She was fucking mortified. "Gah, this is just like that time I walked in on you and Mom. I swore I would always knock first from now on. I guess I couldn't really knock this time though. It was just like *BOOM*, there it is! Jesus Christ," she scoffed, finally peering at me. "I'm still grossed out here. This was not how I planned on starting my morning!"

I held up a hand. "What are you trying to do? Let the whole hotel know? Look, forget it ever even happened, all right? And stop looking at me! Finish up the pancakes!"

"Yeah. Okay. Sure thing, Pops," she snickered, shaking her head swiftly.

I walked into the bathroom and released a heavy breath, silently laughing as I started up the shower.

As the water ran, I gave Chloe a text, letting her know all about my embarrassing mishap.

She responded right back to my surprise.

Little Knight: LOL. Wow. I bet she is flipping shit right now!

I didn't wake up with a hard on for no damn reason. I dreamed of her . . . again.

I had to rub the image of my own fucking daughter seeing me at a vulnerable state out of my head, but when I focused my thoughts on Chloe, it helped. Just thinking about her sweet pussy, her scent that was still on me was enough.

I dropped my boxers, got into the shower, and peered down at my swollen cock. Gripping it in hand, I began stroking lightly. Slowly. Remembering how her soft tongue and mouth felt wrapped around me. How she sucked me like she owned my cock—like she never wanted it away from me again.

Water trickled through my hair as I pressed my left hand on the white tile, stroking harder now. Faster.

I was close . . .

Until the words, _"Eww! Oh my God, Dad! What the hell?"_ blared in my head like a foghorn.

I yanked my hand away, pressing it on the tile wall.

Nope.

I couldn't fucking do it.

I guess that's what happens when you end up in such an awkward situation in front of your kid and it involves your junk.

You can't escape that shit.

Fuck me.

"All right, Dad." After breakfast, Izzy had the handle of her suitcase in hand and a pair of sunglasses perched on top of her head that kept her hair tucked back. "I'm out of here." She smiled broadly at me as I followed her to the door.

"I'll walk you down." I grabbed her suitcase. I was glad she wasn't making a big deal about what happened this morning, though she was still sniggering while we ate breakfast.

"Are you sure you want to stay here?" she asked me when we made it out to the parking lot. She was side-eying me, her lips pressed thin. She was onto me. I knew it.

"It's been a while, Iz. I've missed it here. Feels good to catch a break."

"Yeah." She breathed a dry laugh, popping the trunk of her rental. I tossed in the suitcase and when it was closed, she came up to me and threw her arms around me. I kissed the top of her head and hugged her back. "Wish me luck?"

"I wish you all the luck in the world, Izzy Bear. You'll do great. I know it."

She beamed as she pulled back. I watched her walk to the door and pull it open. When she was inside and had the car started, I tapped on the window.

"What?" she asked.

"Put that seatbelt on."

She laughed. "Sheesh, Dad. I was about to."

"Drive safe. Call me when you get there."

She buckled in and gripped the wheel. "I will. You be safe, Dad, okay?"

There was a look in her eyes before she dropped her sunglasses. I couldn't pinpoint it, but there was definitely some concern there. She was wary about leaving me here alone in Bristle Wave. Here, where she said she hated me. Here, where she knew I'd fallen for another woman that wasn't her mother. A woman who just so happened to be her best friend.

"I will," I assured.

She blew me a kiss, and then drove off. I watched her go until my phone chimed.

I thought it would be Chloe.

I was wrong.

It was Sheila again.

After getting dressed in decent clothes, I heard my phone vibrating on the counter. This time, it wasn't Sheila, but the person I wanted to hear from most at the moment.

A text message.

Little Knight: Still doing lunch? Want to see you again. I'll cook.

Me: Yes, we'll still have lunch.
But you won't cook. I will. I'll bring something by. See you in an hour.

Little Knight: Already, you spoil me

Damn right.

I made my way to the store, already with a meal in mind. As the groceries were getting rung up, my phone buzzed in my back pocket. I fished it out and saw it was Sheila. Again.

What the fuck does she want?

I ignored the call and then sent a message stating I was busy. I knew she wasn't calling about the papers. She was calling to try to start something with me. I knew Sheila, and if she wanted it done, she'd just mail it all back, not call repeatedly. Until she agreed that this was necessary, we wouldn't be talking.

I pulled up to Chloe's house and there was a white van parked at the curb. I took out the groceries and walked to the door, knocking. She answered in no time, sporting a grin.

"What's up with the van?" I asked, walking in.

"The patio roof is leaking. Getting it fixed," she called behind me. I walked into the kitchen and saw the repairman on a ladder, patching it up.

"You know I could have fixed that for you, right?" I called out to her.

"I know, but you have to cook, remember? Plus, I called him weeks ago."

"And they're just now coming today?"

She shrugged and then sank her teeth into her bottom lip. I set the groceries down on the counter and then turned to reel her into my arms.

"It hasn't even been twenty-four hours and I want you again," I murmured in her ear. I felt the shiver hit her. Her mouth pressed on my chin.

"Did you talk to Izzy?" she asked, already breathless.

I drew back a little and gave a small shake of the head. She was clearly disappointed because she pulled away in an instant.

"Theo, why not? You have to tell her. We can't sneak around like before. You know that."

"I know, I know. But she's going off to her audition." I adjusted my jeans. "I don't want her thinking about us when she needs to be focused, Chloe. Let her get that role or believe she did her best, and then I'll talk to her. *We'll* talk to her."

Her lips pursed and then twisted. She knew I was right. Her shoulders relaxed and I stepped forward, planting a smooth kiss on the center of her forehead.

"I'll tell her. I promise. Don't worry, all right? It won't be like last time. You don't have anything to fear, and quite frankly, you don't have much to lose anymore."

"But you do," she replied softly.

I didn't know what to say to that, so I said nothing at all. I turned for the groceries instead. "I will figure it all out. Just trust me. All right?"

She wrapped her arms around me and held me from behind, resting her cheek on my back. "I do trust you, Theo. You know that. I have since I was a teenager," she laughed.

That was true.

I turned in her arms and cupped her ass in my hands, picking her up and planting that same beautiful ass on top of the counter. Like an addict in need of more, I kissed my girl like she was a drug, stepping between her legs.

"Don't worry too much," I whispered when our mouths barely parted. "Just let me kiss you right now. Let me make all that lost time up to you, Knight."

She moaned when my tongue passed over hers. I groaned when her fingers trickled through my hair and she tugged lightly.

I was hard all over again. Ready. Her touch. Her body. Her heart and soul. Everything about her drove me fucking crazy.

How the fuck did I let all of this go before?

Why didn't I fight harder? Why did I walk away?

She tugged me closer, sucking on my tongue, still gripping my hair tight. I gripped the ends of her hair and craned her head back so my mouth could reach her neck. I sucked on the curve of it, thrusting between her legs now, breathing raggedly as my other hand cupped her ass.

"Fuck," I breathed against the hollow of her throat. "You feel so good, Chloe."

Just then, a throat cleared behind us and I pulled back a little, looking towards the repairman. He had on gray overalls, his chubby cheeks red as hell.

I tried hard not to laugh as I stepped back and let Chloe hop down from the counter. Of course she was embarrassed as hell, her cheeks rosy red too.

"I am so, so sorry about that," she apologized with her hands in the air, as if the man would run at any given moment.

"No worries." The man was clearly lying. He was either bothered by it or secretly turned on. I kept my groin pointed in the opposite direction of them. I was hard as fuck and I'm sure he knew it, but I didn't give a damn. "I . . . uh . . . have the roof all patched up. There were small holes here and there but everything should be okay." He glanced over at me, swallowing hard. "If it starts to leak again let me know—well, let the company know. I'm sure they'll send someone out here in a jiff."

I sniffed as I adjusted my jeans and bent down to search for the frying pans.

"Thank you, Bobby. I appreciate that," Chloe responded, mostly ignoring me and my silent remark of snide.

Bobby left with a bob of his head and not one look back, and Chloe rushed my way, tittering. "Oh my gosh, Theo! He was so embarrassed! *I'm* so embarrassed!"

I finally bellowed with laughter, resting my lower back on the edge of the counter. "Must have liked what he saw, huh?"

She tossed her hair back, eyes full of life. "Maybe, but I know one thing for sure: Bobby won't be the one coming back to repair my roof if there's a problem."

We stared at each other, but neither of us could help it. We both broke out in laughter again.

CHAPTER 13

CHLOE

"You're still a great cook," I said after sipping my Diet Coke.

He half-shrugged, chewing the Cajun chicken pasta. "Never stopped."

"Even when you married . . . well, you know?"

He shook his head, fighting a smile. "Nope."

I fidgeted in my seat then, placing my can down. "Do you miss her? I mean, I know you want us to get back on the same page, but what about her? You have to feel *something*."

"I do feel something," he stated calmly, dropping his fork and sitting back in his seat.

"What?" I asked, nervous for the answer.

"Guilty." He exhaled. "I left the papers without facing her like a man. But we'd talked about it before. She kept trying to ignore the subject, calling me crazy, tired—treating me like I was an idiot, really. I was tired of getting ignored so I just went and got it set up.

"When I left the papers on the counter, I knew exactly how she would feel when she saw them. I personally hate hurting people, especially women." He pushed a hand through his hair. "I . . . well . . . I don't know. I just wanted to tell her the truth because her not knowing the truth was eating me alive. I have a feeling she already knows there's someone else on my mind, she's just too stubborn to hear it, and so I kept it to myself. She's a decent woman—doesn't deserve to be neglected because I'm thinking about someone else."

"Wow," I murmured.

"She's upset now, but I think she'll come around. She'll understand this is the wisest choice."

I was quiet for a moment. Watching him—contemplating whether I wanted to know the answer to the question that was on the tip of my tongue.

"Do you love her?"

He blinked slowly. "I care about her, so I guess that means I do. But I'm not *in* love with her. Never fell in love either." He reached across the table for my hands. "You already know who owns the reins of my heart."

I bobbed my head. "I know. I'm just curious."

"And what about you? If that motherfucker walked through that door right now, would you tell me to leave?" He bobbed his head towards the door.

"What? Of course not!"

"You sure?" he mused. "'Cause I would understand. The awkwardness and all. Plus, this is his house too."

"He's not going to come back—at least not anytime soon. He hasn't called in days. I think it would be even more awkward for him to come back after telling me how he truly felt, and also calling off the engagement."

"A fucking dumbass is what he is," he scoffed.

I rolled my eyes, fighting a laugh. His phone started ringing and he pulled his hands away, digging in his pocket for it.

"Let me take this. It's one of the guys calling from work."

I nodded. "Yeah, go ahead. I'll clean up."

He walked around the table and kissed my cheek before answering the phone and making his way to the living room.

I sighed as I picked up some of the dishes. I didn't know what the hell we were doing. Right now, *I* was the other woman—the one that his wife probably knew about and probably despised. These new terms were no better than when I was sleeping with him behind Izzy's back.

I didn't know whether Sterling was going to come back or not. Deep down, I hoped that he wouldn't, and if he did it was probably going to be so he could get his things and never speak to me again.

My Theodore was back, but he was acting as if everything was okay between us—that he had it handled, but I couldn't believe it just yet. I trusted him, I did, but this was happening way too fast and things were way too easy for us right now.

I knew a storm was coming, and it was going to be a fucking hurricane.

It was only a matter of when, and because I loved him as much as I did—because he was the love of my life and I would have done anything for him—I was going to take the risk and walk through the eye of the hurricane with him.

I refused to let go again, not because I was lonely or afraid or stupid, but because what we had was real. What we had couldn't be denied, and I could no longer block the cold, hard truth.

I couldn't fight against it or run away anymore.

I felt alive with him.

Better.

Happier.

Sterling couldn't even make me feel half of what Theo made me feel. And that was the truth.

Later that night, Theo had grabbed one of my movies from the shelf and popped it into the Blu-ray player. I was between his legs, my ear on his chest, my arm wrapped around his torso.

He was quiet since the movie had started.

I couldn't tell if he was actually watching it, or thinking about something else. Closer to the middle of the movie, I finally looked up at him and rubbed his shoulder.

"Why are you so quiet?" I whispered.

He looked down at me with warm, gentle brown eyes. Holding me tighter, he sighed and shook his head left to right.

"I'm wondering if it's too soon to ask you something," he sighed again.

I sat up a little, watching his face carefully. "Ask me what?"

"About leaving from here with me for a few days." He opened his arms and I sat up straight. "I want you to pack some clothes and come with me," he said.

"Where?" I asked.

"I have a few things to do in San Francisco for work, but I don't want to leave you. Summer break is coming soon for you, right? You don't have much work to do at the school right now. I think you deserve a little break."

Oh. I pressed my lips. I was quiet for a moment, looking down at his lap. He tilted my chin so our eyes could meet again.

"If I'm rushing anything, Chloe, we don't have to—"

"No—no." I grabbed his hand, bringing the warmth of it up to my cheek. "You're not rushing anything. I was only thinking how nice it would be to get away from here."

"It would. And you haven't been there before. It'll be a fun and new experience for you."

I nodded. "Okay. Fine." I sat up with a grin. "When are we going to go?"

He smirked. "Two days."

"Such short notice. Are you sure you want me tagging along, Mr. Black?"

"I wouldn't have it any other way, Little Knight."

I laughed, wrapping my arm around him again and leaning in. I pecked his lips and he exhaled, looking down at me as my lips traveled down his neck and to his collarbone.

Before I knew it, he was on top of me with my hands pinned above my head, and the rock in his pants pressing between my thighs. I sighed when his soft lips came to my neck and he kissed me gently.

He took his time, leaving traces of his lips all over my neck.

Tilting his head up, he met my eyes and his mouth pressed on mine. He ground between my legs, making himself harder by the second. I fidgeted, but he still had me pinned to the couch.

"I need to get you away from here," he whispered in my ear. "I want us to escape like we did before. I want us alone—completely alone. No distractions. Nothing to interfere. Just us, baby."

I bobbed my head. "I want that, too."

"I missed the hell out of you, Chloe. I don't care how many times I say it or how annoying it gets hearing it, it's the truth. I missed you." He released my wrists and when he sat up, I leaned forward to unbuckle his belt and then unzip his jeans.

"Whoops." I bit back a smile.

His mouth twitched when he looked down. It didn't take much after that. He knew I was ready.

I knew I was ready.

He shoved my skirt up, tugged my panties down, and then pushed his jeans down. His pants were around his ankles, so I could feel the jean fabric as he bent down. But what I felt more was his cock sinking inside me. Inch by inch, going deeper and deeper. My back bowed, but he didn't let me go too far.

He cupped the back of my neck and worked up a light thrust, his warm breath trickling past the shell of my ear. "Whoops," he mimicked, his voice deep and husky, and I looked up, unable to fight the hoarse laugh.

He pressed his forehead to mine and it was that gesture alone that made me cave. I kissed him whole. I never wanted to let go. I mean, I had him back. He was right in my arms—he was *inside* of me.

He was claiming my body and heart all over again, and I couldn't deny it. I had always been Theo's. Even during our days apart, I was his and he was mine. It's insane to think that nothing about that had changed.

We still loved hard.

We still *fucked* hard.

We still stared at one another with so much passion and ferocity that it would have been impossible for anyone to ignore. There were obstacles we had to overcome, but they could wait. Because right now, in this moment, I was taking *my* man back.

I was holding on tight. I was moaning and sighing and panting and grinding along with him. I was sticky, hot, and wet, and we were one —one all over again.

Around 2:00 a.m., while we were lying in bed, I heard a phone ring. It wasn't mine, but Theo's. He groaned and rolled over.

Picking it up, he blew a heavy breath and silenced the ringer.

"Who was it? Izzy?" I asked, but I could tell by his hunched shoulders that it wasn't her.

"Sheila," he responded dully.

"Oh." I sealed my lips and stared up at the ceiling, unsure of what to say. I couldn't say I was pleased to know she was calling this late at night.

"She's been calling for the past few days. She's trying to talk me out of it," he continued. At least he was telling me the truth.

"Why don't you just answer?" I avoided his eyes when he turned his head to look at me.

"I don't want to be talked out of it. I just want her to sign the papers and be done with it." His voice was a little irritated as he said that.

"She loves you, Theo. I don't think she will just be able to be done with it."

I heard him swallow and then he lied back down. He rested a hand behind his head and stared up at the ceiling with me.

"When we go back, do you think she'll show up?" I whispered. He'd told me earlier that we were going to be staying at their house. I didn't like it, but I figured since he was spending so much time in the house that Sterling and I once shared that I could spare a night or two at his.

"I doubt it," he answered. "She's in Florida with her sister."

"But what if she does?" I pushed.

He looked over rapidly, his eyebrows drawing together. "Then I'll handle it, Chloe." He rolled over, putting his hand on my waist and tugging me closer. "I know what you're thinking, that I'll change my mind about us—or that she'll get me to change my mind. I won't. There's nothing to worry about when it comes to that."

"Are you going to sell your house?" I murmured.

I could see his teeth glisten from the moonlight. His beautiful, full smile. "Would that make you happy?"

I shrugged, but really I knew it would deep down.

"It will be sold eventually. I won't need it."

"Where will you be staying?"

He planted a kiss on my forehead. "Here, in Bristle Wave with you."

I don't know why his statement made me feel so warm and fuzzy, but it did satisfy me, even if just for the night.

He stroked my cheek, putting himself between my legs. "Stop worrying. She won't show up. It will only be for two nights, max. We'll be in and out."

"Okay." I craned my neck so my lips could reach his. He pulled back so I couldn't touch them.

I scowled.

"Do you trust me, Knight?"

"Yes, I trust you," I responded.

His hand ran down my waist and then around to cup my ass. "I only want you. You know that, right?"

"Yes."

"And you know that everything else we have to figure out will be figured out, right? Together?"

"I know. I'm just a little nervous. I guess I'm not ready to face it yet."

He watched me for several seconds, scanning me for the truth.

Then, he finally gave me the kiss I was craving, but with a little tongue. He held the right side of my face and I pushed my groin into his, clutching his hip, keeping him close to my body.

He groaned, and when our kiss came to a brief pause, he murmured, "That's my Little Knight."

CHAPTER 14

CHLOE

Two days later and I was packing up for my trip to San Francisco before the sun had completely risen.

I took Mr. Lint up on the offer of hiring a substitute for the next few days. He was surprised, especially since we only had one week left of school, but the schedule for my students was easy. Simple. They were going to be watching a lot of movies, making popcorn treats, eating ice cream, and answering simple questions.

It was the last week of school, for Christ's sake. I didn't believe in such hard work for the start of summer. They were only kids, and most of their grades were great.

I told Mr. Lint I wasn't feeling well and might have had a stomach flu, and that I needed those days off to recover. He understood and didn't ask many questions at all, to my surprise.

"I have to make sure I'm back for at least the last day of school. I want to see them off, you know?" I picked up my suitcase and started packing the clothes I'd pulled out of the closet.

The sun had just risen. I was so accustomed to waking up early for school that being up before sunrise was a habit. Theo had stayed the night, but he needed to get ready himself so I knew he was going to be heading back to his hotel soon.

He was standing between the frames of my bedroom door, leaning on it by the shoulder. His arms were folded as he watched me, a small smirk playing on his lips. Pushing off the frame, he walked my way and picked up one of my folded sundresses.

"We'll be back before that. You can finish up what you have to do here with your students and then I'll have something else planned for us afterwards. The perfect start to summer. I'm not letting you spend all your time in this house with all *his* shit here."

I shrugged, avoiding his eyes.

"I know you feel guilty about it," he stated. "I know you too well, and I know it's bothering you."

"It would be wrong not to feel guilty, don't you think?" I finally looked up at him. He handed me the dress. I accepted it, placing it in the suitcase and then going back for my sandals.

"Maybe," he mumbled.

I tossed the sandals inside and then turned to grip his shoulders. "But if you think that I'm going to let my guilt stop us from having a good time, then you're wrong, Mr. Black. I'm still going to San Francisco with you, and I very much look forward to what you have planned for us when we get back." I pecked his cheek.

He nodded. "Good." He pulled me closer, his palms drifting down my waist. "That's what I like to hear." He bobbed his head towards my suitcase. "Finish packing. I have to run to the hotel to get some stuff, but when I get back, we can catch some breakfast and then we'll be set to leave."

"Okay. Sounds good."

He grabbed my hand and kissed the back of it.

I burned inside, beaming up at him. I didn't want to pull away and neither did he. But he did eventually, and I watched him leave the bedroom in his dark wash jeans and black T-shirt.

I looked out of the window and saw him hop into his car. And when he left, I couldn't believe the instant desolation I felt. He was only going to be gone for thirty minutes, at most, but every time he walked away it reminded me of how I felt without him.

I shook my head, laughing as I went to the bathroom to gather my toiletries. I was still acting like that college girl.

It was a seven-hour drive from Bristle Wave to San Francisco. As I rode, I was still a little worried about the whole idea, though I refused to tell Theo that.

What if Sheila showed up while we were there? What if she was *already* there?

I fidgeted in the passenger seat several times. The leather was nice, but I just couldn't get comfortable.

A hand landed on mine and I picked my head up, meeting Theo's gentle brown gaze. "You're worrying too much, Chloe."

"Am I?" I watched him carefully before sighing. "How are you so calm about this?"

"Because I know she isn't going to come back. Trust me, she would make it known. I'm only checking in on a few things and packing some of my stuff. That's it. We'll only be there for two nights and then we can go back home to Bristle Wave, where *we* belong."

I liked the sound of that, but even more so I loved how he used the words "we" and "home." It was strange how he knew exactly what I was thinking without me having to say it.

Perhaps I did suck at hiding my emotions.

"I guess I'm just thinking about all the bad things that could happen instead of the good. Like her showing up . . . or maybe she's coming just as we are about to go and she sees us leaving the house together."

"She already knows about you," he informed me, and I whipped my head up, as if I didn't already know that. But the way he said it was different. Like she knew more than just my name.

He pulled his hand away to grip the wheel. The smooth ripple of

the tires on the road proved that he kept them and the car in mainte-
nance often.

"She knows my name and *more?*" I probed. "Like what?"

"That you were Izzy's best friend . . . and that we did things
together to end that friendship. I caught her reading Izzy's diary once.
She asked me about it but I didn't tell her much about it. I lied. Said it
just happened."

"Oh, my God. This is insane then! A death wish!"

He chucked a laugh. "Look, I know you think she's a childish
woman after what we dealt with before, but trust me, she's no fool."

"Well, how do you know that for sure?" I asked and I was utterly
curious. "You hardly knew her—at least, not like how you know me."

He side-eyed me, caught off guard by my statement. His lips
pressed thin and he was quiet again.

When he finally spoke, I was relieved. "I know her enough to know
she wouldn't jeopardize anything—especially her life. She'll move on.
She's six years younger. She has time to find real love."

I didn't respond to that. How could I respond to that? He knew her
a lot more than I ever could, but something still made me wonder if
he was saying that just to make me feel better. He didn't seem so sure
himself.

I stared at the endless road ahead, placing my hands in my lap.

"Let's focus on us," Theo murmured, his hand coming close. "Let's
stay positive." It traveled up and he squeezed my upper thigh. When I
looked over at him, he had a mischievous smile on his lips.

I couldn't help my laugh. "Okay. We'll focus on us."

"That was the promise, right?" He inclined a smooth eyebrow.

"It was." I smiled way too hard before making my next statement.
"I guess next time you'll have to punish me for breaking that promise."

He laughed, a genuine, deep, and sexy laugh. "Now that's something I'm looking forward to."

———————

A hand rubbed my arm.

"Chloe?"

I jolted awake and looked toward the driver's seat. A light smile swept across Theo's lips. His hair was a little messier now, like he'd been running his fingers through it, most likely out of sheer boredom or impatience during the drive.

"We're here?" My words came out in a croak.

I cleared my throat when he nodded.

I looked from him to the house in front of us. It was painted a blue-gray, with white shutters, a cement stoop, and a white guardrail that led up to the wide, red door.

The sun was set now, but I could make out everything: the well-kept bushes and pedicured grass, the bed of dahlias outlining the guardrails. It was beautiful; the perfect home for a married couple. It was almost *too* beautiful.

"Come on." Theo climbed out of the car and shut the door behind him. I pushed out gradually, still staring ahead, unable to pull away.

So, this was the home he shared with her. I must admit, it was lovely, and I envied her even more for it. Able to come home to a place like this, and share it with a man like *him*. That must have felt great, knowing he was home waiting for her, knowing he was probably whipping up one of his delicious meals to share over dinner.

Jealousy seized me, clenching tight in my gut.

An arm draped around my shoulders and Theo pulled me in close, loosening that ball in my belly, but only a little. "You gonna stand out here the whole time or come in?" He grinned down at me, revealing those perfect dimples.

I put on a light smile for him, wrapping my arm around his waist. "Let's go, Mr. Black."

He held me snug and close as we made our way up to the stoop. He took out his keys and released me to unlock the door. When it was open, I felt a swarm of anxiety shoot through me.

Inside. We were really going inside.

I took in a sharp breath as I walked past him. When I was far enough inside, he shut the door behind us and then turned to punch a number into the beeping alarm system.

"It was a long drive. I know those gas station snacks didn't fill you up." He stepped around me and scratched the top of his head. He was nervous about this too—trying to avoid the big elephant in the room, I could tell. He only scratched his head or jaw when he was apprehensive. "You hungry or anything?"

"Sure." I grabbed his hand. "But tell me something . . ."

"What's that?" he asked, stepping closer and looking down into my eyes.

"You're nervous too . . . aren't you?"

"Somewhat."

"Is it because you're afraid she'll show up, or because right now we're in the home you shared with her and you don't know how I'll take it?"

He smirked. "You're too smart for your own damn good, you know that?"

I put on a playful, smug grin. "Just asking."

"I believe it's the latter. I'm not so much worried about her returning as much as I am about you being here." He tipped my chin and placed a warm, full kiss on my lips. "I want to know everything you're thinking, you understand? If you feel uncomfortable in anyway, you let me know. I'll do what I can to accommodate you. You know that."

"I'll try and keep an open mind. Wouldn't be the first time I've done things with you in the home you used to share with a wife." *God, that sounded so bad.*

"No, it wouldn't." He drew me in with a hand gripping my ass, our groins meshing, mouths close, and eyes focused each other's lips. "But I really wish you'd stop throwing that in my face. You could have been my wife a long time ago, and you know it." He caught my bottom lip between his teeth and then released it. "This time, don't run, Chlo. Face the trials with me."

I nodded, but I couldn't pull away from his mouth. I wanted him to do that again. And again. And a hundred more times.

"You want me to kiss you right now, don't you?" he tested, voice like smooth velvet.

I nodded again, quicker this time.

"I bet you do, baby." A smooth laugh vibrated throughout his entire body and then he picked me up, allowing our lips to collide. I draped my arms around the back of his neck and he spun around, storming down the hallway and into the living room.

I didn't pull my lips away. I refused to break the kiss. I absorbed everything he gave, every passing of his tongue. My back landed on something hard, and when I opened my eyes, I realized we were in the kitchen.

I looked over and I was on a counter. An island counter.

Theo worked hard to pull my shorts and panties off as I cupped his face and kissed his forehead. His mouth traveled down, from my chin, to my throat, and then between my breasts. He kissed me there with his soft lips, and then continued down, kissing my pelvis and the valley between my thighs.

Without any words at all, he spread my legs apart and buried his face into my pussy. He clutched my hips and hauled me towards the edge of the counter, tilting my hips so he could eat me in full.

I gasped as I held the edge of the counter and felt the moans he made between my thighs. The vibrations reverberated throughout my entire body, his tongue skimming my nub. I panted raggedly, one hand shooting down and threading through his thick, silky bed of hair.

This . . . this would never get old. Ever.

"Taste so good, Chloe," he groaned as he came back up, trailing kisses up the length of my body. He hovered above me, and I felt his cock poking at my entrance. "I'll take you here first."

He gripped my wrists and pulled me up so I could sit up straight. When my ass was hanging off the counter edge, he pressed between my legs and I showed no resistance at all. He was inside me, and I couldn't help but gape.

He felt so big.

He noticed my reaction and tilted his head, bringing his mouth to the crook of my neck. His strokes built up quickly, and our panting increased. My hands clutched his T-shirt, and I thrust my hips closer, driving him deeper.

"Shit, Chloe. Why do you always feel so fucking good," he asked in between panting breaths. His hands came down and wrapped around my ass. He picked me up and turned so my back could hit the wall, grinding deep and full, and I moaned louder, feeling every inch as he slid in.

"I had a dream about this," he muttered, thrusting. "Right here. Me and you, against this very wall. I was making the sweetest love to you. I was making you *mine*," he sighed, pressing his forehead on mine. "And you were loving it. You were afraid, but I've got you now," he murmured against my lips. He kissed me fiercely and I held him tighter. "I will always be here for you, Chloe. Never forget that, baby."

He lifted his head, pulling his mouth away when I feigned for another kiss.

"Tell me you'll never forget that," he demanded.

"I will never forget it, Theo," I breathed, and he gripped me tighter, supplying fuller thrusts. I felt him grow tense, but he didn't stop. He was close.

"You and me feel too perfect together. We were fucking made for each other."

He held on, and then he released a ragged breath, dropping his face in the curve of my neck. He let out a heavy grunt and I knew he was coming.

He squeezed my ass in hand, planting small kisses above my collarbone, making me feel an endless swirl of heat in my core.

With a big exhale, his large body softened and he rested his cheek on my shoulder. He kissed the tip of my nose when I turned my face in his direction.

"I love you," he crooned. "I really fucking do. How many times have I said it since I first saw you?"

I broke out in a large grin. "Many times," I laughed, poking his nose. "But it's okay. I love you, too."

CHAPTER 15

CHLOE

After the mess we'd made in that kitchen, I told Theo I needed to clean up before dinner. I took a long, hot shower, smiling beneath the stream like a kid in a candy store.

There was a black cotton robe hanging on the back of the bathroom door with a red T on the chest. I knew it was Theo's. Fortunately there wasn't one for her.

I heard sizzling when I came down the stairs.

When I walked into the kitchen, he heard me and looked sideways with a spatula in hand. He did a double take and I bit back a smile.

"I think you're asking for it again." He shut off the stovetop.

"Our bags are still in the car and it was the only thing up there to wear that was in plain view."

He walked around the counter to get to me. "I'll get the bags. Watch the food."

I nodded and he walked out of the kitchen, picking his keys up off the table in the hall and then making his way towards the front door.

When it shut behind him, I maneuvered towards the stove to see what he was cooking.

There were large pink shrimp in a skillet and in the pot was some linguini pasta. Shrimp linguini? Yum.

Twirling around, I started to search for the plates in the cabinets to start setting the table. I found them in the one beside the wine glasses. I pulled two of them down and then grabbed some silverware, deciding to set up the dining room . . . wherever it was.

As I walked around the corner with a small smile, that's when I saw the pictures, hung on the dining room wall. Wedding photos.

I froze, standing on the opposite end of the table, the satisfied smile sliding right off my face. If I hadn't gone so tense, I'm sure I would have dropped the plates, but instead I held onto them tighter.

I know I said I would remain optimistic, but how could I? The pictures were plastered right in front of me. A collage in one abstract frame.

They were hugging. Kissing. Smiling. Laughing. She was so . . . *happy*.

Finally looking away, I set the plates and silverware up and then hurried back for the kitchen. Theo still wasn't inside yet, so I waited, folding my arms and pressing my lower back against the counter edge.

As I waited, that's when I took it all in. The entire home. That's when I noticed her presence had been here all along. It wasn't decorated the way Theo would have had it. It was decorated by a woman. There was a feminine touch.

I chewed on the nail of my thumb, looking from the oven, to the french doors on my left. Outside of them, I could clearly see the aligned flowers. They were a color scheme of purple and pink.

This home was amazing.

But as I looked at each corner of the kitchen and even those french doors, I couldn't help but wonder if he took her there like he'd just done to me? Did they have sex on the counter before? On the dining table or even the kitchen floor? The living room? Or that shower that I'd just used as if it were my own?

A door clicked shut and I looked up. Theo passed by with our suitcases in hand, winking at me before he disappeared. I heard him go up the stairs, a light thud, and then he was coming back down.

"I just have a few things to pack up later tonight after we eat, and then tomorrow I need to check in at the car shop." He came closer, pulling down two clear bowls to dump the food into. "I appreciate you coming, Chloe."

I barely nodded. He put on a gentle display of happiness, winking over his shoulder. He then turned to grab a can of sauce on the counter.

"I already set up the table," I announced, dropping my hand.

"Oh okay. Cool. Well," he shrugged with the bowls in hand, "let's go eat then."

My fork scraped the chinaware as I twirled it in the noodles. Theo was going on about things at his shop—how a guy named Brock was always good with running it while he was away.

"I was thinking about opening a garage in Bristle Wave, too. I have some money saved to start it up. Find a cheap lot, build a small garage, and make another. You know what I named the one here?"

"What?" I asked.

"Black Engine."

I laughed. "That's actually really creative. Fits you. I like it."

"Izzy helped me come up with it." He took a bite of the hot bread roll.

I nodded, but my eyes shifted past his shoulder and above his head. I couldn't stop staring at that damn picture frame. And what was worse—how hadn't he noticed?

Had he grown so accustomed to that frame on the wall that he looked past it whenever he walked by? I was slightly relieved that most of my and Sterling's photos were collected in my phone . . . and most of them deleted now.

"So . . . what do you want for dessert? I have apple pie or brownies. Both come with vanilla ice cream. Your choice."

I met his gaze when he spoke, but the longer I stared at him, the more his smile faded.

Theo's eyebrows drew together and then he glanced over his shoulder to see what I was looking at before. When he realized what it was, he let out a deep, agitated breath.

"Shit." He rubbed his forehead until his skin turned white there. "Is that why you're acting so strange right now? Because of the pictures, Chloe?"

"No," I lied, and I felt my face burn with the obvious fib.

He narrowed his eyes at me before standing up and walking towards the portrait. Lifting it up, he took it off the wall and rested it on its face against the wall. There was something about that empty space on the wall that brought me so much relief.

"What happened to keeping an open mind?" he asked, returning to his seat and digging into his meal again.

"I am," I said quickly. "Well . . . I'm trying."

He dropped his arm, chewing hard as he looked straight at me. "She was my wife, Chloe. We shared this house for over two years so of course there are going to be a few pictures of us here and there. Do I expect you to be okay with them? No. But I took down as many as I could before I left for Bristle Wave. Because I wanted to take you out of that town and bring you here with me. Hell, we hardly ever ate in here unless Izzy was in town. We hardly ate together, period. If I wasn't working, she was."

Dropping his fork, he reached across the table and grabbed my hand. "Don't do this to me. Please," he pleaded. "I'm trying, I swear to God I am. I'm sorry you had to see that. But if you keep bringing it up —if you keep making me feel so guilty about it . . . well, shit," he puffed. "I don't know, Chloe. I won't know what you really need, or want. All I know is that I want us to work this out. I want us to move forward."

"I want the same," I confessed.

"I feel shitty as fuck knowing that I've had two wives already and will probably end up with three later on." He cracked a smile. "But you know what they say? Third time's the charm."

I pressed my lips to smile lightly. It didn't feel like the right time to joke about it. It was too fresh. Too raw. "Don't say that to me. You're not ready for another marriage. You're not even out of your second one yet."

"You think I have to *prepare* to marry you? Chloe, I've been ready to make you my wife for years now. You're the only woman I know that understands me, inside and out. I thought Janet knew who I was —and she knew most things about me—but she didn't know me *enough*. Not like you do."

I looked down at our hands and then over where the picture frame was. "I just want you to be sure, Theo."

"Babe," he mumbled, with a light shake of his head. "I'm fucking positive, all right?" He picked up my hand and kissed my knuckles. "I've never been so damn sure about anything in my life. Being with you is right. It was complicated before, but we loved it. It was special. What I felt for you was real, and it still is."

"I know." I lowered my head. "Will Izzy be coming back to Bristle Wave after her commercial shoot?"

"I'm not sure. She said she'd let me know." He paused. "She knows. I'm sure she does. She refuses to acknowledge it, but she knows who I'm with, and why I wanted to spend more time in Bristle after she left for Orange County. She's been tiptoeing around the subject, too afraid to bring it up herself."

"We should talk to her in person. Together. Air it out. Let her say whatever she has to say, get everything off her chest."

He drew his hand away, rolling his neck. "We can try."

"What do you mean *try*? You said she's changed, right?"

"Yes, but it doesn't mean her opinions won't be just as strong as they were last time and it doesn't mean *you* won't leave again." He sighed, pushed back in his chair and stood up. "I have wine. Do you want some?"

"Sure." I watched him go, stepping around the corner with tight shoulders. I was starting to think it was a bad idea coming here, to this home. In a sense, I was stepping into my own harsh reality by coming here.

How? Because Theo was still married. Sterling still lingered. Izzy's opinion would *always* matter. And we were *not* as ready as I thought for this.

CHAPTER 16

THEO

She tossed and turned all night.

I felt fucking horrible. When I first thought about it, it felt like a good idea to get her out of Bristle Wave for a day or two, and let her see what I'd been doing.

I knew I wanted to bring her back with me once we got off on the same foot, and I also knew Sheila wasn't going to stay in this house, so I took all the photos down before I left—all but one fucking frame that I forgot was there.

The one in the damn dining room. Hell, I hardly ever went in the dining room. Most times I ate alone. Knowing she saw that was killing me now.

As I lay flat on my back, staring up at the ceiling, I could feel her moving. Shifting. Grunting and sighing.

I finally sighed. "Chloe, what's the matter?"

She stopped moving for a split second. Her back was facing me, but then she rolled over to look me in the eye. "Which side did she sleep on?"

I stared down at her. "The side I'm on."

I heard her swallow hard before speaking again. "If I tell you something, promise you won't get mad?"

"You can tell me anything. You know that."

She was quiet for so long I figured she'd changed her mind about telling me. "I . . . can smell her, Theo. *Everywhere*. I can tell she enjoyed being here with you. She's everywhere."

I didn't even know what to say to that. All I could do was stare at her.

"Don't be mad," she whispered, reaching for my hand. "Please. I'm just . . . I don't know. This isn't like how it was with Janet. This is different because, technically, you still belong to her. You two bought this home together. You started to create a life and I feel like I got in the way of that—" She clamped her mouth shut, shaking her head.

I looked away, towards the window where the silver moon was shining through the curtains. Sitting up, I pushed out of bed and walked to the closet. I took down a pair of sweatpants and a T-shirt, got dressed, and then came back, reaching for her hand.

"Come on," I said softly, sitting her up.

"Where are we going?" She looked worried, eyes glistening like I was going to send her back home.

"Away from here. Come on." I tugged on her hand and she warily climbed out of the bed. She followed me out of the room and I let her walk down the stairs before me.

When she was at the bottom of the staircase, she picked her head up to look at me. "Are you upset?" she asked feebly.

"No, Chloe. Not with you."

"So . . . what then?"

"I'm upset with myself. I don't know what the fuck I was thinking bringing you here. I thought that it would be . . . well . . . *shit*. I thought that—" I shut my mouth, my eyes running up and down the length of her. "Hell, I don't know what I thought. I figured it would be an escape, but really it was just like coming back to the place I'd been trapped in for over two years straight with her."

"Where will we go?" she questioned, stepping closer.

"We'll get a hotel. I'll come back tomorrow to pack the rest of the stuff I need."

"Theo—I—" I cut off her next sentence, reaching for her hand and pressing a finger over her lips.

"I wasn't thinking, Chloe. I should have known better. I'm too old to be making mistakes like this."

Her lips twisted behind my finger. She grabbed my wrist and pulled my hand away. "Does this make me frustrating?" she tested.

And I laughed. "No. It makes you smart. And it lets me know you still have self-respect. I see he didn't fully ruin you."

"He didn't ruin me at all," she retorted.

I shook my head. "He fucked you up the day he asked you to be with him."

She stared at me with her wide hazel eyes, but didn't speak. I wasn't expecting her to respond. I wanted it to sink in.

I turned around to pick up my keys from the table and handed them to her.

"Go to the car and wait for me. I'll get our bags."

"You do realize it's almost two in the morning, right?" she laughed.

"I know. But the sooner we get out of here, the better you'll feel." I stroked her warm cheek, our eyes locking. "I want you to be happy around me, Chloe. Nothing less."

"I am happy," she responded. "I'm always happiest around you, Theo."

But was she?

After coming to this fucking place, I was starting to think she was feeling the complete opposite.

We pulled up to one of my favorite hotels, that had a spectacular view of the Golden Gate Bridge.

When I parked, I could feel the relief spreading throughout her body. She looked over at me and stretched her lips to smile.

She just didn't know. I would do anything to see her happy. That house was a free stay, but I'd give everything I had if it meant bringing a smile to my Little Knight's face.

I dropped our bags in the corner once we were inside the suite. It had a great view of the bridge from here; I opened the curtains wider so we could see it. I hadn't turned any of the lights on yet, so the lighting in the room was dim.

Chloe walked forward and peered out towards the bridge. Its lights flashed and the cars driving over the bridge gave it even more life. The water beneath it rippled ferociously.

She sighed, a sound so simple, yet I felt a warmth hit my chest.

I stepped behind her, wrapping my arms around her middle, drawing her in, and kissing the back of her head.

"I love seeing you like this, Chloe. *This*. Not stressed or tossing and turning, just enjoying the moment."

Her head fell back on my shoulder and I looked out towards the bridge. "I'm sorry I made you go through all of that."

"Don't apologize," I murmured. "It wasn't a problem for me. It had to be done. And with this view, I'd say it's worth it, babe."

She turned in my arms, draping hers over my shoulders. Her lips ran feathery light over my cheek, her chest on mine. "It is worth it."

Her mouth was at an angle. All I had to do was lower my head and I would be kissing her.

I did just that.

I brought my face down and kissed my Knight whole. She let out a breathy moan as I picked her up and pressed her back to the glass. I glued my groin between her legs, feeling myself getting so hard for her, all over again.

This woman—fuck, I didn't know what it was. She was still young and flawless, and I was getting older. I didn't know what the hell she saw in me.

It was easy to love someone like her—someone so untainted and simple and beautiful—but it was damn hard to love someone like me. Someone so tainted, ridiculous, and occasionally irrational.

"You'll be mine forever, won't you, Knight?" I rasped against her lips.

She cupped the back of my neck. "Yes," she breathed. "Always, Theo. Always."

I smiled before finishing what I'd started.

Those were the exact words I wanted to hear.

CHAPTER 17

CHLOE

When I woke up, Theo wasn't in bed.

I rolled over and smelled a sweet aroma. My belly churned, and all my senses awakened when I realized what it was.

Food.

I loved t when he cooked for me. It made that sexy man even sexier, knowing he was doing it to please and take care of his woman. I checked the time on my cellphone. It was nearing 11:00 a.m.

That wasn't too bad, considering we'd spent the better half of our night bickering, and then making up, kissing and caressing one another until the break of dawn.

A slice of the sun kissed the horizon when we fell asleep, but now it had bombarded the sky, calling for a great day.

I pushed out of bed and walked to the corner to get my suitcase. I dug through it for an outfit and then went to the bathroom to freshen up a bit. I heard clanging from where I was and grinned in the mirror, imagining him hard at work over the stove, breaking a light sweat.

As I walked out of the bathroom, my phone buzzed on the nightstand. I figured it was Kim requesting an update. She'd been demanding one since she heard I was getting a substitute. I walked quickly to get it, but my smile faded just as quickly as it had appeared.

It was Sterling.

A picture of us was set as his caller ID. I was kissing his cheek as he took the photo.

My entire body went numb. I could still hear Theo in the kitchen moving things around.

My dream man was only a few steps away, waiting for me to join him for a late breakfast.

But I felt awful. I couldn't answer. It could have been an update on Margie, but I knew if it were urgent, he would leave a voicemail or text me to follow up. So I shut off the vibrations and sent the call to voicemail.

My chest was heavy as I got dressed, but I ignored the feeling, walking out and going to the kitchen to meet up with Theo.

He wasn't wearing a shirt, his tattoos on full display, muscles rippling as he bent down and pulled out a batch of cinnamon rolls.

"That smells good," I said, and he dropped the pan and turned quickly to look at me.

"You're up," he noted. "Good morning. I wanted to surprise you with a small brunch in bed. I guess I spent too much time at the grocery store this morning."

I walked ahead and slinked my arms around his waist. "Well, I can always go back."

He kissed the center of my forehead. "You should. Let me make up for my dumb mistake."

"Theo," I scolded lightly. "It wasn't dumb. I agreed to it. I knew where we were going. I guess I just wasn't prepared to actually be *there*, you know?"

"I still should have been a little more considerate, Little Knight." He laughed, shaking his head.

"What?" I asked, tipping my head back, surprised by his sudden change of mood.

"Calling you Little Knight doesn't even feel the same anymore. I think I should start calling you my *Sexy* Knight."

I burst into a fit of giggles. "Sexy Knight? No, babe," I laughed, pulling away and stealing a slice of bacon. "I think I like 'Little' better. It grew on me."

He held his hands out. "Shit, you are my Sexy Knight. Sexy as hell and the whole world should know you're mine." He came closer with heated eyes, wrapping his hands around me and squeezing my ass in his hands. His mouth came crashing down on mine, and I couldn't stifle my moan. I had bacon breath but he didn't seem to mind it one bit.

In fact, he slid his tongue right through my lips and allowed ours to dance together.

"Theo," I laughed between the next kiss. "I taste gross."

"Never that." He cupped my face in his hands and kissed me while I melted in his grasp. He was so perfect in every way, from the things he said, to the way he held and touched me, and even when it came to accepting my flaws.

He didn't expect perfection, but he saw the perfection in me—the same as I did in him. Were we flawed? Hell yes, but that was what made us better. Our flaws were what brought us together in the first place.

When he finally pulled away, he took a step to the left and gestured towards the bedroom. "Now go get back in that bed. Get comfortable and wait for me." I bit back a smile and as I walked by, he spanked me right on the ass.

I yelped and when I looked back he had the most boyish, crooked smile on his lips.

Theo came into the room with a wide black tray in hand. A smile swept across his lips and his brown eyes were mellow and focused right on me.

"Didn't make you wait too long, did I?" he asked.

"Nope. What's on the menu?"

"Cinnamon rolls, an omelet, and bacon. Oh—and orange juice. Can't forget the vitamin C." He carefully placed the tray down on my lap.

I clapped my hands, excited. "You'll eat with me?"

He sat on the end of the bed where my feet were and picked up one off the cinnamon rolls, answering my question without words and winking as he took a bite.

"So, I wasn't sure if you wanted to come to the shop with me. I'll be in the office for about an hour or two to check the books and do a few other things. I can't imagine you want to just sit around there waiting for me."

I chewed before speaking. "I can stay here if you want me to. I don't mind."

He dusted his hands off and looked towards the open window. "There's a shopping center less than a block away. I'll give you some money to go shopping. Let loose. Take some time to just enjoy yourself."

"I've had plenty of time for myself, Theo." I waved a hand. "Besides, I have my own money. You don't have to give me any. You should save it for emergencies."

"I'll leave the money on the counter," he stated, ignoring my last statement, and I rolled my eyes playfully, grabbing the orange juice. I took a small sip and placed the glass back down. "I should leave now so I can get back to you sooner." He licked his lips and watched my eyes. "But before I go . . ."

He picked up my tray and stood. Setting it on the nightstand, he turned to look at me, his brown gaze lingering on my breasts, traveling down the span of my body.

We didn't do much when we got to the hotel last night. Besides kissing, cuddling, and talking about little things, it was an average night. So with that look in his eyes, it was almost like I'd just read his mind. I leaned in closer, and his mouth parted as he ran his thumb over my bottom lip.

The bed dipped as he placed a knee down between my legs, and as he came forward, he cupped one side of my face. It was a good thing he was wearing basketball shorts. They were easy to untie and even easier to get down.

His body grew tense when he felt my skin on his. We broke our embrace with heavy breaths and he reached down, taking my shirt off. I wasn't wearing my bra yet, so when he caught sight of my exposed nipples, he took one of them into his mouth, sucking gently while his fingers slid down between my legs.

He inched my panties aside as he sucked on my nipples, and I felt my core clench tight as his finger pushed inside me. His thumb gave only a little pressure on my swelling clit, but his fingers were doing a number on my body.

He stroked his fingers in and out, teasing each nipple, back and forth, groaning as if I tasted like the sweetest fruit on earth.

I could feel his hard cock on my leg, and with each thrust of his fingers, I felt him growing harder.

"How does that feel?" he whispered on my skin. His breath was warm running across my chest. "Tell me, Chloe. How does it feel when I play with you like this?"

"Good," I whimpered as he added more pressure to my clit.

"Good?"

"Yes," I panted.

"Does it make you want my cock?"

I watched his face, how determined he was to make me come. It honestly wasn't going to take much. Because I was right there—right on the verge.

Or so I thought . . .

When he jerked his fingers away, I frowned. "I don't want you to come yet," he mumbled, stealing a kiss from me when I exhaled erratically.

"No?"

"No. Not around my fingers anyway." He planted one hand outside my head and used the other to get his boxers down. When he sprung free, I felt his hard tip press at my opening, and I ached with so much need.

"I won't go in all the way yet." He hovered right above me, our mouths a hair's breadth away. "I want you to tell me. Say 'Theo, I want you to fuck me' and I swear I will give you the best fuck of your life, baby."

I held him tight. "Theo, I want you to fuck me," I breathed out.

And he took those words and ran with them.

Instead of thrusting deeper, he drew back, brought my body towards the edge of the bed, lifted my feet in the air, and then forced my thighs together. My hips were up in the air, as well as my womanhood, and he leaned forward, his tongue plunging into me.

I gasped, reaching for him, but I couldn't get a good grip. He had my knees near my face, so I was vulnerable to him. Wide open for the taking. A feral sound came from his throat as he slid a finger in while sweeping his tongue over my clit.

My body did things I never thought it could do.

I bucked wildly for him, and he groaned deeper, still eating me. Still taking what was *his*. He pushed my legs higher so he could bury his tongue in deeper. I spread my legs apart a little so I could see him. When I found his eyes, I couldn't help myself.

They were so hard—blazing with hunger. He was ravenous for me, and all I wanted to do was give myself to him, every single fiber of my being.

He ate me until I exploded, and he didn't stop until my moans became whimpers, and small cries for more.

He sat up slowly, his body stacked, muscles rippling. He climbed on the bed, and hovered above me.

Gripping his cock, he started stroking slowly. He was anxious. So hard and ready. So big and perfect.

"Tell me again, Chloe."

"I want you to fuck me," I pleaded.

"Okay," he murmured. "Turn around then."

I turned over just as quickly as he commanded it. When my belly was rested on the bed, he gripped my hips and lifted them in the air. He pressed the tip of his cock at my entrance, and then he drove in.

My back bowed and my mouth shot open as he wrapped a hand

around my throat. His mouth came to my ear, and he murmured, "You want me to fuck you, Chloe?"

"Yes," I panted.

"Okay. I'll fuck you. Don't worry," he worked his hips forward and backwards, building up rapid strokes. "It might get a little rough, but just remember that I still love you, baby."

A pounding noise started, along with the rhythmic clapping from our skin. I dragged my nails through the white sheets, holding on tight as he worked his magic.

"Say my name, Little Knight," he growled in my ear. "Say you love me."

"I love you, Theo," I cried out, as loud as I could. His hand was still wrapped around my throat.

"Fuck," he hissed, kissing my shoulder blade. "I love you, too. I love how good you feel. I love your body. I can't get enough of you. I will *never* be able to get enough of you, Chloe." He released his grip, pulling out and flipping me onto my back.

Shoving my leg up, he slid right back in with ease, and his mouth came down instantly to wrap around my nipple. He sucked each one as he continued grinding.

His body was firm, his growls deep as he tasted me everywhere. "Shit," he growled on the damp valley between my breasts. His lips were glued to me. I could feel his breath drifting over my sweaty skin.

"Perfect pussy," he murmured, dragging his lips up and then crushing mine. "Perfect woman. Perfect *everything*." He shuddered, forehead dropping on my shoulder. He rocked forward, deep, hard, and I knew by the way his body stiffened that he was coming.

I sighed as he rested his face on my shoulder, his scruff rubbing across my chest.

When he looked up, I looked down into his brown eyes and laughed.

"I couldn't help myself, baby. You were so damn wet."

I kissed his cheek. "It's okay," I laughed.

He pulled up, resting on his elbows. He was still inside me, and as he moved, I pulsed around him. His eyes stretched a little wider. "Keep doing that and I'll end up fucking you again."

I giggled.

"I won't be out for long," he assured me.

"Take all the time you need." I rubbed the small wrinkles around his eyes.

He cupped the right half of my face, rubbing my cheek with his thumb. "I meant what I said."

"About what?"

"How much I love you. I love you more than words can explain, Chloe. We're going to figure this shit out. I don't care if it kills me."

"I know we will." I ran the tip of my nose across his. "I have a good feeling this time."

CHAPTER 18

CHLOE

I did some light shopping for about two hours before returning to the hotel. I bought two T-shirts, a new pair of flats (red, so I couldn't confuse them with another color) and a pearl necklace.

I decided to pick up lunch from the Italian restaurant that was on the way to the hotel. To my surprise, they served burgers, so I chose that for Theo and grabbed myself some lasagna with garlic bread.

Theo returned about thirty minutes after I did. Much sooner than I expected, but I was more than happy to have him back.

"How was it?" I asked over lunch.

"Good. Shop's running fine without me, which is what I like to see." He bit into his burger with a subtle smile.

"That's good."

"One of my guys is bringing Ol' Charlie to Bristle Wave for me soon."

My eyes stretched wide. "Really?" I was thrilled, grinning like a wild child. I loved Ol' Charlie. I loved that bike to death. "You'll take me for a ride again?"

He smiled. "I have that and other things in mind."

"Things like what?"

He licked his bottom lip. "You'll see."

After lunch, we walked Baker Beach. It was a warm, breezy day. Hand-in-hand, we walked with not many words spoken. It wasn't awkward at all. We were content. Luckily, there weren't any nude people lying around. Theo found that small fact very amusing before we arrived.

He would squeeze my hand tight when he wanted to silently check in. I would smile up at him, reassuring him that I was fine. When the sun set, we sat by a harbor.

I was between his legs. He had his arms wrapped around my top half, his back against mine. He felt warm. Safe.

"This is us," he murmured in my ear, right before sliding my hair over and kissing the back of my neck.

I looked over my shoulder at him. "Yeah." I looked towards the rippling water and the sun on the horizon. I pushed back a little more and he tightened his hold around me. "This is us. I won't let go if you don't."

"I'll never let go." His voice was firm, but sincere. I knew he meant it. Every word of it.

That night, we didn't make love or fuck or any of what we were good at. We cuddled in utter silence, watching one another. I stroked his cheek as he stroked mine, tangling my fingers in his graying hair as he kissed me gently. Sweetly. Delicately. All over.

We were close, talking to one another without saying a single word. Before I knew it, I'd fallen asleep in his arms, to the comforting sound of his beating heart.

I fell asleep with a smile on my face. I fell asleep with the man of my dreams. The man I loved. The man I had never forgotten.

My sweet, beautiful Theo.

———

When we got back to Bristle Wave the next afternoon, Theo didn't take me straight home or to his already-booked suite. He took me to the docks. And when he met up with Dane, who handed him a set of keys, that's when I knew what he had planned for me.

He was going to take me for another ride on Dirty Black.

That boat—*God, that boat.* It held so many memories. That boat was what really gave us our foundation. We made so much love on it. We listened to so much music and drank so much. All we had on Dirty Black was each other and having each other felt like everything we ever needed.

Theo came back in my direction after collecting the keys from Dane and said, "I know what you're thinking. Not today. Tomorrow."

And I squealed. I squealed so loud and jumped into his arms. I forced my lips on his and he laughed under my unanticipated kiss. I was surprised we didn't fall into the water from the collision. But he was a strong man. And swift too.

I was so happy to have him back in my life again . . . but we both knew that when it came down to us, happiness didn't last always.

Little did I know our happiness was going to be interrupted sooner rather than later.

CHAPTER 19

THEO

After dropping some of her things off at home, I brought her back to the suite I'd been cooped up in for nearly two weeks now.

"I'm thinking about getting another place here," I announced as she turned off the blender. "Something simple. Two bedrooms. A nice view of the docks and the ocean."

"I like that idea. When?" she inquired, pouring the smoothie into a cup and then dropping a straw into it.

"Whenever I get the house in San Francisco on the market again. Once Sheila signs those papers, I'll let her know either she can keep it and stay there, or I'm selling it."

I shrugged. It sounded so fucked up, but I couldn't stay there and I knew she wouldn't, with all we'd done there, so there was no choice but to sell it.

She dropped down on my lap, sipping her strawberry concoction. "Whatever you decide to do, you know I'm here to help."

"I know." I pushed a lock of her hair back. "You ready for tomorrow?"

She grinned. "More than ready. I'm going to pack some sandwiches, drinks, and cards—all that good stuff. I'll make a run to the store tonight. Oh, I also need to call my boss, let him know I may need another day." She paused and thought on something, lips twisted. "How long will we be out there this time?"

"As long as you want, Knight. There's no rush, but we won't just be on the boat this time."

She sat up, eyebrows puckered. "No? Where else will we be?"

I laughed. Only laughed.

She smacked her teeth and narrowed her eyes. "Theo," she whined. "Where?"

"You'll see. There's no fun if I tell you, now is there?"

Her eyes rolled, lips pressing around her straw again. "Fine," she said after her sip. "You're lucky I like surprises."

After she made her grocery run, she was back in no time.

I was exhausted from the drive back, so I told her I was going to make a few calls to the shop and my lawyer and then lay down.

She finished up during the middle of one of my calls. Stepping up behind me, she brought her hand around, running it down my chest and over my stomach.

I peered over my shoulder with the phone glued to my ear. She smiled lightly, grabbing my hand and mouthing the word, "Hurry."

I winked, nodding, and then gestured towards the bedroom. I wrapped the call up quickly but when I entered the bedroom, she wasn't there. I heard commotion in the kitchen, ice being shuffled around. Kicking my boots off and then tugging off my jeans, I laid down, releasing a heavy sigh.

Exhausted wasn't the word. I hadn't had a full night's rest since coming back to Bristle Wave. I could have blamed myself for hounding the woman I love, but I refused. Having her back was worth the lack of sleep.

I had to admit, though, I was getting a little too old for this shit.

Chloe finally came to the bedroom with a cup of ice in hand. She shut the lights off, but before she did, I spotted the faint smile on her lips.

"Chloe?" I called. I could see her coming closer. She climbed on all fours on the bed, maneuvering between my legs. I didn't fidget, not even when I felt that cold cup hovering over my chest.

"I want to try something," she whispered.

"Like what?"

"Something new. With you. I read it in a book once. The guy really got a kick out of it." She put the cup to her lips and took one of the ice cubes in her mouth, still watching me.

"You still read those dirty books?" I chuckled.

"Mmm-hmm," she mumbled, mouth full. After placing the cup on the nightstand near my head, she brought her face near my upper chest.

The ice landed on the crease between my chest and she dragged it down, over my abs and to my navel with her lips. That mixture of fire and ice woke me right the hell up.

I was no longer tired. I was alert. Fully alert.

"Shit, Chloe," I groaned. She picked the ice back up with her lips and started cold kisses back up to my chest, then dragged them down again, past my navel this time. Her fingers wrapped around the waistband of my shorts, and she tugged. I tilted my hips to assist.

When they were near my ankles, she took the ice further down, and *goddamn*. There it was. Her cold mouth hovered right above my cock. She stalled, and this time I fucking fidgeted.

I was ready. Hard.

From the moonlight, I saw her eyes flash up to meet mine, and then she went to work. Her mouth wrapped around the head of my cock, and I hissed through my teeth, the pleasure too fierce. She sucked me in, length by length, the ice melting, sliding down to my balls.

"Fuck," I groaned. It was a sensation that not even I had encountered. Ice and a blowjob. Neither Janet nor Sheila had done this to me before.

But Chloe? My young, sexy, fucking amazing Little Knight had given me something new, and I was damn proud of it.

With my hands behind my head, I staggered on my next breath. Up and down, up and down. She went slowly at first, swirling her tongue, doing magic tricks around it with her hot little mouth and the cold ice trickling down on my balls.

I was throbbing when she took my entire cock into her mouth, wanting so badly to grab her hair and tug on it, but she was doing her own thing. She was giving me an experience and I didn't want to ruin it by being greedy.

I stayed cool as she swirled her tongue, twisting her lips and the ice around my pulsing cock. I couldn't help the tightening of my core, or the way my balls grew taut as she lapped her tongue around them too, letting the ice melt and coat my sack.

Her mouth came back down on my hard dick, hot and wet, and she moaned, causing a vibrating sensation that felt unreal.

I felt myself wheeze when her hazel eyes bolted on mine. The look she gave me was so fucking sexy, like she was hungry for me. Never going to get enough.

Fuck. I was close. *So close.* No teeth, just the flickering and prancing of her velvety tongue. She moaned around me again. That's when I realized the ice had completely melted. It was gone, so she took my cock in deeper, until she damn near choked on it.

My eyes rolled back. "Fuckkk, Chloe."

That was it. That was all it took.

Just like that, I bucked and my hands came down. I held the base of her skull as I came deep down her throat. She drank every last drop as if it were sweet—like she longed for the taste of my come.

I shuddered as she drew her semi-cold tongue back up to my tip and lightly suckled on it, and when she pulled away and the air hit my cock, I shuddered again with way too much satisfaction.

"Ah, shit," I moaned, flopping back on the pillows. A fucking moan? I never moaned.

She grinned as she climbed on top of my lap, only wearing one of my white T-shirts. Her nipples were straining against the shirt. She was ready for another round today.

"How was it?" She smiled hard, like she already knew the answer to her own question.

"Fucking amazing, Chloe. I've never had that done to me before."

"Really?" Her smile grew wider.

"Never."

"So, I finally gave you a first at something?"

I laughed. "Yeah, you did. And it's a first I will never forget."

She kissed my forehead. "This time, I taught Mr. Black something," she teased, smirking, and then climbing off the bed.

I couldn't help the laugh that rumbled out.

"I'm going to take a shower," she announced. "I know you're tired, but it would be nice if you joined me."

I groaned, flopping back again and planting my palms on my face. "You're serious right now, aren't you?"

"As a heart attack, Mr. Black."

I busted out laughing as she sauntered to the bathroom, tossing her shirt before she'd even entered. When the door was partly closed, I sat up and shook off the weariness, but something vibrated behind me.

Her phone was on the nightstand.

I took out another pair of shorts to wear after the shower, doing my best to ignore the vibrating. It stopped, but started ringing again seconds later.

I walked to her side of the bed and checked the screen.

Sterling.

Of course it was that motherfucker calling. He always stepped in to ruin shit—to ruin my life. And always at the worst time.

I had the urge to silence it, to delete and block his worthless number, but I couldn't touch it. I couldn't make the decisions for her, no matter how badly I wanted to. It was her cellphone, not mine. But I was damn sure about to squash whatever the hell was going on right now.

I headed towards the bathroom, spotting her through the opaque glass, washing her hair and body.

Look at her. That fucker didn't deserve her. She was too much for him. Too mature. Too beautiful.

She was mine. He wasn't getting her back. Fuck that.

I opened the glass shower door and stepped in behind her. I grabbed my soap, watching as she rinsed the suds away. When it was gone, she let the water run over her face and then stepped back to wipe it all away with her fingers.

I couldn't bite my tongue about it anymore. The longer I watched her, it made me wonder.

"Why didn't you tell me Sterling's been calling?" I finally asked. Water ran over her naked, wet body, making it even harder for me to be angry.

She froze for a moment, avoiding my eyes. "How do you know he's been calling?"

"He just called before I came in here. Twice. Have you two been talking?"

"No," she stated earnestly. "No, Theo." She grabbed my hand, blinking with damp eyelashes. "I've been ignoring all of his calls. I don't want to talk to him . . . mainly because I don't know what he wants." She swallowed thickly, looking down. "I know his mom is sick —the woman that was my father's caretaker." My back stiffened. I opened my mouth to say something about that but her head shook as she continued. "He could be calling about that, but he hasn't left any voicemails so I don't know. I'm thinking maybe it's not her—that maybe he's just trying to talk things out about us. But I don't want that. I don't want him trying to come back. I don't want him to make this harder for us. For *me*. I guess I'm a coward trying to take the easy way out." She smiled, only a little. It was a worried smile.

Relief. Sweet fucking relief.

"Damn." I studied her, how her lips fell flat. She squeezed my hand tighter, but I pulled away and used that hand to tip her chin so our eyes could meet again.

"His mother was good to your father. What if he's calling about that?"

She lightly shrugged. "I don't want to answer."

"I know." And I could understand why. I didn't want to answer Sheila either, fearing that she might try to step in and break us apart. I didn't want anything or anyone intruding right now. Things were going well. Too well.

Look at us. We were afraid of our own damn demons—trying to hide from them instead of facing them together like we should have been doing.

"But you're right," she sighed. "So I will call after our trip tomorrow to check in. If it's not about Margie, I won't let the conversation carry on."

"Sounds like a good idea." I pulled my hand away, stepping closer. With my lips pressed to her forehead, I inhaled the rich scent of her vanilla shampoo. "We can handle this," I murmured.

She nodded. "I know. I'm just scared, I guess."

"Of what?" I tipped my head back to see her fully.

"I don't want *us* to end again. I'm afraid." Her voice cracked as she said, "It could be worse this time."

I cupped the back of her neck. "We won't." My forehead pressed down hard on hers. "Do you hear me? We won't. We fight and we win. As long as we fight . . ." I trailed off. Her eyes were so damn hopeful, so desperate for relief. For an answer. "As long as we don't give up on each other again, as long as we take this second chance and protect it, nothing is going to tear us apart. You're mine, you hear me?" I held her a little tighter. She bobbed her head. "Mine, Chloe." I crushed her lips with my own, hauling her closer. When our mouths parted, I said, "I'm never letting you go again. I don't care what kind of fight I have to endure. You're worth whatever battles I have to face and whatever scars I end up with because of them."

She smiled softly and then rested her head on my chest.

She had no idea what kind of hell I would go through for her. Through fire and thick flames, I would walk. Through the smoke and cinders, I would push through just to save her. To be with her.

That nightmare I had was coming. I could feel it. It was building up, and it was only a matter of time now before it swarmed me.

But instead of letting her walk away like she did in that terrible, horrifying nightmare, I was going to go after her and keep her.

CHAPTER 20

CHLOE

Sterling didn't call again that night or in the morning when Theo and I were packing up the car, ready for our boat trip. He wore a smile all morning, like he wasn't going to let anything get him down today.

I wished I could have done the same, but I found myself thinking about our current situation.

Theo: still married, filing for divorce, not final.

Me: Feeling guilty. Somewhat ashamed. Fresh out of an engagement.

What were we thinking? I think the truth of the matter is that we *weren't* thinking much at all. We were just *doing*. Izzy technically still didn't know about us, though Theo had a feeling she may have. Sheila was probably furious, ready to destroy me, and Sterling's behavior was starting to worry me. I didn't want Theo to know that, so I kept it to myself, but I was worried. Only because I was afraid he was calling to bear bad news again.

When Theo tossed the cooler full of drinks in the trunk, both alcoholic and non-alcoholic, I tucked my hair behind my ear and pressed my back against the passenger door.

"Theo, I want you to promise me something," I said as the wind tousled my hair.

"What's that?" He stood up straight, dusting off his hands and shutting the back door. He was wearing black and white board shorts and a white T-shirt. His hair hadn't been gelled or brushed. He had the perfect, slightly gray bed hair. I had to admit, the gray made him sexier.

"When we go on the boat, I don't want to talk about Sterling or Sheila or even Izzy. I don't want there to be any downtime for us to start thinking about that stuff. I want us to be so occupied with each other that all we can think about is us and what we want." I stepped closer to him, grabbing his hands. "Can you promise me that?"

"You know I can," he responded, voice gentle. "That was going to happen, regardless." He flashed a crooked smile, revealing those dimples. The sunlight danced off his eyes, the wind tangling in his hair too. Such a gorgeous man. Beautifully flawed, but perfect to me in every way.

"I hope so. Better make it a good one, too. I have to go back to school tomorrow. You won't see me all day."

He rubbed my cheek and then kissed my forehead. "Oh, it's going to be a good one." He flipped his wrist to check his waterproof watch. "Come on. I wanna get out to sea before it gets too hot."

We both jumped in the car, strapped in, and he drove to the docks. During the drive, we were hand-in-hand. I smiled over at him and he returned a half-smile, gripping the wheel and speeding up along the winding road that led to the docks.

He finally let go when we arrived. Parking his Chrysler, he looked over at me and said, "I hope you're ready for today. It just might overwhelm you."

"Overwhelm me?" I laughed, grabbing the door handle. "Well, now I'm even more excited to know what this surprise of yours is." Tossing a wink over my shoulder, I stepped out in my strappy sandals and sundress, looking right over the top of the car at Dirty Black.

There he was. Waiting for us.

Theo started grabbing the coolers and I picked up the bags with the towels and sunscreen in them. "You know, I find it kind of weird that all the things you own that have an engine are all *"he's"* and not *"she's."* Isn't it a guy thing to name their cars and boats after a woman?"

He laughed like he was truly amused by that statement, dragging the cooler on the wheels and pressing his key fob to lock the doors. "I thought about it a few times. I don't know. I guess it all goes way to back to my mom. She used to have a car named Bucky. Bucky was our old reliable car when I was young—the kind of car that broke down every week, but would start right back up just in time so I wouldn't be late for school or her, for work. Whenever she used to talk about it, she'd say *he* and not she. I guess it runs in the family. Tradition thing." He shrugged, lips pressing. "Who knows?"

"Maybe it does. Now that I remember, Izzy's car in high school was named Paul, after Paul Walker."

We both laughed. "Yeah . . . that sounds about right," he continued laughing.

We stepped onto the boat and it wobbled a bit with our added weight. He dropped the coolers near the sitting area, in the shade. I placed our bags down on the deck, in the sun so the towels could get a little warm to lounge on, and Theo walked towards the steering wheel, stuffing the keys in and cranking Dirty Black up.

He started up effortlessly.

I sat down in the chair to his left, smiling up at him as he placed a pair of sunglasses on the bridge of his nose, shielding his eyes.

"You ready?" he asked, quirking a brow, with a small smile playing on his lips.

I held two thumbs up as he gripped the wheel and put the boat in reverse. "Born ready, baby!"

CHAPTER 21

CHLOE

I could feel the ocean spray on my skin as I stood in front of the guardrail, letting the wind ruffle my hair. The boat wasn't going too fast or too slow, just a comfortable speed.

I gripped the silver railing, inhaling the salted air. This was my home. I had grown to love the ocean, even during the storms. Having the ocean in my backyard gave me serenity. During the times that I just needed to be alone, I would walk that very beach.

I would put my feet in the cold water and think . . . think of Theo and the past. About how imperfectly perfect we were. The kind of match we made. About how he touched me, kissed me, and told me that he loved me.

I would never forget the day he snuck into my bedroom when I came home from college, just to tell me that he loved me. I thought about the first time he said those words every day.

The boat finally began to slow down and I realized Theo was making a right turn. Some land appeared, along with a tall wall of jagged, auburn rock. I glanced over my shoulder, but he simply smiled, taking us closer.

There was a shore. A beach.

He stopped the boat when we were closer to shore and docked it to keep the boat in place.

"Theo, where are we? What is this?" I hadn't realized how far we'd actually ridden to get here. It took nearly thirty minutes to reach this destination. Last time, we went less than five minutes out from Bristle Wave and we stayed on the water.

"This," he said, voice dripping with delight, "is your surprise." He walked toward the steps, where the exit of the boat was and flicked his fingers, gesturing for me to follow.

I didn't hesitate. I was too curious and excited to find out exactly where the hell we were.

He helped me off the boat and my feet landed in the shallow blue water. With my hand still in his, he led the way up the shore and onto the pristine, white sand. There were no footprints, no trace of human life, other than ours.

He made his way towards the jagged rocks, walking a few feet down until a small hole in the rocks appeared. The entrance was carved by nature, the edges of it smooth and slick with mist.

Theo kept walking. We were going into a cave. It grew darker, but only a little. There was light inside this cave, coming from small holes above that allowed the sunlight to filter in.

I looked over at him, but he kept his gaze ahead, as if he knew that whatever he was looking for was close.

And then it appeared.

He didn't have to announce it for me to see.

Because it was right there.

So beautiful. So full of life. Simply amazing.

A gaping hole was formed in the ceiling of the cave, rays of gold showering down on the water below. There was even more sand here, the clear, blue water rushing up to the small shore. It was a beach.

A *hidden* beach.

It was incredible, and for a moment I held my breath, squeezing Theo's hand, unable to form the right words.

I finally felt him looking my way, but I couldn't pull away from this view. The water tunneled to shore and then retreated. The waves were gentle, and the water looked deep enough to swim in.

I took a few steps forward to see where the water was coming from and there was another entrance. This entrance was big enough to fit *Dirty Black* through, but I wouldn't have risked it. The edges of it were much sharper than the one we came through by foot.

But through that gaping entryway, I could see the entire ocean. I could see boats from a distance and seagulls flying by. An infinite supply of blue water.

"Holy shit," I breathed. This place . . . it was . . . it was *everything.*

"Does that mean you like it?" Theo's dimples were on display when I turned to face him.

I was speechless. I could feel my head shaking and my pulse in my ears. I could feel the excitement and joy coursing through my entire body, but I had no words. I couldn't explain myself enough in that moment to let him know that I loved it.

I loved it so, so, *so* damn much.

This surprise? It was epic. Truly fucking epic.

He scratched the top of his head, nervous as I stared at him, mouth agape. I realized I still hadn't spoken, so he did.

"Do you remember when I took you out on the boat for the very first time and you asked me what I did whenever I sailed out alone?"

I barely nodded, clamping my mouth shut.

"Well . . . I came here. I found it once with Dane. Three times I visited this place, but being here alone wasn't really fun—peaceful, but not fun. It was lonely. So I didn't come here anymore after that third time. But I did make a promise to myself that if I ever fell in love again after Janet, that I would bring her here. And I would show her a good time. I would make it the best day of her life . . . one she will never forget."

My mouth parted. I wanted to speak—wanted to scream. So many words were on the tip of my tongue, ramblings like: *Thank you. I love you so much for bringing me here. I can't believe this place. It's beautiful! Such an amazing man with a big heart. How have I been living without you?*

He sighed. "If you don't like it or think it's too much, we can go. We can stay on the boat—do something else to occupy ourselves and forget we ever came here—"

"No, Theo," I murmured, focused on him. "No. Are you kidding me?" My laugh was hoarse and raw but genuine. "I . . . I *love* this. I love it so much. This place?" I held my hands out, spinning around in my frilly blue cover-up dress. "It's *perfect*, babe. So damn perfect."

Relieved, he put on one of his boyish, lopsided grins and then he said, "Well what the hell are you standing over there for? Come here. Show me you really love it."

I laughed a laugh that made my entire body feel tingly, and then rushed into his arms, fastening them around his neck. My mouth crashed down on his as he gripped my waist and picked me up in his strong, inked arms.

Clasping my ass in his hands, he groaned and then sighed, allowing me to thread my fingers through his thick hair and French kiss him. The passion burned inside me for him. I didn't want to let up or stop.

In this cave, alone with him, it felt like some sort of small haven. A *safe* haven. Like nothing could touch us. No one could see us. No one could disturb or shame us. Nothing could penetrate our love.

So you can bet your ass I didn't stop, because I had no reason to let up. I kissed him until his arms became tired and he had to lay me on my back on the cool sand. I felt it getting in my hair, on our skin, but we kept going.

Not too much later and he had my dress shoved up and my bathing suit bottoms down to my ankles, his board shorts down to his. I could feel his firm ass as I slid my fingers down and clutched it— could feel his tip at my entrance, anxious, thick, and ready.

I gripped his hips and forced him inside me. Both our mouths were touching, but they parted as he plunged deeper.

And deeper.

And deeper.

When he was completely inside, he flashed a small white smile, his eyes narrow and calm, and said "I want to share the rest of my life with you, Chloe."

Then he dropped his face to the crook of my neck, kissing me like he couldn't get enough of my body. And he stroked, so full and deep that my nails sank into his warm skin.

His hard body against mine was more than enough to put me over the ledge. He held the back of my neck with one hand, his mouth on my chin as I tilted my head back and breathed out my pleasure.

He pumped a little faster now and I gasped, holding on tighter, listening to the water crashing in, meeting the shoreline, feeling the distant rays from where we lay, burning bright and true.

"It's always been you, baby," he whispered against the shell of my ear, voice ragged and gruff. "Always you, Little Knight."

Moments later, after our mouths connected and he rocked inside me, we exploded. We shattered together in that beautiful, hidden cave. I screamed his name as loudly as I wanted to because no one but him could hear it.

He groaned louder than I'd heard in a while, holding the back of my neck tight, his muscles tensing.

He brought his mouth down on mine as our bodies writhed and came undone, kissing slowly this time. Passionately. Still giving light thrusts as he emptied himself inside me.

I broke the gentle kisses to clasp his face in my hands. I studied his eyes, his handsome face, the small smile that lingered on his lips, and how truly happy he was with me, right here, right now.

"You are mine and I am yours," I whispered on his lips. "And as long as we remember that, I know we'll be okay."

His face softened, but he didn't say a thing, only kissed me all over again with his warm lips, showing me how much I truly meant to him.

CHAPTER 22

THEO

We spent the better half of our day inside the cave, sitting near the water with our towels behind us. The sun was perched high in the sky —the perfect day for this. Here. With her.

We swam around in the shallow part of the water, closest to the shoreline for a while. I wasn't sure what aquatic life actually came in these parts, but it seemed safe enough. Like any regular beach, only inside a cave. As long as we didn't go too deep, I figured we were fine.

She had music playing from her portable speaker, the song 90210 by Blackbear blasting out, laughing about something she remembered about one of her students.

I had her gripped in my arms, the water sloshing between our chests. When her head fell back and her laugh came out shriller, I smiled. She was so beautiful.

Fuck, this girl was everything to me. Everything and more. I hadn't felt this happy since Isabelle was born, and that was over twenty-five years ago.

I didn't feel this way with Janet.

Definitely not with Sheila.

But her. I don't know what it was about her. Maybe it was because I could remember how she was there for me during some of my darkest times, helping me up to my bedroom, taking care of me when she could have just ignored me from her home on Primrose.

Janet would have left me in the garage until I pulled my shit together and Sheila . . . well, she wouldn't have known what the hell to do besides nag me.

But even at the mere age of nineteen, Chloe Knight was there to save me. She was there to pull me out of my dark, dangerous spiral to hell. She brought me back to life with her small kisses, her sweet giggles, and the heart that was made of pure, solid gold.

I'd never met anyone purer. Never thought a woman so simple and loving could care for someone as fucked up as me. But she did. She cared, and she showed it every single day. The fact that she could make me harder than a rock was another upside. A great one, in fact.

"You know," I started when she finally settled her glee, "when you left, I wanted to hate you."

She blinked rapidly, her face going board straight. "*Did* you hate me?" she whispered, sliding out of my arms and landing on the ocean floor.

"No," I replied. "Of course not."

And she flashed a little smile of relief, lowering her gaze, letting her thick eyelashes touch her cheekbones.

"I knew I wasn't going to be happy again without you. Not completely. Not like how I feel right now. I felt so goddamn empty the past four years, Chloe. Empty and hollow and . . . useless. Like . . . if I didn't have you, what was my purpose? Why move forward when I couldn't even come home to your smile or warmth? Why bother trying?"

Her lips pressed as she brought her gaze up again. "I know . . . and I'm so sorry, Theo."

I shook my head. "Don't be. I think I know why it happened."

She was a mildly confused now. "Why?"

"To make us stronger . . . better. Despite what's going on back at home, I feel like our connection has grown a lot, almost to the point that I'm astounded by it. Because I know that if I fuck up, it could destroy us."

Her damp eyelashes fused together. She shut her eyes for a few seconds. "You won't fuck up," she assured me, holding my waist and drawing me closer. "You know how I know?"

"How?"

"Because we are going to settle this together. We're going to talk to Izzy whenever she has the time and I'm going to go and tell Sterling the truth. And as for Sheila . . . well, if you need me for that too, I'll be there. I won't run or hide." She laughed about something, her head moving left and right in a light shake. "I didn't want to talk about them while we were out here, and listen to me?" She lightly scoffed.

"So?" I stroked her cheek. "This is different. You're being optimistic and that optimism is exactly what we need right now." Her grin was contagious. "Come on. Let's go eat and have some drinks. Relax on the beach for a little while. We can still make this about us."

She bobbled her head like a child. "I like the sound of that."

We ate, listening to music and the sound of crashing waves. She had a few fruity alcoholic drinks while I sipped on the bourbon in my flask. She found it amusing that the flask was custom-engraved to say, *"It's Mr. Black to You."*

"Who made that for you?" she asked, biting into a carrot.

"Izzy. It was a Christmas gift. It was a little joke she made when she brought one of her friends to San Francisco once." I read over the bold red letters. "Her friend called me *Theodore* the first time she met me—my full damn name. I had to scratch my head when I heard it and Izzy could only laugh when I said to her, 'It's Mr. Black, but nice to meet you.'" I laughed. "Funny, she hasn't brought that friend back since then." I ran a hand over my damp hair. "As a matter of fact, she hasn't brought anyone around in a while. No friends. No boyfriends, which is good news by the way." I rolled my eyes at that and Chloe smacked her teeth, swatting a hand at me.

"She can have boyfriends, crazy!"

"Not around me, she can't." I placed the flask down and she started drawing circles in the sand outside her towel.

"Why do you think she hasn't brought anyone around? You think it might be because of me?" she asked.

"What makes you think that?"

"I don't know." She hesitated, avoiding my line of sight. "Maybe, deep down, she's afraid another one of her friends might fall for you. She doesn't want to go through that again. I mean, you are hot, Theo. Hot as hell. I think sometimes you forget that."

I scoffed. "I'm an old man that just so happened to fall for my daughter's former best friend. Was it planned? No. Would I ever do it again with another one of her friends? Fuck, no. Do I regret what happened between us? Hell, no."

She blushed at that, twisting onto her knees and crawling towards me. "I guess you are an old man now, huh?" she teased, eyes trained on my lips. "Your gray hair looks good on you, though. I wouldn't change a thing."

"Yeah, yeah. That's what you say now. But when I'm sixty and you're forty—"

"I will still love you," she said, louder than me, so I couldn't finish my sentence. "I don't care about the age. I never have. I love you because you're *you*, and I wouldn't have my Theodore Benjamin Black any other way."

All right. I admit, that one snagged my heart a little.

I grabbed her upper arms. "Come here," I chuckled as I pulled her on top of me.

She yelped as I squeezed her ass in my hands, but she didn't hold off on kissing me. She molded against my body, sinking between my legs, combing her fingers through the silver hair that I somewhat hated, but dealt with because it came with age.

But if she loved it, I'd keep it.

Because I was hers.
Forever hers.

CHAPTER 23

CHLOE

The ride back was peaceful.

I was tired, but it felt good to have the golden rays of sunset on my skin, the warmth covering my bare shoulders and legs while the wind and ocean spray caressed me.

We'd left the cave with smiles bigger than when we'd arrived there. We left with our hearts on our sleeves, beating in unison. I kept feeling him watching me as he pulled the anchor up and drove away from our little safe haven.

I felt eyes on me again, and I glanced over my shoulder to look at him. He was holding the wheel and, as expected, his eyes were glued on me. A smile graced those full lips, his eyes mellow.

"I love you," he mouthed.

I fought a smile, heat creeping up my neck and to my cheeks. "I love you, too," I mouthed back.

His smile—so damn childlike and handsome. Even for his age, he looked so young. Like he had no worries in the world; I knew that the reality was that he had many.

I looked towards the ocean again, drawing my knees up to my chest. Dirty Black rocked and swayed, but the sounds, they were serene: the sloshing of the water hitting the boat, the seagulls, and the wind rushing past my ears.

There were many times in my life where I felt utter happiness, but this moment—this quiet, serene, beautiful moment . . . well, this was it.

This was bliss.

I never wanted to let it go.

I would hold on for as long as I could, as tight as my muscles and fingers would allow me.

This was our joy. Our foundation. *Our* life.

Despite what was in store, I was so glad we were taking it back again.

We had everything unpacked from the car and were back at Theo's suite.

"I need a shower, badly." I rubbed my hair and grains of sand landed on the floor.

"Well go ahead," he gestured towards the bathroom. "I'll unpack the leftover food so it doesn't spoil, and come join you in a second." He dropped his bag on the floor, coming my way. When he was close, he nudged me against the wall, grabbing my hand and bringing it up to kiss the back of it. "Did you enjoy your surprise?"

"I did." My belly filled with heat. "It was perfect."

"The perfect day," he murmured.

"Date," I corrected. "It was a date, and it was the best one I've ever had."

"Hmm . . . I didn't think of it as a date. It just felt like another day with my sexy Knight."

I burst out laughing as he ran the tip of his nose up my jawline. When his lips came up to my earlobe, I shuddered, even more so when he kissed me there.

When he brought his lips back down and they brushed across mine, I sighed, hooking an arm over his shoulder. He clutched my hip and picked me up, sinking between my legs when my back hit the wall.

His lips claimed mine and I moaned, my fingers touching the hair at the nape of his neck. He groaned, holding my hips tighter, his breaths shaky, like it was hard for him to resist.

"I don't wanna end up making you dirtier." His forehead pressed down on mine.

"That's what showers are for, right? I'll wash up like new."

He vibrated with laughter, kissing me again. As his hand slid up to my hip and beneath the waistband of my bottoms, a throat cleared from somewhere. It wasn't either of us.

It was light. Girly.

"Um . . . *Dad?*"

I knew that voice. There was only one person in the world that called him that. And when it registered . . .

HOLY. SHIT!

Theo jerked away from me like I was a hot skillet. When we heard the sound of Izzy's voice, I felt my chest tighten with fear. He lowered me to my feet and turned as quick as lightning to face her.

Her head was slightly tilted, but she didn't seem confused at all by what was going on. She looked from him and then over at me. She watched me for the longest time, and then released a shaky breath.

Theo and I stayed motionless. I was hardly breathing.

Not this again. We still hadn't told her. I knew we should have before we got deeper. I knew it. We shouldn't have stalled. We should have just confessed before she left.

I looked away, staring down, as Theo took a step towards her.

"Isabelle, what the hell are you doing here? I thought you were in the OC?" Theo asked, still shocked.

"I *was*," she replied, putting emphasis on the word. "But we wrapped up for a temporary break." She paused. "Good news is, the directors are easy to work with this time."

"Oh . . . *shit*." Theo ran his fingers through his hair, fidgeting on his feet. We were all quiet for the longest time. But, of course, Izzy didn't allow the awkwardness to swallow us whole.

She, of all people I'd ever met, hated awkward moments.

She walked past us, where we stood in front of the wall near the bathroom, and dropped her purse down on the table in the corner. She looked around the hotel, as if searching for something else. I wasn't sure what.

My heart was pounding so hard. Dangerously hard. I was certain Theo could hear it from where he stood. The drumming was drowning out all other sounds.

"Okay," she started, holding her hands up, ready to strike. Her brown hair was braided into a fishtail, her cheeks flushed red. Perhaps I wasn't the only one that was embarrassed to no end.

"Izzy," Theo pleaded, stepping forward with a hand out. "We were going to tell you once you got back. I promise."

"Oh, I'm . . . I'm not *mad* or anything, if that's what you guys are thinking." She cracked a smile and my eyebrows drew together as I took an inch of a step to Theo's right to get from behind him. "I stopped by to visit because you told me you were still here. I got in with the room key I had. Maybe I shouldn't have been so quiet coming in—or probably should have knocked first. I was just hoping I could surprise you." She forced a small smile. "I . . . was hoping I wouldn't walk into something like *this* though."

Theo stared, but said nothing. He was waiting for her to lash out, same as I was. Waiting for her to yell, or scream, or throw a tantrum, like she did when she found out about us the first time.

But she didn't.

Instead, she walked towards the couch and sat on the arm of it. Theo walked closer. I took a step ahead as well, but kept my distance, just in case she decided to spring up and claw my damn eyes out at any given moment.

"What's the matter?" he asked her, like he knew something was wrong.

She twisted her lips and looked around before lowering her eyes and pinning them on me. "Do you really *love* her, Dad? Or is this just some cry for attention?"

He was quiet for a moment. When he looked my way, I could only press my lips with a slight shrug.

"You know, I—I can go if you guys need to talk in private—"

"No." Her voice was hard and serious as she cut me off. "Stay." She swung her eyes over to Theo again. "Dad, answer the question."

He blew a heavy breath, picking his hands up and then dropping them as if they were dead weight. "Yeah. Yeah, Iz, I do love her. I never stopped loving her, even when we were apart. It's not a cry for attention. She's it for me."

She thought on that before speaking again. "Did it kill you not to be with her . . . because of me?"

He sighed. "Everyday, Iz. But it wasn't your fault. Things just . . . happened. Things that were out of your control."

"Hmm." She sat back and stretched her legs. As she looked out of the window, she let out a small, bitter laugh. "I used to wonder why you loved her so much—why it had to be my *best friend* you wanted so much. I don't know what it was about the two of you, but it made me so upset, because in my head, you were like a father to her, too. Back then I would have rather you been alone than with her. That's how selfish I was. How inconsiderate I *used to be*."

She peered over his shoulder at me and I winced, still without words.

"That's what I *used to* think. But I understand now." Standing, she walked around Theo to come to me and I took a step sideways when she was less than a foot away.

"I'm not pissed, Chloe. I'm not even angry or shocked. I'm . . . just . . ." she trailed off, and I could see her eyes welling up. I looked over at Theo for a clue, but all he could do was hike his shoulders up and hold his hands out. He didn't know what to do either.

"Look, I know what it feels like to love someone that you know you can't have," she continued. "I know how amazing it feels to have that alone time—like that person understands everything about you. You only want him and nobody else. All you can think about every single day is him. You want to forget about him and move on . . . but you can't, because reality cuts in and you remember that he was never yours to begin with. And that making him yours would cost so much on both ends."

She released a ragged breath, her eyes pooling with tears.

"I hate myself for what I said to you, Chloe. And I really came here because I couldn't *not* say anything, you know? I knew my dad would be with you. Why else would he stay in Bristle Wave, you know?" She let out a raw laugh as she glanced at him. His mouth twitched. "I know he still loves you. He kept hinting at it with me, trying to get me to talk about it, but I wouldn't budge. Only because I didn't know what to say. I could tell he was worried because he didn't want to hurt me by making the same choice again. But . . . I'm not hurt.

"The only thing that hurts me is that I interfered with what you guys shared. It guts me knowing both of you ended up with people you didn't even want. You care for those people, but you don't want them. Not the way you want each other."

She grabbed my hands and my entire body lit up. It was her first time touching me in years. She smiled warmly and then hauled me in, hugging me tight around the neck.

My eyes welled with tears and I gave a quick look over her shoulder at Theo. He stared like he couldn't believe his eyes, but then dropped his head, exhaling. He was so relieved.

And I was astonished. I never thought in a million years I'd be hugging Izzy again, but I was. And I cherished it. I wrapped my arms around her in this moment because she needed me. She needed *us*.

And knowing that caused quite a few tears to shed on my behalf. I didn't know what was up, or why she'd become so sentimental. This wasn't the Izzy I knew when I was twelve, or in high school, or even in college.

This was a different Isabelle Black. A . . . *broken* one.

"I'm sorry," she sniffled over my shoulder. "I really am, Chloe. You were my best friend, and because I was so selfish and judgmental, I ruined what we had."

"No," I cooed. "No, it's okay, Izzy." I grabbed her shoulders and studied her eyes. "It's the past. Okay? You know I would never hold something like that against you. If anyone's to blame, it's me."

She tucked a loose strand of brown hair behind her ears. Her face was red, streaks of tears lining her cheeks.

"We were going to tell you," I murmured. "We just . . . didn't know when. Or how, really. We didn't want to upset you."

She sighed. "Trust me, I am the last person that can be upset about this."

"I would understand if you are, even a little bit."

"I'm not, babe. Not now. I promise." Her smile was sincere. An exact replica smile of her father's.

"Are you okay, though?" I asked. It seemed like something was bothering her. Her eyes, they were sad. She was tense. She didn't look happy at all. Something was definitely wrong.

"I'm as great as I'll ever be," she assured me.

"Did you get the role?" Theo asked behind her.

"Oh—yes!" she beamed. "I wanted to tell you that in person." She turned to face Theo. "I did great, Dad. It was awesome. They loved me. I can't wait to go back. They're paying for my stay and everything when I return."

"Well, that's good, Iz. I'm proud of you." He put on a pleased smile for his daughter.

"Besides, um, making out or whatever—" she cleared her throat. "What else were you guys planning on doing today?"

"Not much," Theo responded. We were just going to hang here. Order in."

"Oh, no way." Izzy scoffed and then reached for my hand. "Dad, Chloe and I should catch up. Like, really, *really* catch up." She looked over at me. "What do you say we go to the mall or something? Doesn't close until eight. Remember how we used to get cinnamon pretzel poppers and share them?" Her eyes lit up like they were made of stars.

I laughed because I could remember it very well. I loved our teenage mall trips. That was back when we thought we had it all figured out. Boy, were we wrong. "I would love that."

"Good." She clasped her hands. "I'll go get my suitcase out of the car. You look like you need to get ready so go ahead." She waltzed past me but stopped as she gripped the door handle. "Oh—you don't mind if I steal her from you for an hour or two, do you, Dad?"

He held his hands in the air innocently. "Keep her for as long as you need, Izzy Bear."

She let out a small squeal. "Good. I'll be back!"

She took off in an instant, exiting the hotel room, and when the door was shut behind her, Theo walked my way, a light smile on his lips now. "Well . . . that didn't turn out to be the nightmare I was expecting."

"I know right," I whispered, grinning. My heart was still beating so fast. I was truly excited about this. And shocked. "We'll only be a few hours, I'm sure."

"Take all the time you need. Let her get to know you again. Get to know her again. Start over."

"I can tell something's wrong with her. She looks . . . down. I don't know." I waved a hand, sighing. "You know when she gets around to telling me what's going on with her, I *can't* tell you. Best friend vow. That was our number one rule. Don't tell the parents *anything*, whatsoever, even if we just so happen to date one of them. Only time to tell was if one of us was kidnapped or something."

He looked amused, eyebrows tilting. "Oh, trust me. I remember how you two were. I won't even bother pushing for answers. I'll let her tell me when she's ready." He kissed me on the center of my forehead. "Just make sure my Izzy Bear is okay. Make sure she's happy. And make sure she actually understands our situation." He hesitated, looking me hard in the eyes. "As her father it's . . . well, shit, it's hard to talk about stuff like that. Love and shit. All that girly talk, she did with her mother, not me. I can tell her that I love you, but telling her why and how we started is just . . . awkward as hell, you know?"

"Maybe she won't want to know the details." I patted him on the cheek. "One thing at a time, babe. If it comes down to that, I'll try and explain, but I'm pretty sure she gets it. She's not a little girl anymore."

"Hell, she'll always be my little girl, no matter how old she gets." Wrapping his arms around me, he drew me in and then exhaled. I felt his warm breath run through my hair. I listened to his heartbeat as I rested my ear on his chest. It was pounding with relief. "I'm glad everything is turning around for us."

"Not everything," I sighed. There was still Sheila and Sterling. Sterling, I felt like we could handle because I hadn't heard much from him lately. I didn't know what I was going to get from him once I called and got around to telling him the truth—that I was in love with Theo, had been for many, many years, and that I couldn't really be there for him anymore.

That was a phone call I was seriously dreading.

And Sheila . . . I wasn't so sure. She seemed like the biggest threat and obstacle right now. We knew her time to barge in was bound to come.

CHAPTER 24

CHLOE

Izzy didn't talk much about herself during our trip to the mall. She asked more about Theo and me, how we were doing. If we felt bad about it. So many other deep questions that were tough to answer.

I kind of knew what to expect with Izzy. She liked to dig deep for answers, so I gave them to her in blunt honesty.

"Are you in love with him?" she asked.

"Yes. I have been since I was a senior in high school."

"So weird," she laughed and then popped a pretzel into her mouth. "Do you think he was in love with you back then?"

I pressed my lips. "Um . . . I wouldn't say in love. Maybe he felt *something*, but nothing quite that deep yet."

"When do you think he felt that way—in love with you, I mean?" She narrowed her gaze.

"He told me when I came back home to help my dad while he was sick. We were a few weeks in. He snuck into my bedroom—"

"He snuck into your bedroom!" she sputtered, utterly amused by this.

"Yes," I giggled. "I thought it was sweet. He told me that night that he loved me. And . . . I don't know. For some reason I believed him."

"Because you felt the same," she stated. Not a question. A statement.

"Yes."

She took a sip of her lemonade, waving a hand and sitting back in her chair. "It's still a little . . . weird, I guess. I mean if you were some other chick that I didn't know, I wouldn't find it weird at all. Apparently Dad has a thing for younger girls." She half shrugged. "But . . . it seems freaking legit. Seriously, the fact that he wants to divorce Sheila just to be with you again . . ." Her head shook rapidly. "That takes balls. And love. Lots of it."

I sat up a little when she mentioned Sheila. "Do you think she'll sign the papers?"

"Oh, she'll sign them. She has way too much pride to chase after him or beg." Her tone was confident. I found reprieve in that. "But Sheila's a total bitch. She's, like, the complete opposite of Dad, which is why I *know* she won't make this process easy for him in the slightest."

"A bitch?" I repeated, blinking wildly. "How?"

"What? Dad hasn't told you the crazy-as-fuck stories about her?" She looked me over and my eyes stretched a little wider, demanding answers. When she saw that I was completely clueless she sat up again, dropping her pretzel back in the cup. "She's the reason they're even married—giving him ultimatum's and shit. It's why I've never really tried getting closer to her. Wait . . . he really hasn't told you about *anything* she's done?"

"No," I mumbled.

Her face scrunched a bit. "That's . . . weird. I guess he doesn't want you to know about that side of her. He doesn't want you to worry. Damn it." She looked away, towards the restaurants lined up in the food court. "I've probably said too much then."

"No, Izzy. As a matter of fact, you haven't said enough." I grabbed her hand and squeezed it, forcing her to look at me again. "Tell me what she's done. I need to know everything about her if I'm going through this with him."

Her eyes were just like his when she knew she was in trouble. She lowered her gaze, focusing on my cup of grape soda. "Chloe, I—" She paused. "Chlo, I really think you should talk to him about this. You know I love gossiping, but not when it comes to my Dad. Plus, he'll get the story right. He's only told me the stories over the phone right after they happened. I might . . . I don't know . . . mix up the details or something." She shrugged hard, like she really didn't know the full story. But I knew she did. Theo told me he called Izzy at least every other day to check in with her, and if he didn't call, she would.

Their bond was strong. She knew, but I didn't want to push or force the secrets of her father out of her because she was right. It wasn't her business or story to spread. Theo could tell me himself, but I wondered why he hadn't already.

"Oh, come on. Cheer up, Chlo." Izzy stood and walked over to grab my hand. "Let's go shop around. Talk about something else—like how your teaching is going."

I pushed my lips together, standing when she tugged on it. "Sure. That sounds good."

But deep down I was impatient. I didn't want to shop or talk about my career and myself. I wanted to get back to the hotel immediately and get some answers out of him.

I knew how Izzy liked to exaggerate things, so maybe it wasn't a big deal, but as she passed me weary glances on our way to *Forever 21* while asking me about the school, I figured perhaps she wasn't exaggerating. That perhaps Sheila was a good cause for concern after all.

CHAPTER 25

THEO

I heard the hotel door open from the bedroom. Izzy was laughing a girly, lighthearted laugh I hadn't heard in years. I smiled, gripping the edge of the door, but not walking out yet.

"We should go out tomorrow, too," she said, her laughter dying. "Maybe we can get our nails done or something. I'm sure I need it." I glanced over and Izzy had her hand up, checking her cuticles.

"Yeah. I could use a good pedicure," Chloe responded. "It'll have to be after school lets out, but we can definitely make that happen."

"Great." Izzy looked sideways and I stepped out, arms folded as I smiled at the two of them from where I stood. "Well, I booked a hotel for myself. I know you two need your . . . privacy." Her smile was a bit uneasy. I could tell it still made her uncomfortable, knowing what we were really doing behind closed doors, but she was trying and as long as she was, that's all that mattered.

"Oh, Izzy, stay as long as you want!" Chloe waved a dismissive hand, side-eyeing me. "I'm sure we won't really need privacy tonight. I have an early morning."

153

"Oh, no, Chlo, I can't. I have some scripts to go over and some emails to check before bedtime. I will be here tomorrow as soon as you come by, though. I swear it. You have my number." Izzy glanced at me nervously and my brows dipped. Why was she in such a rush? Most times she procrastinated having to catch up on what needed to be done.

Chloe's lips pulled down as Izzy gripped the doorknob and smiled at us. "Dad, I'll see you for breakfast tomorrow?"

"Yeah, sweetie," I said. "I'll be here."

She gave a wary smile.

All right. What the fuck was going on?

Izzy pulled the door open and walked out, glancing back once at Chloe with a hard, serious look before taking off. When the door clicked shut behind her, Chloe didn't even bother looking in my direction. Instead she marched for her tote bag in the corner and slung it onto her shoulder.

"You should get me home. It's getting late and I have a few assignments to get together before class." Her voice was tight. She glanced up when I didn't say anything, and when I came closer and extended a hand, she held up her own, stopping me in my tracks.

"Theo . . . please. I should get home."

"What's wrong?" I asked, looking her over."

"Nothing, I'm fine." I could tell she was lying. Her arms crossed tightly over her chest, her own little shield.

"What is it? Sterling calling you again?" I took a step forward, face serious now. "Did he say something to you?"

Her eyes narrowed as she picked her head up. "What? No! No, Theo. It's not Sterling this time. It's you!"

"What? What about me?"

"We're supposed to be doing things right this time, Theo. I trust you and you trust me. That's what we're supposed to do, remember? Not keep secrets from each other, especially about things that obviously should be discussed."

"What—Chloe, what the hell are you talking about?"

She blew an agitated breath. "Nothing. It's nothing." She waved a hand.

I paused. I couldn't escalate whatever the hell was going on by pestering her for answers. So I took the easy route. The longer I made her hold it in, the more willing she would be to tell me.

So I said, "Well since you don't want to be an adult and tell me, I'm taking a shower. I'll drop you off after I get out. Just wait for me."

She scoffed and dropped down on the couch, rolling her eyes and staring through the window that revealed the ocean. I watched her, hoping she'd break, but she didn't.

So I got in the shower like I said. It was the longest shower of my fucking life. What the hell could it be? Izzy had to have told her something while they were together—something that probably had me looking like a complete fucking jackass to Chloe.

That was one thing I didn't miss—their gossip. They chirped like birds whenever they had something juicy to talk about. When I got out of the shower, she was still sitting in the same spot.

Sighing, I strolled to the bedroom, taking out some clothes to wear from my suitcase. I heard footsteps as I slid into my boxers and then into basketball shorts.

She was right between the frames of the door, when I glanced back. No bags strapped around her. Just that same guard up again, her arms folded and face solemn.

"What haven't you told me about Sheila?" she demanded. She glared like she knew something I didn't. Or maybe she knew nothing at all, but knew there were a few things I hadn't told her.

And I hadn't yet . . . for a reason.

CHAPTER 26

CHLOE

Theo rubbed the towel through his hair. "What do you mean? I've told you pretty much everything about her."

"Have you really?"

His eyebrows narrowed. He seemed utterly confused. He looked at me from head to toe, and when he brought his eyes back up and locked on mine again, his shoulders sagged and he released a gradual, heavy breath.

"Shit," he grumbled. "What the hell did Izzy say to you about her?"

"Oh, nothing . . . just that she's a total bitch, and that she may or may not have forced you into marrying her." I took a step forward. "I thought that's what you *wanted*—to marry her. Why didn't you tell me she forced you into it?"

His head shook but he said nothing.

I threw my arms in the air. "Seriously, Theo! What don't I know about her? What are you trying to hide?"

"I'm not hiding anything!" His voice was mildly agitated now.

"So why did Izzy tell me she'd make the divorce hard for you? I thought you said she'd agree."

"She will agree." He slouched down on the edge of the bed.

"Okay." I held my hands out and took another step forward, glaring at him. I had to remember that I couldn't get angry. In order for him to tell me I needed him calm. *I* needed to be calm.

So I walked closer and then knelt down on the floor, in the gap between his legs. He pushed his hands through his hair, dragging them over his face.

"Theo." My plea was soft. I grabbed his wrists to stop his rough hands.

When he finally opened his eyes and looked into mine, he whispered "I'm sorry, Chloe."

"For what?"

"Not telling you everything from the start. I should have. I was going to. I was just—well, shit. Like I said before, I know how she is. She'll sign the papers, but I also know deep down she isn't going to make this easy. She's going to try and make it a fucking nightmare."

I squeezed his hands tighter, even more worried now. "But how? There's not much she can do. You didn't have kids together. You have your own career and she has hers. So what she gets a little of your money in the end? I'm sure we'll be fine."

"No, Chloe. That's where you're wrong. She won't get a *little bit* of my money if shit works in her favor. She'll probably wind up with a lot, and I'll end up broke, losing all the money I saved up." I swallowed hard. "I had to add Sheila as co-owner of Black Engine. The loan I needed was too big for me to get alone, with my income back then. I was between jobs, working for people when I moved there instead of for myself. With me still paying off Izzy's student loans, her car, and the mortgage in San Francisco, they weren't going to approve me unless I had a co-signer."

My grip slacked on his. "Oh."

"This happened before we were even married. She knew I needed a fresh start, and that I wanted to start up my own shop, so she offered me a deal. She said she'd sign with me and give me my dream, just as long as we got married by the end of summer. She'd been talking about it a lot before. I kept avoiding the subject. I wasn't ready to be married again—especially to her. I'd just met her. But after what happened with you and me, I felt like I didn't have much else to lose .. . so I did it.

"But she took advantage of the situation, and I was a fool not to consider the consequences. She wanted to be part-owner of my business, as well, not just the person signing off so I could get the loan. The loan is almost paid off. I've made it a profitable business, and she knows it. She knows how the books run, how much I'm making a week. She knows I don't have to work every day because business is *that* good. She does interior designing, which only gets her money every few months. Big chunks here and there, but it runs out fast with her. She's a big spender. She shops . . . a lot. Sometimes for shit she doesn't even need. I'd hate to say it but . . ." He trailed off, wary now. Looking at me with an unsure gaze.

"What?" I asked. I pushed up to my feet and sat beside him. "Tell me, Theo."

"She's almost like Trixie in some ways, just older. More mature, but still desperate for attention, and definitely selfish at times. When we planned the wedding, she didn't care about what I wanted. She didn't care about any of my ideas or even how expensive it would be. She planned it all with her sister and mother. She was a bridezilla. She didn't even invite my mother to the wedding, and I asked her many times if she'd sent the invitation because I saw her making it out to her. She swore she did, and I figured mom just hadn't received it or got it too late and couldn't RSVP, but I worked on Sheila's car once, cleaned it out, and saw Mom's invitation in her glove box months after the wedding date. She'd never sent it."

"What?" I hissed. I was disgusted. "Why would she do that?"

"Because Izzy is right. Sheila's a bitch. She didn't want anyone changing my mind, or making me think twice about going through with marrying her. She's manipulative and controlling, and if shit doesn't go her way she throws a fucking tantrum about it. She hasn't called for two days and, I admit, it has me worried. It means she's probably planning something. It won't be good."

I watched his eyes glaze, not with sadness but with anger. He knew this—all of this—but didn't want to tell me. And I understood why. He didn't want me worrying.

Because right now I was panicking. She had control of the situation. She could have all or most of his money if she wanted— if she played her cards right.

"She could accuse me of some bullshit that isn't true," he went on. "And they might believe her. That's how great of a liar she can be."

"Then you'll get a lawyer. A good one. My father knew a ton of them and I still have their numbers in my address books. I can reach out to them," I insisted.

He shook his head. "If they're as good as you say, it'll cost too much, Chloe. I'm better off saving what I can now with the guy I already have."

"Who cares about expenses? You have the money, Theo. You can fight against her. I can help. My dad left me a great deal of money before he passed away. I haven't touched it much because it's my rainy day fund, but I don't mind taking some out to help you."

He peered up at me. "Stop, Chloe. You don't have to do that. Besides, I can't fight her if I don't know what she's up to."

I blinked rapidly. "So . . . what are you saying?"

His lips pressed. *Silence.*

"That you want to go meet her?" I whispered for him.

"It would be the wisest thing to do. Talk it out with our lawyers. Make sure she's calm. I will be able to tell if I need to gear up or if I can relax about it and just prepare for a small dent in my pocket. If I need heavier gear, then we'll talk to the lawyers your father knew."

I pulled my gaze away, staring down at my lap now. He tilted my chin just as quickly as it dropped and put my eyes on his again.

"She won't win," he murmured, tightening his grip on my chin.

"If you see her and she tries to kiss you or—"

"She won't."

"How do you know?"

"Because I won't let her get close enough. Besides," he smirked. "She'll smell you on me. She'll know you've been around. I'm sure of it. Should make her want to keep her distance."

"Theo, this is serious. If you go see her and it backfires, or she gives you another ultimatum to stay or she'll ruin your life, what the hell do I do?"

I shot up to my feet, and he did the same. "Chloe, would you stop?" He watched me pace the room while raking frantic fingers through my hair. "That's not going to happen. It's starting to sound like you don't have faith in me now."

I looked over and he cocked a brow, demanding a response to that statement. "I trust you," I said firmly. "It's *her* I don't trust. Izzy says you tolerate her. She feels like she owns you, and I see now it's because she has partnership of *your* company."

He sighed again. "Chloe, just calm down and come here."

My lips trembled, but I walked towards him. He tugged me into his arms and his warm skin pressed on mine, his lips on my forehead now.

When he tilted his head back to look down at me, he murmured "I was with her for four years, Chloe. I know enough about her to know better. I know that when she starts to shoot her guns, to have my cannons ready. If you think I'm going to go down like some fucking pussy, you have me mistaken for Sterling. Look, I've talked to my lawyer. He told me it would be an easy and simple case, if I do my part. He's working on getting my name off the contract for the shop. All I have to do is pay the bank $10,000 by the end of the month and then change the name of it."

"How are you gonna come up with that much money in such a short amount of time?"

"I have an account she doesn't know about. A security box at the bank. I've saved money from way back, when Janet and I were married, just in case a time like this would come. If I'm adding it up correctly, I should have over $65,000 in there. I have a rainy day fund, too," he smirked. "But it was really for Izzy in case something happened and she needed help."

I gasped. "Really?"

He nodded. "Well, that's great then! But how will paying the loan and changing the name of the shop get her out of it?"

"I'm the sole proprietor of the business. In the contract for Black Engine, she is only co-owner as long as the shop has that business name. All I have to do is pay off that loan and relaunch myself. I will change the name of my company so she won't have any ownership over the new one. She can have the Black Engine name, whatever profits are left from it, but I know she won't bother keeping it running under her own name if I'm not running it anymore. It's a loophole we found. It's risky, but we think it will work. Right now she is considered an owner via investment in Black Engine, but if I return her investment, which paying off the loan will do, change the name and get a new business license, the contract we signed together will most likely become null and void. I can keep my garage, but I'll have to wait a while, get a new name, if she decides to keep the Black Engine name. I'd rather see it run to the ground than let stay it afloat for her benefit, or to use to manipulate me. The whole thing may confuse customers, and I could end up losing some money the first few months from the expenses Black Engine has, but it's a risk worth taking if it means I can spend the rest of my life with you."

I couldn't help myself then. I blushed and smiled way too hard. "So you've had this planned before you even told her you wanted a divorce?"

"Yes. And it's a good thing the contract is freestanding. Means nothing is set in stone and it can be disputed. The house and all the other shit . . . well, for all I care she can keep it and if she doesn't, I'll sell it. I don't care as long as I can get my name off the mortgage."

"And you're sure she won't win?"

"I'm about 99.9% positive. She can pull her stunts, delay the process for investigations and whatever else she can scrape up, but she won't get very far." He revealed those beautiful dimples. "My lawyer worked out some of those kinks."

I smiled. "I hope you're right, Mr. Black." I looked towards the door, lips pushing together. "When will you go meet her?"

"Within the next two weeks, maybe. I have to call her. Is that okay with you?" I bobbed my head. He kissed my cheek. "Good."

"Maybe I should go with you?"

He thought on it, head tilting a bit as he watched my eyes. "You can come," he murmured. "But if things get too tense, you can't run away. I need you there for me. I need you to fight with me."

"And I will."

"Promise."

"I promise," I whispered, and then kissed the light scruff on his chin.

"That's my Little Knight." He twirled me around and I landed gently on the bed. He climbed between my legs, his groin meshing with mine, and I wrapped my arms around him, hauling him closer, kissing him deep.

We could do this. We could win.

CHAPTER 27

CHLOE

The following afternoon, my eyes burned with unshed tears. I may have been being a little dramatic, but it was harder than I thought, seeing my students off on their last day of school.

Of course, they were filled to the brim with adrenaline and joy, now that summer was here, rather than the small amount of sorrow that lingered inside me, but it was okay. I was proud of them, and certain I'd see them roaming the halls again next school year.

"I have waited so long for this," Kim sighed as she leaned against the wall with me, watching the students nearly scream their damn heads off with excitement as the final bell rang.

"I don't know. I'm kind of sad," I admitted as they whizzed toward the exit. "They're leaving me for another teacher that may or may not know a little more than I do. I almost feel cheated."

Kim laughed, folding her arms. "Hey, be glad they aren't coming back. It means you did a great job teaching them." She looked over at me with a tilted smile. "I haven't heard much since you skipped out for that trip with him. How are things with the silver fox?"

"Oh, they're great, Kim. Great with him, and Izzy too. I'm actually meeting her in about an hour so we can get our nails done and catch up a little."

"Ooh, sounds like things are getting serious again," she said, eyes lit with excitement.

I couldn't fight my laugh. "Maybe. But there's still a lot for us to handle. With Sterling, and Theo's wife." I rolled my eyes just thinking about it, collecting some of the papers on my desk and stuffing them in a folder. "As soon as that's out of the way, we're free. I don't think Izzy minds so much anymore. She's not acting too weird about us or anything so I think that's a start."

"It is. Sounds like you have it all planned," Kim noted.

"I just think by us moving slowly, taking our time this time, that it helps. Last time it was—I don't know. Rushed. Lusty. Unfinished. This time, there are fewer interruptions. We don't really have that fear of someone barging in on us like before and losing each other. And even if someone does, what the hell are they gonna do, you know?"

She nodded with a smile. "I hear you, girl. Well, let me know how your nail trip goes. I'll be in my classroom trying to get my shit together so I won't have to come back to this hellhole more than I need to this summer. You'll call me?"

I nodded with a smile as she started towards the door. "Of course I'll call you. We'll meet soon to catch up too. I promise!"

"Oh, please, take your time! I want my details deep, filthy, and long, just like I want my men when I bring them to bed. There's no rush!"

Around 4:30 that afternoon, I was being seated in a plush leather massage chair in a salon close to the ocean and slipping my feet in bubbling, warm water.

This nail salon had a great view of the beach, overlooking the docks, where we could see the boats coming and going, some of the sailors and ordinary people climbing on or off their vessels.

I grinned as I spotted Dirty Black at the end of the docks, its black sails lightly flapping with the wind. That boat had created so many beautiful memories for us.

"What are you over there grinning about?" Izzy's voice cut through and I looked over at her, still smiling as she plopped her feet one by one into the swirling water.

"Nothing," I laughed. "Just thinking."

"About Dad?" she playfully taunted, tilting a curious eyebrow.

I fought the smile that wouldn't go away. "Maybe."

"You know you don't have to lie to me, right, Chlo? I mean we used to tell each other everything. Literally *everything*. I . . . want to get back to that. Minus the details about the sex and stuff, because that would be weird as shit to imagine."

I giggled. "Yeah, it would be." I sat back as the woman grabbed one of my feet and smiled at me from beneath her facemask. As she started to lightly massage them with a foot scrub, I said, "So . . . how have you been? I mean—it's been years. I need updates, chick! Theo told me you went on a trip to India two years ago?" I was prying now. Theo told me that, and also the fact that she didn't come back as the same woman that left him two months prior.

"Oh." Her face dropped as she focused on the old yellow nail polish on her toes. "Yeah, it was great. So beautiful there. It was a meditation and renewal trip. A way to cleanse and replenish your spirit, you know? I realized after that whole encounter here with you, Dad, Sterling, and Trixie, that I had been a complete bitch. I mean, I have never spoken to my dad like that before and didn't think I'd ever become that spoiled, selfish brat, you know? But you want to know what really triggered me to go on that trip?"

"What?" I asked as she studied her lap.

"Well, I had this crazy dream about my mom. It was right after I graduated from college and lived with Dad and Sheila in San Francisco, before I moved back to New York for my job. I . . . uh . . . I don't know. It was so strange. I was in this field of blue grass—her favorite color. There were white flowers and I was wearing all white. I saw a bright gold light appear in front of me and her face appeared. When I saw her standing in all that white and shining with gold, I just broke down. I sobbed as she walked my way with the gentlest smile. But she came to me and held me until I stopped. And she whispered in my ear, all the things that I should have known. That she loved my dad, but more like her best friend rather than a lover. That she loved him for giving her a daughter—me. That she didn't blame him for the night that she died, because he was really tired from working all day and she knew that. She insisted that he go home early that night. She blamed herself for not going home with him. But all this time I'd been blaming Dad, because if he would have waited for her after her party at the bakery, he could have protected her. Saved her. She wouldn't have been gutted by those thugs." She let out a deep, shaky breath. "She would be here now. But I thought about it—that if she was still here, would they have been happy now? As happy as my father is to this day? Because I tell you, Chloe, I have never in my entire life seen my father so happy. I've never seen him shine so much while around someone. He wasn't like that with Mom, and definitely not with Sheila. It's only you." She waved a hand. "I mean, yeah he has that fatherly glow when he sees me after a few weeks, but no. With you, it's different. And I saw it that day that I came back to Bristle Wave for the Fourth of July a few years back, but I ignored it. I saw it when we came back here a few days ago and ran into you on the beach, but I still wanted to ignore it."

I watched her as she picked at her cuticles. I had no words. No thoughts.

"Anyway . . . after that dream—which was super vivid by the way—I looked up ways to recharge. To renew. I wanted to become better, not only for myself, but for Dad too. I couldn't keep putting up a guard against my own father, you know? He's all I have. I needed . . . help. So I did my research and found out about this meditation retreat in India. After I did a little more digging, I made it an official thing. I was going and I was going to come back a better person. A new person that saw the world differently."

"And you did," I murmured. "Theo says you've changed a lot—in a good way."

"I mean, it helped some. I spent some time alone and meditated with a personal guide, who helped me clear my head on most things. He was a really nice and wise guy." She glanced over, as if nervous to speak now.

"What is it, Iz?" I asked softly.

"Well . . ." She sat up a bit and I did too, giving her my undivided attention. "They assigned me to meditation classes that were two people per trainer every three hours. And I was stuck with this guy named Cameron Hughes. He was sweet, funny, and easy to talk to—a surgeon. Cameron made the trip ten times more fun for me. Since we were partnered for meditation, we pretty much did everything else together. We met up for breakfast, lunch, and dinner. We walked around the resort and mostly had small talk about our lives. I told him I'd just graduated and was getting into acting. He said he worked long hours at the hospital and needed a break from the real world." She swallowed hard, rather painfully. "I thought that was great, you know? He was bettering himself, just like me. It was something we had in common. We wanted to cleanse ourselves—be better people for the real world. At first it was just a friendly thing between us, you know? We had our sessions together to meditate, we continued eating meals together so we didn't end up being the loners. We laughed—a lot. Talked about things I probably would only talk about with you. I figured a guy like him wouldn't tell my secrets. He didn't know where I lived or who I really was, and I didn't even know if what he'd said to me was true either. But it was fun. The mystery of that was exciting.

"We had one free day there where we could do whatever we wanted. I decided to go to the spa, get a massage, a facial, and then go back to my room and read up on future scripts for auditions. It was around midnight when I got a knock on the door. It was Cameron, so I let him in. I don't know why I was so happy to see him, maybe it was because he had brought along a bottle of wine that he wasn't even supposed to have, or maybe it was just his presence alone that made me happy." She giggled.

I did as well.

"Anyway," she went on, sighing heavily, "I got us some paper cups and we drank while eating some of the snacks they brought to our rooms every day. It was light and innocent, really. He talked about his free day and how he had gotten this amazing massage and then walked the resort to think, swam at the salt-water pool, and then came back to his hut to take a nap. I told him about my day, how simple it was, but then he caught me off guard with something." She pulled her gaze from mine. "He told me that he had been thinking about coming to my room all day. I told him where it was a while back, just in case he wanted to practice meditating, breathing techniques, or anything of that nature. He caught me completely off guard that I spit all over him. Literally, red wine all over his white shirt. I panicked then and rushed for some towels to help him clean up. But when I came back to the room, his shirt was off. And I couldn't breathe, Chlo. It's like . . . my whole guard went down. All of my self-control went flying out the window. I was stupid to pretend I really wanted to help him clean up. I mean, his chest was a little damp from the wine. But I helped him wipe it away and before I was done, he grabbed my wrist, pulled me closer, and told me he *wanted* me. And . . . I didn't hesitate. I let him kiss me and then take me. I let him take me on the bed, and against the wall, and even on the floor. He stayed the night and I felt . . . whole. I couldn't explain it but I knew I didn't want him to leave and I was glad we had a session together the next morning."

"Wow—Izzy, I—that's great, right?" I smiled bright.

"No." My smile failed me. "I don't know. Something about it felt wrong, even though all at once it felt right. I knew it was bad, but it's like while we were there, nothing else mattered. I mean, we hardly knew one another. We were in an entirely different country, no one to stop us. No one to interrupt or tell us it wouldn't last. It was just us and it was so perfect. Like a dream or some kind of romantic movie."

That sounded familiar.

"We had sex all over that damn resort," she continued. "Got couple massages, fucked in the pools late at night after they were closed." She sighed, and the woman painting her toes looked up rapidly, eyes wider now. Izzy laughed, embarrassed while holding her hands up.

"Sorry," she murmured, and the woman pulled her gaze away, finishing up her paint job.

"Anyway," she went on, looking over at me. "I knew it was going to end soon, and he did as well. Two months we were alone together, doing shit we shouldn't have been doing. We were in my bed together on our last night and I asked him if he would keep in touch with me when he got back. He told he would—*swore* he would. He promised he would even try and see me one day. I gave him my number just in case, but I should have realized then that he didn't give me his and it was most likely on purpose. The last day there, we kissed goodbye and I thought it was only *for now*. At the airport, I was so desperate to see him again that I found him on *Facebook* and sent him a friend request.

"When I got back home I felt so rejuvenated. I felt amazing and truly refreshed. Really, like a brand new person. Remade. I was hoping to hear from him within the next few days, but I didn't. Then two weeks passed, and still nothing. Not a single text. Not a call. Nothing." Her head dropped. I could see her eyes glistening. "Another month and still nothing. Two months," she huffed, "nothing. So I finally decided to check his *Facebook*. He had finally accepted my request—I don't think he knew it was me—and that's when I finally saw that he was married. Had been for six years. And he and his wife had two kids together."

I stared at her, not expecting that one. "Oh my goodness, Iz." I grabbed her hand. "I'm so sorry."

"No. It was my fault," she murmured. "I should have known better than to trust an American man that I met in another country. It was just a fling for him. He was free of his wife and kids and he took full advantage of that. But to me it was much more. I mean I've never shared so much time with just one guy. I've never gotten so deep with someone until him. I told him things about me that I shouldn't have. Things about you and Dad. When the reality of it set in, I realized he'd only told me what he wanted me to hear. How he wanted me. How he was thinking about me. It was all bullshit and I should have known, but I was so blinded by his beauty, his personality, and our uninterrupted time alone.

"You know, I tried messaging him on Facebook to ask him why he didn't just tell me he was married with kids? It showed that he saw my message, but he didn't respond. And then the next day I tried to check up on him and we were no longer friends. I think he saw it was me, the girl from the resort, and blocked me. He never knew my real name. He just knew me by Izzy."

"Wow. What a fucking dick," I snapped.

Her smile was painful. "I deleted my account after that. All of my social media accounts. I changed my number. I wanted nothing to do with him and I never wanted to see or hear from him again."

Damn.

"The resort was great, but I was never going to go there again. It wasn't a regret, but more of a disappointment. But I guess that's what I get for believing his lies. For thinking I was really *that* lucky. That was two years ago. I've tried dating since then but I can't trust anyone enough for it to last."

"That was shitty of him to do, Izzy. You can't blame yourself for his actions."

She was quiet for a while, almost too quiet and too still. She didn't move. Didn't blink. Just stared down at the woman applying a clear coat of nail polish to her toes.

Theo was right. Something was bothering her, and it was *this.* She'd fallen in love with a married man and he'd crushed her, because he'd lied and manipulated her.

I felt so sorry for her. I didn't even know what the hell to say to her in that moment. All the words kept getting lodged in my throat. How was I supposed to make her feel better? What was I supposed to say?

"I get what happened between you and my Dad now . . . at least I think so," she finally said quietly, chewing on her bottom lip. "I shouldn't have been so harsh. Instead, I should have put myself in your shoes." She huffed a laugh. "I think it's funny how that all worked out. Karma is one hell of a bitch, huh?"

"No," I cooed. "Hell no, Izzy. Don't say that. You fell in love with him. That's not Karma. That's life."

"Exactly, but if I hadn't been so bitchy, self-centered, and close-minded about the idea of you and my dad . . ." She gasped a little. "I just thought it was so gross and dumb. Like, what the hell would he want with my best friend? A girl my age? A girl that was like a *sister* to me? I figured he was going through a mid-life crisis or something like that." Her eyes became glassy as she threw a frustrated hand in the air.

I couldn't look away, which gave me the urge to want to cry too. But I kept it together for her, because this time I was her shoulder to cry on. She needed to let this out. She'd been holding it in for so long, I could tell. I was certain this was the first time she was saying all of this aloud.

"But after you left, I spent more time with him. And I realized that while I was there and didn't know about you and him yet, he was so much happier. He was smiling. He was full of life. He laughed and joked and hardly spoke of Mom—at least, not in the negative way like he used to. He was . . . remade. And afterwards, I was still too selfish to think it was because of you. I convinced myself that it was just sex between you guys—some pointless, stupid act on your part."

Her lips smashed together. She was fighting her tears, hard. She was on the verge. I knew it. That hadn't changed. They were going to fall soon.

"But then you left because of me. And he became so miserable and quiet, and made every conversation we had hard to continue and mostly awkward. He was always checking his cellphone, like you would randomly call or text him one day, but you never did. He would walk alone, and not show back up for hours. He would get so drunk. I realized then that I would have much rather seen my father happy and alive and remade, than like he was during that time without you. That's why I wrote you that letter. Too afraid to face you, so I wrote it. But I'm glad I did. It made me feel somewhat better." Her smile broke through the falling tears. "Even with Sheila, he wasn't completely happy with her. In all honesty, I felt like he was trying to make something of it with her for me, but it wasn't working. I could tell he was forcing it. He was faking it. He didn't want her. He cared about her, but didn't want her. He'd settled for someone like her because he wanted me to be happy and to have a family to come to and he wanted to forget about you. Prove a point or something that maybe it was just a summer fling. But I was wrong. So, so wrong."

She reached over and touched my arm.

"After my trip, I knew exactly how he felt when you didn't call. I checked my phone constantly. My *Facebook*. Months went by. And then they rolled into a year. Still nothing, even though I knew he was married and all. I just figured he hadn't completely forgotten about me. But I saw more photos of him and his wife and that was the day I decided to I delete my account. I just . . . felt broken. Because he was smiling so big and looked so happy with her, but only months ago, he'd told me he needed me and wanted me. I should have known it was a lie. He was just another man, alone during a trip, wanting to have a good time. I was stupid to think it was actually something. I needed a cleanse of the mind and body, like my meditator had told me in India. Stalking him on *Facebook* had become a toxin. I had to get rid of it. I needed to start over, so I put my career first and I worked hard to get gigs. Granted, they paid only enough to get the bills paid, but it was better than nothing. It was my dream, and I was making it happen —still am making it happen." She smiled appreciatively. "I don't hold anything against what you and my dad have. If anything, I'm *happy* that you guys are making it work again. He's happy. You're happy, and we all deserve happiness, no matter where it comes from. Who am I to stand in the way of that?

"I wanted to deny it, but the proof was there. It was real and true and still is. I thought Mom was his soulmate, but apparently I was wrong. I guess after seeing them together for so long, I couldn't picture him with anyone else—especially you," she laughed. "But I don't control fate or how the stars align or any of that other spiritual bullshit."

I laughed, she giggled.

"So, you don't have to worry about me. Okay? I can tell you love him and you have for years. You know him, probably way better than I ever could." She watched me carefully. "Just don't . . . leave again. Okay? Don't hurt him again by walking away. I think right now is when he needs you the most. He acts all macho-man around you, but deep down I know he's just as nervous as you are about everything—from what I will think, to getting through this divorce with bitchy Sheila, and what it will be like once he's finally free from it and spending all of his time with you."

"I won't, Izzy. I wouldn't do that to him again," I told her.

"Promise?"

"I promise."

She smiled and then reached over to hug me around the neck. "I hope you can forgive me, Chloe?"

"Of course I do," I sighed. And I really meant it. I'd never been angry with Izzy. Hurt? Yes, but never angry, because I understood. I'd betrayed her trust. If anything, I was the one that needed forgiving.

We were moving forward now. Trying to make something work out of this, and I was so happy she was accepting the truth.

She was right. This wasn't a fling. This was real and true and it was never going to fade.

CHAPTER 28

THEO

I could hear their voices as I sipped my coffee. Chloe and Izzy bustled through the door moments later, just like old times, laughing about God knows what.

"I take it you two had fun?" I inquired, stepping around the corner as they dropped their purses on the couch.

"Oh, Dad, it was great," Izzy sighed. "I feel *so* much better. Getting that pedicure was much needed."

I looked over at Chloe who simply shrugged, grinned, and then sipped on her iced coffee. I returned an identical grin.

"You guys eat anything?" I asked.

"We had cheese danishes from Starbucks before we got here." Chloe lifted her cup in the air and shook it so the ice could rattle. "I think I'm good for now." She walked towards me. "I have something to do really quick."

"And what's that?"

"A phone call. I need to call and settle some things with *you know who*." She made a face and sighed.

"Who? Sterling?" Izzy called from the kitchen.

Chloe looked over my shoulder at her. "How'd you know?"

Izzy half-shrugged. "Had a hunch. What can I say?"

Chloe fought a laugh, pulling out her cellphone. She kissed my cheek and started for the balcony but I caught her elbow before she could step out. "Let me know how it goes. You hear me?"

"Yeah, I hear you," she whispered, studying my face carefully. "I wouldn't hide anything from you, Theo. You know that, right?"

"I trust you. Not him."

"It's okay. Just let me handle this and I will be back to tell you everything."

Reluctant, I pulled away, but nodded. She twisted around and slid the glass door shut behind her, placing the phone to her ear and tucking a lock of hair behind the other, already exasperated.

Footsteps sounded, and Izzy popped up beside me, releasing a small huff. "It'll be okay, Dad."

I looked down and her eyes met mine. "What makes you think I'm worried?"

She snorted. "Who do you think you're kidding? You're sweating like a pig in a slaughterhouse."

I rubbed the sweat from my forehead. "It's the coffee. Makes me hot." I walked towards the kitchen, dumping the rest of it in the sink. As I did, I heard Izzy coming towards me again. When I looked up, she was already watching me.

"You know," she rested her elbows on the counter, planting her face in her hands, "I can tell when something's up, Dad. With you and her. She trusts you and I know you trust her. You don't trust *him*, which is pretty understandable. She told me he's been calling, and so has Sheila." I folded my arms at the sound of Sheila's name. "My belief is that it will all work out. Last time it didn't . . . because of me. But I'm not standing in the way this time. No, if anything I'm here to help. I don't want you going back to Sheila the Witch. I'd much rather hang with Chloe than her. But promise me one thing."

"What's that, Iz?"

"Promise me that if you guys get hitched one day or whatever, that I won't have to call her *Mom*."

I burst out laughing and she joined me, winking before pulling away. It was like her to always put a smile on my face, but even so, my smile slipped away as Chloe slouched down in her seat, roughly pushing fingers through her hair.

She was frustrated now, and I wanted to go right out there, snatch the phone away, hang up, and say to hell with him. But this was something she needed to do, for herself. She hated guilt; it always ate her alive. Her guilt was the reason we'd parted ways in the first place.

"Fine," Chloe said as she pushed out of the chair and yanked the sliding door open. "Fine, Sterling. Next weekend."

She hung up, grimacing at her phone now.

"What? What'd he say?" I asked, meeting up to her as Izzy sauntered into the bathroom. She avoided my eyes until I tilted her chin and forced her gaze on me. "Chloe. Tell me."

Her lips twisted and pressed all at once. She was worried.

"He . . . wants us to get re-engaged"

CHAPTER 29

CHLOE

"What?" Theo barked. "To fucking hell with that shit! He isn't calling anything back on! He's the one who left!"

"Don't worry. I told him we aren't. Of course he asked me *why* a million times and I told him I just don't think it's meant to be."

Relief struck him. He released a ragged breath and took a small step backwards, but before his feet settled, he came closer, cupping the right half of my face and staring into my eyes. He knew. He always knew. "Wait . . . what else aren't you telling me?"

"He'll . . . be back next week, and he wants to talk in person. I . . . need my house, Theo. I can't avoid it. All of my things are there, and so are his."

"Okay. Well, then we'll get your stuff out. I'll buy a storage unit for you somewhere."

I shook my head. "I should talk to him first before I just start packing and leaving. It's the least I can do. I mean his mom is the one who took care of my Dad and now she's dying."

His eyes were glassy, as he murmured, "I understand." But when he pulled his hand away from my cheek, I felt empty. "When will you go?"

"Next weekend. I'm not sure when he'll be back but he said he'd let me know. So . . . I'll talk to him. Tell him the truth in person."

"Shouldn't I be with you?" he asked.

"Do you really think that's wise?" I laughed.

He forced a small smile. "I guess not. I'd probably end up punching him in his face just for the hell of it."

"Exactly," I giggled, "and the last thing I need is for you to be arrested. Look, you're not too far away. I'll call you if I need anything. I'll even let you drop me off there."

"If I drop you off, I'm waiting outside. I'm not leaving." His jaw ticked. He was serious.

"Sure. That's okay with me."

His shoulders sagged and he slumped down on the couch. "Okay—all right, fine. Go see him. Let him know, but after you talk to him, it has to be done. Once it's over, I don't want him having anything to do with you, and I don't want you having anything to do with him."

"Theo." I snaked myself onto his lap, kissing his warm cheek while he pretended to still be pissed. But I knew the kiss made him melt a little inside. I knew because goosebumps swept over his arms. "He won't after I meet him there. I'm all yours, remember? You know how I will feel if I don't at least speak to him face-to-face."

"Yeah, I know, I know. That soft little heart of yours can't handle that kind of guilt or regret."

I dropped my forehead on top of his shoulder and passed a soft laugh. He vibrated with just as much laughter and then he tilted my chin again, bringing my face up and pressing his lips to mine.

"Do you trust me?" I whispered.

"More than anyone." His voice was gentle and deep. He hauled me closer. "You trust me?"

"More than anyone," I repeated, and his eyes went mellow, small wrinkles forming around them.

"That's my Sexy Little Knight."

I laughed way too hard at that one, and as I did, Izzy stepped around the corner and said, "I'm going to pretend I didn't just hear that."

The next day, I think one of my worst nightmares had come to life.

The storm was coming full circle now, closing in on us, ready to rip our happiness to shreds.

"What about burritos?" Theo asked as he shut the door behind him. He was going over dinner options for the night.

"That actually sounds really good right now." He came in my direction, linking an arm over my shoulders and walking towards the elevator.

"Burritos it is."

On our way down, he nuzzled my neck. "Theo? Seriously?" I laughed. "Didn't you have enough in the hotel?"

"What?" he crooned with a shrug. "We're alone. No one's watching."

I pointed at the camera above. "That's where you're wrong."

"Who cares? If they are, let 'em watch. Sure they're bored in those cramped up offices anyway. Let's make their day."

I burst into a fit of giggles as he continued his nuzzling. He was only messing with me, but I felt myself getting hot for him by the second. Ready, all over again.

"Oh—shit," I sighed when his soft lips brushed my chin. "I forgot my purse."

"You don't have to pay for anything." He planted a hand on the wall above my head. "I've got it."

"Yeah, but my classroom keys are in that purse. I have a few last-minute things to grab today before they start locking up the school.

"Right." He nodded, and the elevator chimed. When the doors shot open, he walked out, but held the doors open to hand me his room key.

"Thanks," I laughed. "I'll meet you at the car. Bring it up front!"

"Hurry." He slid his fingertips into his front pockets and walked away coolly, like all eyes were on him. I'm sure all eyes were on him. He was delicious. Who wouldn't stare at a fine specimen like him?

It was a quick ride up. I grabbed my purse and then hit the elevator again, having to wait a little longer this time to get back down.

I pressed the button for the lobby, and as soon as I was down, I walked out and rounded the corner, going towards the exit. But that's when I saw Theo. He was talking to someone.

A woman.

I stepped to the left, behind the thick white pillar, before either of them could notice me, narrowing my eyes when she hissed at him.

Just then, I realized who she was. The blonde hair. The blue eyes. It was Sheila. I could hear everything from where I hid.

"So this is where you've been hiding?" she asked. "You were ignoring my phone calls so I had to find you myself. Looked through the credit card records. Saw you were staying here." She looked around. "What's so special about this place, huh, Theo?"

"Why are you here?" he snapped, purposely ignoring her questions.

"You know why I'm here. We never talked about this."

"Yeah, because you never wanted to sit down and talk about it with me like a civil adult. You kept ignoring me."

"So you just disappear?" she ground through her teeth.

"What the hell did you think I would do? Stick around? Wait for you to want to listen to me?" He shook his head. "No. That's not how a marriage works."

She swallowed thickly as a few people walked past them. "Are you doing this because of *her*?" she hissed.

"Who?" he retorted.

"The girl—the one you wrote that letter to while you were in the basement. Yeah, I saw it when I organized down there a few months ago."

"I don't know what you're talking about," he muttered, looking away.

She laughed a bitter laugh. "Of course you don't. God, you never do. Maybe that's why I didn't want to listen. Because you never make yourself clear, Theo. Hell, maybe this divorce is a good thing. I didn't realize I had married a coward and dumbass." I frowned, ready to step right out and shut her the hell up . . . but I didn't. I stayed away. For Theo. *Not* her. My sudden appearance would have worsened matters. Sheila looked around. "Is she here? I bet she is."

"I don't know who you're talking about." Theo folded his arms tightly over his chest, jaw ticking now.

She sneered, taking a step closer to him. "I know she is. Hey, maybe I can use that in court. Say you were cheating on me with a girl half your age."

"You know damn well I never cheated on you, Sheila. You can say what you want, but we're separated. What I do during my personal time now is none of your goddamn business."

"Thinking about another woman while married to me is cheating in itself," she snapped back.

He scoffed. "Really? You're going to stoop that low now?"

"I'll stoop as low as I have to if it means I come out of this clean. You're not getting out of this easily, Theo. You agreed to this because you had *nothing* left. I took you in and brought you up, and I can easily snatch that away and ruin your life again. You and that *whore* you're seeing behind my back will have nothing by the time I'm through with you."

My fists clenched tight. "That bitch," I hissed.

"Sheila, I'd advise you to get the *fuck* out of my face and go to Florida with your sister—if you were even there to begin with. You came all this way to pick a fight and unless you want to lose and end up with hurt feelings, I suggest you leave. Right. Now."

"What? Did I hurt *your* feelings by calling her out? What else would a girl sleeping with her best friend's dad be? She's nothing but a no-good, disgusting whore that didn't respect her relationship with her friend enough to stay away from the likes of you." She scoffed and when I peered over, she had a finger jammed into his chest. "You know what, I'm out of here. You enjoy your time in this wasteland.

But when it's time for us to settle this, I hope you're ready to pay up because I am *not* backing down until I get everything I want."

She glared at him for several seconds—him with his fists clenched at his sides, jaw still pulsing—and then, before I could process it all, she twisted around and stormed towards the exit.

I took a step over, seeing her climb into a silver Mercedes parked up front and driving off without looking back.

Theo stood in the middle of the lobby, fists still clamped. I sighed, cooling myself as best as I could, and then walking out to meet him. Grabbing one of his balled fists, I loosened it and then looked him in the eye.

He avoided my gaze. "Sorry you had to hear that," he grumbled.

"No, it's okay," I murmured. I was glad when he loosened his fingers. "Wow, I knew she was a bitch, but I didn't think she was *that much* of a bitch," I laughed, but there was hardly any amusement to it.

"Yeah." He shoved his fingers through his hair. "Fuck her. Let's get out of here before she decides to pop back up. We need to get the hell out of this hotel period. Stupid of me to think she wouldn't try and find me through my card records. She's reaching now, stooping low. Guess that means I should be getting ready to gear up, huh?"

He squeezed my hand and walked towards the revolving doors. We didn't see any trace of her in the parking lot. We figured she was gone for good. I hoped she was.

She was trying to deliver a message, but Theo noted that she was scared herself. He saw the panic in her eyes—the fear that he would be leaving and had the possibility of taking everything that was his.

He said that she hated being without. Her parents were wealthy but chose to stop taking care of her years ago when her father grew ill. She had a good lawyer, but like I'd said before, we could find one even better if need be.

It's funny. Theo didn't seem so concerned after that encounter. The only thing truly bothering him were the names she called me, but he said deep down he could feel it. She was losing. She had no case to make and nothing outside of the agreements to claim.

All was fair in the contracts. He had even signed a prenuptial agreement with her for his assets, just in case something like this happened. He was already giving her more than she deserved outside of the agreement. She needed to back the fuck off and accept them already.

CHAPTER 30

THEO

The week flew by way too quickly. Izzy stayed two more days before taking off again to Orange County for filming. Chloe and I spent the majority of our time in the hotel—*all over* the hotel.

I couldn't keep my hands off of her. My young Knight, shining in her armor. There for me like never before. She didn't dare leave my side. She wanted to spend the rest of her summer with me, and I was more than okay with that.

Of course, there was another disturbance and it was her dick of an ex, Sterling.

It was also Sheila. She was coming back sooner than expected, which meant that next week, I would have to drive to San Francisco and discuss things with her face-to-face.

Chloe said she was okay with tagging along and being there, but I knew deep down she wasn't. She wasn't cut out for shit like this— conflict and debates. She was the mediator, the type to try and settle things the right way.

As much as I wanted her to stay, I needed her to come. I needed her support, just in case shit decided to go haywire.

"Have you heard back from your lawyer?" Chloe asked after I told her we would be meeting Sheila sooner.

"He called yesterday. He's close to finishing up. He should have the contract for me soon. I mailed him a check. Everything is pretty much good to go."

"What are you going to call the new franchise anyway, that is, if you have to change it? I was kind of digging the Black Engine thing." She wrapped an arm around me as we continued our stroll on the beach.

"I don't even know, but I'm sure you'll help me come up with something."

She grinned up at me. "I'm sure you'll figure it out before I do."

We spent most of our time tangled up, breathing deep, fucking and loving. Time seemed to sweep by with her. It's funny how slowly it dragged by during the years without her. I hated waking up in the mornings, thinking about what she could possibly be doing with another man. Just the thought of it made me angry enough to clench my fists, and I'd have to force myself into workout gear just to jog it off. I'd hit the gym way too many times, trying to pump out the stress. It hardly worked. Not even working at the shop distracted my mind long enough to forget about her.

I had hoped that one day I could just wake up and not have her on my mind. Just one day where I could go to the store or clean the house or even ride Ol' Charlie without a single thought of her.

It was fucking impossible. She was a part of me. She'd snatched my heart right out of my chest and ran away with it. It had been hers ever since that first day in the park, when I took her in the grass, when she was so young and beautiful beneath me. Never had I found someone so flawless. Never in a million years did I think I would fall in love with a girl half my age.

But with her, it happened, and the only regret I had was that I walked away on the last day I saw her instead of staying—instead of *fighting.* I'd made a dumb choice by marrying Sheila, and now I was dealing with the consequences.

But it didn't matter because the reward was going to be worth it.

Chloe and me, taking on the world. Living like we should have been all along—in love and carefree. Doing what we did best. Making each other happy. Making up for all the lost time. Enjoying the powerful love we shared.

If that wasn't enough for a man to look forward to, I didn't know what was.

Before I knew it, it was fucking Saturday. Chloe's cellphone rang, and we both knew who it was before she even checked the Caller ID.

"I'll get my keys," I grumbled, pushing off the bed and walking to the kitchen. I heard Chloe answer the phone with quick responses and then she was in front of the kitchenette with me. She gently grasped my elbow and stepped up to my side.

"If you don't want me to go, Theo—"

"No, you need to. It's fine."

"I know you don't like him," she muttered. "Probably should have gotten more things sooner instead of waiting until today."

I shrugged. "It's fine. You can't bring all your stuff here, right? Get what you need. We'll figure the rest out later." I paused, upper lip twitching. "But you're right. I *don't* like him."

"It's easier this way. It won't last for more than thirty minutes, I promise."

I pressed my lips as she looked up at me with glistening hazel eyes. Cupping a hand on the back of her neck, I tugged her closer, tilting her chin so I could reach her lips.

Fire burned through me as I kissed her, sliding my tongue through her full lips, tightening my grip on the back of her neck, tasting the strawberries she'd just eaten on her tongue. She moaned as my other hand gripped her ass and I forced her lower half closer, gluing her body to me.

"I need to fuck you before you go over there," I rasped, picking her up in my arms. She yelped as I marched towards the couch and placed her on her stomach. I didn't hesitate pulling her skirt down or hoisting her shirt up. I unbuckled my belt next, unbuttoned my jeans, and shoved them down to my ankles.

Without me having to command her, she knelt on all fours, resting her face on the sofa and lifting her ass in the air. I could see her perfect pussy though the small gap between her thighs.

So pink and perfect.

I was hard as fuck, stroking my cock as I rested one knee on the edge of the couch and knelt behind her. I gripped her waist, gliding in with ease, listening to her moans grow thicker and louder until I was completely inside. Balls deep.

Fuck, she was so tight. So tight and always so wet.

"I want him to smell me when you walk through that door. I want him to know," I rumbled as I leaned forward and pressed my lips to her ear, "that you have *always* been mine. And his appearance doesn't change *shit* about that. When you go there, Chloe, I want you to remember the way I'm about to fuck you. I hope you blush when he mentions me, so he'll know you're thinking about my cock being inside you. So he'll know that you will *never* be his again."

She writhed as I drew back and slammed in again. My cock was so hard inside her, despite the fact that we'd just done it less than an hour ago. I could feel her pussy pulsing around my length, her wetness coating every single inch.

She moaned louder, my name spilling from her lips. I ran my fingers through her hair, tugging on the ends, forcing her head back.

"Oh, Theo," she whimpered. "Babe, are you—*oh, yes*—are you jealous?" she asked, out of breath.

"Fuck yeah, I'm *jealous*. He's not taking what's mine again." And knowing it caused me to thrust a little harder. I wanted her to feel me when she got there. I didn't want the sensation leaving anytime soon. I wanted her legs wobbly and weak when she got there, so she'd remember what caused it.

Me.

Not him.

Never him.

Me.

"So good," she sighed.

And I smirked, but as she pushed back, circling her pussy around my cock while I stroked, I clenched her hips.

"Fuck, don't do that, baby. You'll make me come too soon. You know that gets me every time."

She glanced over her shoulder, grinning playfully, and then she did it again. And again, pushing back and circling her hips in tight little circles while clenching her tight, slick pussy around me.

I spanked her ass and she moaned even louder, her fingernails sinking into the couch. Moving, faster, listening to our clapping skin and her shaky, high-pitched moans.

She squealed my name like she would never forget it, and that was all it took to bring me over the edge. I stilled, gripping her thin waist and coming so deep inside her sweet, tight pussy.

"Fuck," I groaned, my head falling back. She clenched my cock again, drawing out all of my release. "Shit, Knight." I fell forward, on top of her as she collapsed. My face was on her shoulder, my cock on her ass now. "You always feel so fucking good."

She turned her head to kiss the tip of my nose. "Just so you know," she laughed softly, "I won't forget this. I don't even want to go anymore. I already want more of you."

I couldn't fight my smile.

Good. That was exactly what I wanted to hear.

CHAPTER 31

CHLOE

"Theo, you have to let go of my hand." I looked over at him with a small smile.

His eyes swung down to our interlocked fingers. "Shit. Right. Sorry." He pulled his hand away and mine was hot and slick with sweat.

We were sitting in front of my house, and Sterling's two-door blue Honda was parked in the driveway, as expected.

"Hey," I cooed when he didn't pull his gaze away from Sterling's car. "It will be quick, I promise. Okay?"

"I should go in with you."

"Theo, I love you, but your temper is horrible," I teased. "I think it's best you stay out here and let me handle it."

He put on a crooked smile, hunching his shoulders. "All right, all right. Fine. Twenty minutes, Chloe. Not thirty. Not twenty-five. If it takes longer than that I'm coming in."

"I have to pack up some more clothes too so I may need that extra ten minutes."

"Yeah, okay. Fine." He released a ragged breath, slouching back in his seat. "But I'm waiting right here in front of the house."

I laughed. "And that is more than okay with me." I grabbed the door handle. "Don't stress, okay? I'll be right back."

He shut his eyes, exhaled, and then nodded. "Kay." I started to push out but he caught my elbow and I looked back. "Hurry before the sun is completely down. I have a surprise I want to show you."

"*Another* surprise?" I grinned.

"I think you'll love this one a little more."

"Okay. I'll be right back. Sit tight."

He reluctantly pulled away and I climbed out of the car, shutting the door behind me and walking towards the house with my keys in hand. When I met at the door, I drew in a deep breath, looked over my shoulder at Theo's car, and then stuffed my key in the lock, unlocking it and stepping right in.

The living room, dining room, and kitchen lights were all on, making it appear brighter than usual inside. "Sterling?" I called.

"Yeah!" he shouted from the kitchen. "I'm in here."

Eyes narrowed, I walked with caution. It was then that I smelled something in the air. It was a fishy scent. When I made it into the kitchen, I could smell the tilapia cooking. There was a bowl of pasta on the island counter and two wine glasses, as well as my favorite sparkling wine too.

Great. Just great. This was going to make it even harder for me to tell him. He'd cooked, cleaned—*what the hell was he thinking?*

"Oh—hey, you!" He looked over his shoulder with a broad smile, still frying the fish. Hell, he'd even shaved and cleaned himself up.

"Um . . . what are you doing?" I asked, folding my arms and leaning against the wall.

"Cooking," he chuckled, dumping the fish on a plate. "For you."

"Wow . . . uh . . . you should have told me you were going to do all of this, Sterling. I wasn't planning on staying for very long."

"Oh." He dropped the spatula and spun around, looking me over. "Plans tonight?"

"Yes."

"Ah." He bobbed his head way too many times to count. A nervous habit. Then he pointed to the island counter where the wine and glasses were. "I bought your favorite. Thought we could start over. Make up, you know?"

"Sterling, I really don't think we should," I responded nervously, rubbing my elbow. "I mean, things have settled, and I've accepted what you said. About us and Janet. It's fine. You don't have to feel bad about telling me the truth."

"Come on, you don't even want to try again?" He laughed an uneasy laugh. "I cooked, Chloe. Cleaned up a bit. I wanted to make it easy for you tonight. Look," he sighed, taking a step closer. "I know I fucked up before. I was being stupid and trying to find an excuse for how I felt. The truth is, I am over Janet. Have been ever since I met you. I think about her a lot, yes, but that's not what was really bothering me, you know? It was Mom, and her being sick and all. I'd found out weeks ago, and I'm sorry I took so long to tell you. I couldn't get leave from work until just recently, which stressed me out even more. It was just . . . I don't know. I was frustrated. With life. With everything."

"Why didn't you just tell me that from the start, Sterling? Why say it was Janet?"

"Because I knew that would make you keep a little distance from me. I wanted to go alone. You didn't need to see Mom like that. She isn't well."

"So she's still alive?" I asked, pushing off the wall with concern.

"Yes, but not doing so good. I left to come and work things out with you. She told me I was stupid for letting you go, and you know what? She's right. So I'm back for now. I'll be leaving to see her again tomorrow, but I'll be back."

Shit.

"Do you think you can give me the name of the hospital?" I asked, nervous.

"What for? You can just ride with me. It's not that far," he offered, picking up a piece of fish and eating it.

"No, Sterling, I don't think that's a good idea. Look . . ." I pushed my hair back, exhaling. "I'm not here for dinner or anything even remotely romantic. I'm here to talk about the engagement. We aren't calling it back on. I just . . . can't. I shouldn't. It wouldn't be right to keep this going when I don't even want it to."

He stopped chewing slowly, brows furrowing a little.

"Don't get me wrong, this is sweet and I appreciate it, but I can't, Sterling. The past few days you were gone made me realize that you were right. We aren't meant to be. I was trying but . . . that's it. Just *trying*. It didn't feel like enough, you know?"

"Oh. Yeah . . . sure. I guess." He was avoiding my eyes now, scratching the back of his head.

"I came to tell you that and to pack some of my stuff. I have a hotel booked so you can stay here and get what you need until you leave. If I stay it will be a little awkward." I probably should have mentioned Theo, but he already seemed bummed enough. I mean, he'd put together this dinner for me. I didn't want to put him down in the dumps any more than I already had.

"Right. Um . . . *right*." He dusted his hands off. "I get it." He huffed a laugh. "I guess it's sorta my fault. I shouldn't have been so shady."

I didn't say much, but my nod gave it away that, yeah, he shouldn't have kept me in the dark. Theo was outside waiting for me—the love of my life. I wasn't going to change my mind this time or let my guilt steer me.

I felt bad, yes, but he brought this on himself. We were never in love. We just cared for one another and I knew deep down that he knew that too.

"Shit." He turned and gripped the edge of the counter, shaking his head swiftly. Shakes of disappointment and regret.

I took a small step backwards, taking this as my opportunity to start packing some of my things so I could go. I headed up the stairs and as soon as I made it into my closet, I pulled down a suitcase and packed some of the dresses and jeans I had in the closet.

I took down a few blouses and some of my sandals, and then stuffed some pajamas in as well. I already had my toothbrush, but I needed my other hair and facial products.

As I collected them and brought them back to the duffle bag on the bed, I looked over and then gasped, spotting Sterling standing between the frames of the bedroom door.

"Shit," I gasped clutching the heart of my chest. "You scared me."

"Sorry," he murmured. He looked paler now, than he did in the kitchen. I didn't look at him for too long. I had nothing more to say. I felt like I was being a bitch, but I had to stay strong. I couldn't falter.

As I zipped up my bag, Sterling walked towards where the vanity was. He looked at my jewelry in the holders and then I heard him take a hard swallow before he picked something up and lifted it in the air.

"When did you take it off?" he asked, voice sullen.

"A few days ago," I lied.

He said nothing.

Why is he making this harder than it needs to be?

"Do you mind me asking who you have plans with?" He clutched the ring in hand.

"Kim," I lied again.

"That her car parked at the curb?"

"Yep." I forced a smile. "She got a new one."

"Doesn't fit her," he noted. Theo drove a black Chrysler. No, it didn't fit Kim, but who cared? Theo's windows were tinted. I knew Sterling couldn't see through them, but I was almost certain he knew it wasn't Kim. "Chloe," he pleaded, "are you sure about this? I—I can do better. I can try. I mean, I know I haven't been the greatest fiancé lately, but I want us to try and work it out again." He paused, watching as I placed my suitcase down on its wheels. "You can't just give up. We can't. We *shouldn't.*"

"Sterling, I'm not giving up. I'm doing the right thing for us." I stood up straight. "I know you're not over Janet. You say it but . . . you're not."

He looked away then, eyes glistening.

"I really don't want you to let this stop you from doing anything. We can be friends." I smiled, making my voice lighter. I knew Theo wouldn't have liked that I said that, but I also knew Sterling wouldn't call once he figured out that I was leaving, and not coming back. That

I was moving forward—well, backwards in a sense. "Anytime you need to talk, I'm here."

He kept his eyes away, looking everywhere else but at me.

"I get it. I'll . . . uh, pack my things then. Find a new place to stay." His jaw ticked. I couldn't tell if he was angry or just upset. "I'll probably be in and out to make sure I have it all, but don't worry about me just showing up. I'll let you know beforehand."

"Okay." I started for the door. "If you . . . need anything, I'm here. Just remember that, okay? We can talk about what we'll do with the house later."

He shoved his fingers through his hair, glancing sideways. "Yeah . . . sure."

I walked to the door, peering over my shoulders. I felt horrible now, but I couldn't linger. He'd have taken it as a sign of weakness, and tried to make a move. And I couldn't because Theo was waiting, and the sun was almost set.

I felt Sterling's gaze on me as I walked towards the stairs. When I took the first step, he was looking at the ring again, brows stitched. I didn't know what the hell he was thinking, but I wasn't about to stick around and find out.

I trotted down the steps, grabbed a Diet Coke from the fridge, and then hurried for the front door. I was out in no time, taking in a deep breath of relief as I made my way to the car. I tossed my bag in the backseat, and then climbed into the passenger seat.

Theo was already looking at me, brown eyes swirling with concern. "So?" he inquired.

"He didn't take it well, but I think he understands." I cleaned off the top and then cracked open my can of soda.

He put the car in gear and sat up in his seat. "Good. Better that he makes it easy for you." He drove away with a smug look on his face.

"What's that look for?" I asked.

"You weren't even in there for ten minutes. You made it quick."

"Easier to do than I thought," I sighed. "But I feel bad. He cooked and bought my favorite wine. He was going to try hard this time. I could tell."

He glanced over as I took a sip of soda. His hand touched mine and our gazes met when he squeezed it. "It's done," he murmured. "I know you probably hate disappointing him, but it had to be done. At least he knows the truth now."

I nodded and jerked my gaze down to my lap. That was a secret I'd keep with me. Sterling didn't know the whole truth—that I was officially leaving him for Theo. If I'd said that, it would have proved him correct even more.

All I wanted was Theo, and I'm sure that would have hurt to know more than just settling it with a gentle breakup and never seeing one another again.

CHAPTER 32

CHLOE

My concern for Sterling's well-being made me somewhat forget about the surprise Theo had mentioned before I'd gone inside the house.

We didn't go back to the hotel, but instead Theo kept driving on the interstate until we were driving down a hill and onto rocky gravel.

"Where are we?" I asked, curious now.

He winked but said nothing. Moments later, a house appeared. It was a two-story home, built with dark green shingle siding and a porch made of smooth wood, the railings painted a glossy white. Tall palm trees were planted outside the home, the bushes trimmed neat.

Two garages were attached to the left of the home and Theo parked in front of one of them. Shutting the car off, he sat back in his seat and looked ahead with me.

"Whose place is this?" I asked.

He smiled. "Ours."

"Ours?" I gasped, eyes stretching wide. "What?"

"Well, I mean, right now it's mine. My mother helped me get it—

she even let me get the keys early. I'm hoping that within a few weeks or months or whenever the time is right, we can call it ours. I already put a down payment on it, and got approved for the mortgage. Turns out I could buy another house, now that I've paid off the loan to the bank for my garage. Once I get the house in San Francisco sold, and you handle yours it will be . . ." He stopped talking, trailing off lightly. The leather of his seat crunched as he shifted. "Too much?" he asked, gesturing towards the house.

I blinked at him before grabbing the door handle and pushing the door open. Theo climbed out just as quickly as I walked along the cement driveway, breathing in the warm air, studying the yellow daisies planted along the driveway and by the front door.

He didn't say anything as I walked towards the porch. I made my way up the stoop and when he was right beside me, I said, "Open it."

He pulled out a set of keys from his front pocket and then put a bronze key in the lock. When he twisted it and the lock clicked, he pushed the door open and stepped back, letting me go inside first.

His eyes were soft. Mellow, with a hint of worry. Was he afraid I wasn't going to love it? I walked inside before I could answer that question myself.

The floors were made of mahogany wood. There was no furniture. A chandelier hung in the dining area, the walls painted a light shade of gray. It was completely vacant of furniture inside.

I continued forward, and there was a wide-open space that revealed the outdoors. When I got closer, I realized there wasn't any glass. It was just a long, rectangular walkway, but the doors had been pushed open.

A breeze hit me and I glanced back. He stood by the door, his fingers in his front pockets.

I kept walking until I was through the open space and on the wooden deck. It was unoccupied, but the view . . . the view was absolutely breathtaking.

I thought the view we had from his hotel was great, and even the view from my backyard, but this was another level of beauty. The home wasn't sitting right on the beach. We were on a cliff, over-looking the ocean. The railing was made of glass and outlined with wood. I heard my feet moving forward, my hand gripping the rail.

I was smiling. Hard. The minimal heat from the sunset lingered on my skin, the breeze still flowing.

Before I knew it . . . I was *crying*.

The tears were hot. Blazing hot, but I didn't swipe them away.

Complete.

Never had I felt so whole. I wanted to burst with joy.

Footsteps sounded behind me and then a large pair of arms wrapped around me. Through blurry vision, I could see the tattoos on his tan skin, the tribal wave he'd gotten for me. I could feel the warmth of his hands as they pressed on my waist. I saw my tattoo—the boat. Matching with meaning.

"It's not too much," I said when he kissed the crook of my neck. "It's perfect, Theo. So damn perfect."

Without words, he spun me around, cupped my face in his large hands, and kissed me. I threw my arms over his neck and he picked me up, sitting me on top of the rails as he pushed between my legs.

He groaned and sighed, a noise catching in his throat. It wasn't a noise of pain or sorrow; it was one that would stick with me forever. A small whimper, one that proved he would do anything and every-thing for me.

All of the emotion had caught up to me on this day. Going from feeling guilty to feeling incredibly grateful. All this from one man. It couldn't get better than this.

"It's perfect," I repeated, a grin breaking through the kiss as I bobbed my head.

"I'm glad you think so." He rubbed a line of my tears away with the pad of his thumb. "But there's one more thing I want to show you." Stepping back, he grabbed my hand and helped me off the guardrail.

He led the way through the living room and through a beautiful, modern kitchen made of chrome and black tile, and then he opened a door.

It led to the garage.

He flipped a switch to turn the light on and I couldn't help myself. This house was a great surprise, but nothing could surprise me more than seeing Ol' Charlie parked in the garage, waiting for us.

"Oh, Theo," I laughed, clasping my hands. "This is the best surprise yet!"

"Got him while you were at work. Brock brought him down this morning. Picked up the keys to the house too. Thought I'd show you what kind of future we can have once we get through this fight—that it will all be worth it in the end."

It felt like my face was about to split in half. If words could make knees quake, then mine were probably about to crumble to pieces.

I stood on my toes and kissed him harder than before, my fingers curling in his navy blue T-shirt.

When the embrace had settled, he pulled away and picked up a pink helmet from the shelf. "How about a ride before it gets too dark?"

I accepted the helmet. "I would *love* one."

The ride was liberating.

I'd never felt so free.

So alive.

My arms were locked around him as we rode on Ol' Charlie, through Bristle Wave, rumbling past Dane's bar as a few people he knew waved at him, and on the single street by the beach.

When the sun was barely in sight, he parked the bike on a pier, planted his feet on the ground, and then grabbed my hand. He helped me climb off first and then he propped the kickstand.

We stood on the pier, side-by-side, my head resting on his chest, and it remained that way until the sun fully sank. Until it was dark and there was nothing but the velvety night sky, the silver moon, and the twinkling stars surrounding us.

He didn't have to speak for me to know how he felt.

199

His silence spoke volumes. The look he gave me, how his eyes sparkled from the moonlight and stars, was enough.

In his eyes, I saw the words *I love you.* In his eyes, I saw a wonderful future I could create with him. In his eyes I was lost, and if being lost felt like this, I never wanted to be found again.

CHAPTER 33

THEO

She was too eager to wait. She wanted to move in right away, so we spent most of the week moving furniture out of her *old* house.

The furniture was still in good condition. We brought along her sofas, the dinner table, and the bed frame and headboard from her bed. I refused to bring the mattress she shared with Sterling. Fuck that. I ordered a brand new one for us to break in. I didn't want his presence anywhere in my house.

It'd been several days and still no word from Sheila, but there was an email with the new contract from my lawyer, about opening up a new franchise.

Things were picking up. I felt better than ever, especially now with us in this house on the cliff, waking up every morning to a view of the beach. The breezy air. The peace and quiet.

On Friday morning, I decided to make Chloe some breakfast. We'd moved most of what we needed for the time being. She brought along some more clothes to fill the closet. Of course we had no washer and dryer yet, but we made trips to her house for clothes that needed washing. We were going to get that last.

I guess it was a good thing she still had the home, but it did tick me off when she had to go back alone, knowing that fucker could stroll in at any given moment and be alone with her.

I hated the idea of it, but with the contracts, and endless phone calls with Sheila's lawyer and mine about the divorce, I couldn't always drop her off. She was a woman now, with her own car, and I had to understand that, but I hated sending her off without me. I hated knowing he could pop up to try and manipulate her again.

As I cooked to music by The Rolling Stones that Friday morning, I glanced over at the clock. It was nearing 11:30 a.m. She was usually awake by now, most times before me. As I whisked the eggs, I looked over my shoulder, hoping to hear her coming down.

Nothing.

I dumped the eggs in the skillet, scrambled them up, and then shut the stove off. After washing my hands, I was making my way upstairs. The door was still shut, and it creaked lightly as I pushed it open.

She was still in bed, her brown hair like a curtain over her face. She was breathing deep. Still sleeping, apparently.

"Chloe?" I called, sitting on the edge of the bed and rubbing her thigh. She rolled sideways, turning her back to me. I fought a laugh, stepping around to the other side of the bed. "Chloe? You hungry?" I asked, stroking her hair back. She groaned, shifting and then peeling one eye open. "Breakfast is ready. It's almost twelve now."

"Twelve?" she repeated, rolling onto her back. "How? Feels like I didn't get enough sleep at all." Her face was pale. She sat up sluggishly. "I don't think I can eat right now, babe. My stomach isn't settling too well. I think it was those oysters last night. Seafood always does this to me. I told you! That restaurant had a three star rating for a reason. Four stars or more for seafood from now on."

I grabbed her hand and helped her out of bed. "Go ahead. Wash up. I'll go set up the table and find something to settle your stomach."

She bobbed her head, her hair bouncing, staggering towards the bathroom and shutting the door behind her. When I heard the faucet start, I made my way back down the stairs and grabbed some plates to set up.

As I started, bringing the blueberry muffins and eggs to the table, I heard her footsteps.

She rounded the corner, frowning as she stared at me. "Hey. I was just about to look for some medicine—" I was about to finish, until her eyes stretched wide, she cupped her mouth, and dashed for the downstairs bathroom.

"Chloe!" I called. "Shit." I set the last plate of food down and hurried after her. The door was already shut and locked behind her, but I heard gagging. The toilet water sloshed. Another cough and gag. Knocking, I called her name again. "You good in there?"

"I'm—" Another splash.

I pressed my back against the wall, staring at the door. I listened to her vomit again and then groan in agony. "I don't think it was the oysters. If it was, I would be sick too," I called from where I stood.

"I don't know what else it could be. The shrimp and crab was fine." She slightly gagged. "Ugh—why does it smell so bad out there? What did you cook?"

So naïve. I knew this would happen, just not *this* soon . . . and I wasn't even sure how the hell I felt about it. But I knew. I'd experienced it before. It was something I was never going to forget.

"Chloe, baby," I laughed, walking towards the door and pressing a hand on it. "I think you and I should take a little trip to the pharmacy."

"For what?" she asked, sniffling. "Medicine?"

"No. For this little thing called a pregnancy test."

As soon as I said that, I heard the toilet flush and then the door was yanked open. Her eyes were even wider now, her face still colorless.

"Theo, I am not pregnant. I can't be! I'm on birth control."

"I've seen birth control fail plenty of times before, babe—not to me, but a few friends here and there. The stories never end."

She looked me in the eyes, her body going still. "Theo, I—"

"Me. You. Pharmacy. Now. Before we talk about it, let's make sure."

I wrapped my arm around her shoulder and helped her out of the bathroom. "There's one right down the street. Won't take long."

"Shit," she hissed. "What if I am?" she asked as we started up the stairs. "I mean, shit, Theo, we haven't even settled your divorce yet. You have all this stuff on your plate already. This is a bad time —and Izzy—"

"Izzy will probably be over the damn moon. She's wanted a sibling for years now. Janet swore she wasn't going to have another. Izzy was hard enough to handle." When I said that, she cracked a smile. I was glad to see it. "We don't know anything for sure. It might actually be the seafood, but from my experience, I'm betting money that it isn't the seafood, but something better."

"Better?" she asked, stunned as she tugged one of her shirts on. "How is growing a baby better, with all you're going through?"

"Because it will be coming from my Little Knight." I cupped the back of her neck and kissed the center of her forehead. "That's a dream come true right there."

She bit a smile, but didn't say anything.

And she didn't have to. The look in her eyes—that look she gave me—was more than enough for me to know that maybe she'd dreamt of the same thing too.

CHAPTER 34

CHLOE

"You aren't nervous about this? I mean, this changes a lot, Theo. Babies are *huge* responsibilities."

"I know they are. I think I did okay before, though." He laughed. I could tell he was trying to keep his cool about this too. I honestly wanted to freak the fuck out. "Look, if you are, you are, and we'll handle it. If not . . . well, I guess that's okay. As many times as I've been inside you since we've reunited, I will be very surprised if you aren't though."

"Right." I waved the stick in the air. "Well . . . I'll let you know in, like, three minutes?"

He nodded with a light press of the lips. "I'll be waiting in the living room."

When he walked off, I shut the door behind me. My heart was pounding, my fingers going numb as I ripped through the paper and pulled out the stick.

Dropping my sweats and panties, I sat on the toilet and brought the stick down.

After the job was done, I capped it, sat it on the back of the toilet, flushed, and then washed my hands.

And then I waited. It was the longest three minutes of my life.

At first, there was only one line. One bold, thin line. My heart steadied in rhythm . . . until another line appeared right beside it. Fainter, but it was there. Two lines.

POSITIVE.

Holy. Shit.

CHAPTER 35

CHLOE

There were too many thoughts—too many feelings overwhelming me.

The bottoms of my feet hit the cool wood as I stepped out of the bathroom. With the stick in hand, I continued my walk, unsure of how I felt.

Should I be excited or upset?

Should I be regretting this?

Should we have been more careful?

I took the final step it took to get around the corner and Theo was sitting in Janet's red recliner, finishing up his muffin. I stared at him for several seconds before making my appearance known.

What will this change? I loved what we had now, and one thing I knew for sure was that kids brought stress. Kids aren't easy to handle. With all we had going on, would he even be able to take care of them the way he wanted to? If the divorce backfired, would he spend most of his time trying to figure it out . . . away from me?

He sat there like he had no care in the world, which made me wonder if I was panicking for no reason. He already knew how babies could change things. Maybe it wouldn't change much for him. Maybe it would make our bond stronger.

I hoped.

Finally clearing my throat, Theo picked his head up in an instant and then shot to a stand, a smile spreading across his lips. Was he expecting good or bad news? Hell, was me saying *yes* going to be the good or bad news to him?

"Well?" he probed, wide-eyed.

I waved the stick in the air as I took a few more steps into the living room, unable to form words. I wanted to tell him right away—I really did. I wanted to blurt it out just to see his reaction, but something about it terrified me.

Theo wasn't the type to run away from his problems, but what if this caused him to panic? What if this was too much? What if he never expected to have babies with me—or to have another child again?

"Shit, Chlo. Come on. Your silence is killing me here," he laughed nervously, dropping his hands to his waist. His smile was crooked. He wasn't sure whether to grin or frown.

"Two lines," I murmured. "It's positive." I didn't blink. I didn't want to miss any of his reactions. "And I—I'm sure it's yours," I went on. "Sterling and I haven't slept together in the same bed for months. We've hardly even touched so . . . I know. I got my period before you first came back. Only person I've done anything with since then is you."

His mouth twitched. "I—I know," he laughed hoarsely. "I believe you."

"So?" I pushed, swallowing hard. "What are you thinking?"

"I'm thinking," he started as he walked in my direction and pushed his fingers through his silver-shot hair, "that I just might be the luckiest man on the fucking planet right now."

My thundering heart sped up ten more notches. I broke out in a grin and Theo hurried my way, picking me up by the waist. I hooked my legs around him and he lightly shook his head, not in disbelief but in complete awe.

"This is the best news I've gotten in years," he laughed. "Shit,

Chloe, I—" He struggled for words, smiling way too hard. That beautiful, adorable smile. I understood his speechlessness. I was at a loss for words myself, so instead of letting him continue the search for something to say, I wrapped my hands around the back of his neck and kissed him. Hard. Deep.

I could still feel my pulse in my veins. I could feel his heart beating against mine. It was good news for him. *Great* news apparently. I'd never seen him so happy. When our lips parted, he was smiling so damn hard I thought his face might break.

"My Knight, carrying *my* baby." He carried me to the couch, placed me on my back, and then leaned forward and cooed to my belly. "You hear me in there? It's your daddy, and I'm never going anywhere! I love you to death already!"

"Wow. Now you're really Daddy Black," I giggled as he kissed me below the navel, his lips brushing my skin, tickling me. "Theo!" I laughed.

He picked his head up, brown eyes bright.

"Are you sure about this?" I asked. "I mean I know it will change a lot between us. I know it wasn't planned or anything . . ."

"Fuck the plans and society's rules." I sat up and he took a seat right beside me. "That's *my* baby in there and you're my woman. I don't regret a damn thing. Will shit change? For sure. But it's always for the better. Always."

My face grew hot, cheeks spreading wide as I formed a smile. I rubbed my stomach and released a heavy breath. "This was something I had always fantasized about, you know? Finding the perfect guy to have my kids with. Feeling this way—on top of the world. Like nothing can stop us now."

He leaned forward, placing a soft kiss on my lips. "Nothing will *ever* stop us again, baby. You have my word."

CHAPTER 36

THEO

There were no words to describe how I felt.

The happiness—that emotion that swells up inside you, to the point that you feel like you'll burst if you don't let it out.

My baby. She was carrying *my* baby.

My Little Knight was everything to me, but this? This may have been the best thing to happen to us yet. She thought there was going to be stress, but fuck that. There wasn't going to be any more stress. No more worries.

With her carrying my child, no one would touch her again. No one would threaten her, and if they did, they had better start running because I would be coming for them. I would hunt them down until I found them and make them regret ever doing something so stupid—crossing the wrong man.

That was my baby in there. Mine.

And she was mine. Only mine.

What more did I need?

Later that night I got a voicemail. It was a voice that ruined the good news I'd just received.

"Theo, it's Sheila. I'm boarding my flight to San Francisco right now. I'll be there for a few days. Come within the next day or two. It's time to talk about the divorce with our lawyers in person. Hope you're ready."

I frowned at my phone as Chloe rested her head on my arm. "You still want me to tag along?" she asked.

"Hell yeah. I'm not leaving you here."

Her head tilted. "We shouldn't tell her that I'm pregnant. It might make things a little more complicated. Maybe I can come, but while you two discuss the divorce and the contract, I'll wait outside or something. Cause less of a distraction."

"You can do whatever you want, Chloe. But you're coming with me to San Fran regardless." I grabbed her hand and kissed the back of it. "I think we've got this one. She didn't sound too pleased. She almost sounds . . . defeated," I laughed. "She lost. She probably only wants to talk about selling the house. If it sells, she wants to keep the furniture and shit. She might even ask me for a loan so she can stay on her feet for a while."

"And will you give her one?"

"I figure it's the least I can do. Better that she doesn't feel completely down and broke. Maybe she'll move back to Florida with her sister. I really don't care as long as she stays the hell away from me."

She shook with laughter. "That would be nice."

Yeah, and easy.

Too fucking easy.

CHAPTER 37

CHLOE

By morning, my Theodore was a mess.

He made phone call after phone call, which left me having to pack up most of what he was bringing, as well as my own stuff.

I was mostly finished, but there were a few things I had left behind that I wanted to bring along, like my good jewelry—just in case I happened to run into Sheila one-on-one. It was a childish thought, but if she were to see me and figure out who was, I wanted her to find me beautiful and mature. Not some young girl that she'd assume didn't know much of anything and had stolen him away.

I also needed to bring my Kindle with me. It was going to be a long ride and I had a lot of reading to catch up on.

By the time I finished packing what we needed and got some lunches together for the ride, it was about an hour after noon.

"I know what the papers say, Phil. The prenup should help. Will she agree or not?" Theo asked, frustrated as he paced the bedroom.

I grabbed my car keys and when he heard them jingle he looked sideways at me. His eyebrows shot up, his eyes asking me where I was going.

He'd gotten even more possessive ever since the news. Last night, I felt him watch me sleep. This morning, he didn't leave my side until his lawyer called and forced him to check his emails for information.

I honestly found it kind of sexy—the fact that he didn't want to leave my side for even a second.

"I'm making a run to the house," I whisper-hissed. "Forgot a few things. I'll be right back."

He frowned and lowered the phone. "I'll go with you."

"No—Theo, please. Take care of your calls. It'll take me less than thirty minutes. I'll be right back."

He was iffy about it. He looked me over twice before giving an averse nod, slouching down on the edge of the bed. "Don't take long," he murmured, bringing the phone back up to his ear. "No—not you, Phil. Continue." He shot me a small smile and a wink and I kissed his forehead before taking off.

When I pulled up to my house, I was relieved that Sterling's car wasn't in the driveway. Good. He wasn't here and probably hadn't been back since that night I saw him.

I hopped out of the car and locked it behind me with the key fob. None of the lights were on inside, the way we left it.

I hurried up the stairs in search for my Kindle. It was exactly where I left it on the nightstand, along with the charger. I tucked it beneath my arm and then went towards my jewelry, picking up a few of my favorite pieces and stuffing them in the pocket of my purse. I could get the rest later.

My gaze dropped to where the engagement ring was and I sighed. He left it. I noticed as we were moving that all of his things were gone. All of his clothes, his soap, and cologne. In fact, it didn't even smell like him anymore.

Sighing, I turned around and walked out of the bedroom, down the stairs, and to the kitchen to check for water. But as I entered and flipped the switch on, that's when I saw him.

He was sitting right at the island counter on one of the stools. His eyes pulled up to mine and I gasped, taking several steps back.

"Shit, Sterling! What the hell are you doing? Why were you sitting in here with the lights off?" He didn't respond, and I frowned a little. "I guess you're still mad?" I folded my arms and still he didn't speak.

"How long has he been back?" He finally spoke, his fingers drumming on the countertop.

"What are you talking about?"

"You know exactly who I'm talking about, Chloe. Don't play stupid." His jaw ticked, those eyes of his growing a shade darker.

"Sterling, I have no idea what you mean." I was lying. I had a clue, but it was no longer his business with whom I was with or what I was doing. He jeopardized our relationship the day he walked out on me.

"No?" He stopped drumming. Then he lifted his elbow and shoved a filing folder that was beneath it, across the counter and towards me.

"Open it. I think you'll know exactly what I'm talking about since you can't seem to think right now."

I opened the folder, eyeing him as I did. He was acting strange and had to be drunk, high, or both. It wasn't new to me.

When I pulled out the contents, I couldn't believe my eyes.

Pictures.

All of them.

I flipped through the photos of *Theo* and Izzy. And then I stopped on one of the photos he had of me. We were on Theo's bike. My arms were clung around him, my chin well rested on his shoulder as he rode with sunglasses on.

"How the hell did you get these?" I snapped, flipping through and finding photos of him and I in San Francisco. Walking into the hotel. Coming out of it. Laughing. Smiling. *Happy.*

My heart sank.

"I was waiting for the day he returned. I had a feeling he would."

I tossed the photos back at him and they scattered all over the counter and the floor. "I don't know what you're talking about or what you're trying to prove, but I'm leaving now."

He pushed off the stool and walked around the island counter, catching my elbow before I could get out of the kitchen. I grimaced at his hand, snatching my arm away.

"He probably thinks I'm the bad guy, when really he's the one that just shows up and takes the women I love right away from me. With you, I admired you at first sight, Chloe. It wasn't love, but you were smart and beautiful, and I *wanted* you." He was close now, his voice soft, but dark. He stroked my cheek with the back of his hand and I shuddered. It was cold. "I wanted to make you happy because I knew he never would. He only cares about himself—"

That's not true," I snapped. "You . . ." My throat felt thicker, dryer. "All *you* care about is yourself. You always have. It's not my fault you can't keep a woman. It's not my fault you're so fucking unreliable."

He scowled when I said that, one eye twitching. "Tell me, Chloe. How was it anyway? Did he make you feel like a woman again? Did you feel bad and dirty?" He was ridiculing me now. "Did he fuck you so good that you completely forget about me because I tell you . . . that's the same shit he pulled with Janet. That's why she tried to leave me for good that night. He whipped his scrawny little dick out and worked his manipulative magic. That's when I knew Janet was weak. That's how I know *you* are weak—running back to *him!*"

"Oh, fuck you, Sterling!" I pushed off the wall and stormed for the front door. "If anyone's weak, it's you. You're a pussy—still stuck on women that barely loved you. And it's no wonder," I scoffed, looking him over. "You're a fucking joke. How is anyone supposed to take you seriously when you talk like that to them? When you run away from your problems instead of facing them like a real man!" I wrenched the door open and pointed a stern finger at him. I no longer had any sympathy for him. I was done. "You should pack all of your shit and get the fuck out of here now. I will handle the house." I shook my head, disgusted with him. "I never want to see you again. If you show up here again, I will tell him. And I mean it."

His upper lip twitched. "Don't think this is over, Chloe. It's far from it. He doesn't fucking deserve you."

"*Fuck you,*" I snapped again.

And with that, I slammed the door behind me, hurried to my car, and climbed in. I started it and pulled out of the driveway, but before I could put the transmission in gear and drive away, I saw him standing at the window, peering out of it. Watching me.

His eyes were narrowed, his jaw tight.

He was angry, I could tell. But he was no longer my problem. Not after the way he spoke to me.

He was still that creep that watched me from the windows when he came to visit that summer.

Maybe I'd been wrong about him this entire time. Maybe he didn't care. Maybe he was only with me to try and prove a point to Theo— that he could take me just as easily as he took Janet.

Maybe . . . he never loved me to begin with. Maybe it was all just a stupid, pointless scheme so he could feel like the better man. *Disgusting prick.*

Sad thing was, I was never going to find out the answers to any of it.

CHAPTER 38

CHLOE

I hurried into the house and locked the door behind me as soon as I was back, checking the windows to make sure no cars pulled up after me. For all I knew, he could have followed me.

Fucking jackass.

"Hey," Theo called as he walked by with the phone to his ear. "You okay?"

"Yeah," I breathed, spinning around with a strained smile. I lifted the Kindle and charger in the air. "Got my reading device and some jewelry in my bag."

"Good. We'll be set to leave in the morning. We'll have to leave kind of early though. I have to be at my lawyer's office by three."

"Yeah," I panted. "That's okay with me."

He nodded, studying me with slightly furrowed brows. He lowered the phone a bit and asked again, "You sure you're okay? You look a little sick."

"I'm feeling a little queasy," I said, smiling. *But not from the baby this time.*

"Go lay down. I'll join you when I finish this call." His nostrils flared then. "Our lawyers. Going over settlements. All money-related of course."

I shrugged a little and walked towards him, kissing his cheek. "I'm sure it will be okay. I'm still here to help."

He winked, and when he turned his back I hurried up the stairs. Shutting the door behind me, I sat on the edge of the bed and raked a trembling hand through my hair. I had to tell Theo about what'd just happened, regardless.

The photos.

His shit-talking about Janet and me.

But it couldn't be right now.

Right now, he had to focus on what he had to deal with in San Francisco.

But afterwards, I would tell him. Sterling was becoming a hazard and I had too much to lose to handle it alone.

CHAPTER 39

CHLOE

This ride seemed to be much quicker than the first time we came.

Perhaps it was because of all of the thoughts running through my mind. I was fatigued of course, but my main concern was for Theo. If Sheila didn't accept the negotiations today, there was no telling what could happen.

She was delaying the process, which was going to make it a little tougher for us to move forward at a steady pace. It was kind of hard to move onward when she kept barging in.

When he parallel parked in front of a large building with silver windows that was in the heart of the city, I drew in a full breath. We were here. He didn't have to say it for me to know.

He shut the car off and then sat back in his seat. "She's in there," he murmured.

"Yep. Just waiting to emotionally murder you, huh?" I side-eyed him.

He was smiling. "You know you don't have to come in."

"I want to. I won't be close by but I'll wait in the hall or somewhere comfortable."

He licked his bottom lip and then scratched his head. "Okay. But I'm not sure how long it will take." He pulled out his wallet and handed me a debit card. "I just got this. Only under my name—not that damn card we shared. If it starts to get too late, go book a hotel. You already look tired. You should be resting right now, not worried and stressing about this."

"I'll only go if you come out and tell me to. Otherwise I will stick it out."

"Take the card, Chlo. Get food and whatever else you want." I grabbed it and put it in my wallet.

"Are you ready?" I asked, voice hesitant.

He gave a broken smile. "As ready as I'll ever be." He took a long inhale and then exhaled. "Come on. Let's get this shit over with."

We walked into the building, Theo not as confident as I'd hoped. He said we'd already won, but even he knew that anything could backfire and change at any given moment.

The building was clean and neat. There were many lawyers in suits, as well as clients walking around, and I wondered if they were all victims of divorce or something else. Many women were there, some crying. Some smiling. The ones that were crying made the hair on the back of my neck stand up.

Theo rounded a corner and when he came to a black door with the name Phil Hunter on it, he knocked. The door was pulled open almost immediately.

To our luck, it was only Phil, a thin man with hair grayer than Theo's. He looked older than him by about five or six years. He wore a navy blue pinstriped suit and a tie to match. If there was one word I could use to describe him . . . narrow. He was as thin as a pencil. Thin nose, small eyes, and really thin lips.

"Good to see you, Theo," Phil said, extending his arm and shaking it with a light smile.

"You too, Phil."

Phil nodded and then looked down at me. I forced a small smile.

He extended a hesitant hand. "And you must be . . . ?"

"Chloe," I filled in for him, shaking his hand.

Phil swooped his gaze over to Theo again. "Girlfriend?"

"Yes," he answered quickly. "Where are they?"

"In the conference room down the hall." He paused, looking between us. "Look, I don't want to be the bearer of bad news here, Theo, but in order for this to go as smoothly as possible, Chloe will have to wait here or in the lobby. Sheila is already causing a fuss about the negotiations. She thinks they're unfair. With your girlfriend here, she'll hunt for more—use it against you as much as she can, in court if it comes down to that."

"Chloe wasn't planning on joining us for the conference, Phil. I agree that the smoother this can go, the better."

I nodded my agreement.

Phil looked so relieved. "Okay. Great. Well, Chloe, you can wait in my office then—if you'd like. If you need anything, there is a coffee maker in there, some ginger tea set up, and the bathroom is just down the hallway there." He motioned Theo toward the conference rooms. "Let's hope this doesn't take too long." He clasped his hands and pressed his lips together to smile. "Let me just grab my folder and briefcase."

When Phil turned and walked into his office to gather his things, Theo stepped up to me and placed a damp kiss on my forehead. "Remember what I said. You get tired or anything, go book a hotel nearby. With Sheila, there's no telling how long we'll be in there."

"Okay. I hear you. Just do what you have to do." I knuckled his chin. "You've got this."

His smile was faint. He placed a swift kiss on my lips and when Phil returned, he pulled away and walked down the hallway with him, towards the conference room.

Sighing, I walked into Phil's office and decided to make a cup of ginger tea and as I set it all up, my only hope was that Theo would come out of this unscathed and free.

That's all I wanted for him.

Freedom.

CHAPTER 40

CHLOE

Four hours now. It'd been four long hours and none of my e-books were distracting me, not even the pregnancy novels I'd downloaded. The pacing in the office wasn't helping, nor were the cups of tea and crackers.

I felt jittery all over, my nerves on end, so I sat again.

I had to hold out. I knew he wouldn't have minded if I left, but I was here for him, whether he knew it or not. The sun was already sinking. It was starting to get late. I knew better than to be nosy, but the only person that would know who I was, was Theo and Phil.

The conference rooms had windows you could see through. Plus, I needed to go to the restroom. Placing my Kindle on the coffee table, I pushed out of my chair and walked out the door, down the hallway and towards the restrooms.

Before I could get to them, I saw Theo sitting at a round table in a room with gray walls. Beside him was Phil, who was talking on his behalf, and across from his was . . . Sheila.

Her hair was curled to perfection. She had on a red silk blouse and a pencil skirt. I couldn't tell what kind of heels she wore, but I knew she'd dressed to impress for a reason.

Trying to get him to see what he was losing.

Theo sat there, scowling at her, fed up. He didn't give a damn about her looks.

I wasn't sure, but it seemed she was smirking.

I could hear Phil droning on as he spoke to her lawyer. And then I heard him ask, "How much are you seeking exactly, Mrs. Black?"

"Don't call me that anymore, please," she responded rapidly, sitting back in her seat with a frown. "It's Sheila Ruth. Just call me Miss Ruth." Her Jersey accent was thick.

"Okay, *Miss Ruth*," Phil continued, impatience lacing his voice. "Is there a set amount?"

"I've only got fifteen thousand in a private account. Don't have much more than that," Theo grumbled.

"Well, that sucks, doesn't it? I guess that means you have to stop skipping days at the garage and actually work now." Her grin was smug. I frowned, and when I did, Theo's gaze shot up. He spotted me and sat up in his seat a bit, but his gaze didn't linger. He pulled away before Sheila could notice and figure out what he was looking at.

"I need more than that if I'm going to make a living for myself again. You want me to sign off on the shop and not be co-owner, I need something in return. Otherwise, that shop you run is the only income I'll be getting. Designing offices and homes doesn't cover enough anymore and you know I can't ask my parents for it right now with my father being sick and all."

"Well, not if he stops working and pulls his rights to the shop's name, *Miss Ruth*."

She whipped her gaze over to Phil. "What are you talking about?"

"Well," Phil slid the papers across the table, "this is a new contract. He's paid the loan off, so he doesn't owe any more on it. He's also willing to sign over his ownership of Black Engine, meaning that you can keep the shop and its name all you'd like as sole owner, but that business will be on your hands, not his, if you want it to keep running. Here," Phil said, pointing to a highlighted section. "The contract states clearly that either owner may pull from the company at anytime they see fit. That means you'll be held responsible for Black Engine if you decide to keep your name on the contract and he doesn't."

"Let me see that." Sheila's lawyer snatched up the paper, propping his glasses on the bridge of his nose and reading over it. Theo watched him carefully with a smirk.

I smiled with him.

When the lawyer whispered something in Sheila's ear, she shook her head and scoffed. "I can't do that. I don't know shit about a how a mechanic's shop is supposed to run!"

"We know you don't," Theo said. "Which is why you should take the deal. I'll give you whatever money I have to spare, but I can't give more than the fifteen, Sheila. If you try and keep your co-ownership of Black Engine, I will pull my name and you will be on your own. You will drown in debt and have to close shop eventually if you try to keep it and you'll lose even more money. Let's not make this anymore difficult than it needs to be."

Theo glanced up a bit and bobbed his head at me.

I nodded, turning and walking to the restroom with a sneer. From the looks of it, they'd trapped her in a corner and she had no way out. Of course she could keep trying to go for more money, which would fuck Theo over in the end, but we all knew she would be quick to pull her name from Black Engine before Theo. She couldn't handle what he'd created. She knew nothing about that line of work.

Theo had already said he'd spoken with his employees and would take them with him if anything changed. Hopefully he wouldn't have to change a thing.

I went into a stall, slightly relieved, but only slightly. After I was finished, I stepped out and went for the sink, but then the door swung open and in *she* walked.

She was about the same height as me, I realized, taller with heels on. She seemed flustered now, her blond eyebrows drawn together, but of course she was still beautiful. Stunning, really. But I was never going to admit that out loud. Dropping her purse on the counter, she dug into it and pulled out a tube of lipstick.

I felt her glance over at me as I pumped out some hand soap and started washing my hands. I was sure she had no idea who I was, so I pretended I didn't know her either.

Well, that's what I figured, until she said, "Hmm. You're a lot prettier in person than I thought you'd be."

I shut the water off. "I'm sorry?"

"Chloe, right?" she inquired, applying a coat of the red lipstick. "Yeah, it's you. I've seen you in a few of Izzy's photo albums. You were young—a little girl." She looked me over in the mirror. "But not so much anymore, I see."

"No, I guess not." I looked away and walked towards the paper towels to dry my hands, apprehensive now.

"You know you deserve better than him, right? You're young with your whole life ahead of you. What do you want with him anyway?" She popped her lips and then capped her lipstick. When she stood up straight, she twisted around to look me in the eyes.

"I don't think that's any of your business," I responded.

Before I could walk out the door, she spoke again and I paused, not daring to look back at her. "You know, I knew he was in love with another woman when I met him. He had that sadness about him. Like no other woman in the world would ever be enough and I thought I could change that. But I didn't. And still can't. I guess if anyone is to blame for this divorce happening, it's me for thinking I could fix such a sad, broken man like him." Her nostrils flared a bit.

"Why are you telling me this?"

"Because you seem to be the only person that can talk some sense into him. And if talking to you will get me what I want, then so be it." She dug in her purse and fished out a tube of mascara. "So this is what you can do: tell him that I will settle with fifty-thousand dollars, the furniture from the house, and the car he bought me is mine, and I will leave him alone for good. I know he has more than fifteen grand to spare. I'm not an idiot. He's clearly lying. I won't take it to court if he agrees. I will relinquish my ownership to his shop and he can be happy or whatever the hell else he wants to be with you. I will accept the other negotiations he set up. As long as I don't walk out of this divorce in a slump, he'll be fine."

I swallowed thickly, glancing over my shoulder. She had that same smug look on her face, like she knew I would go running to tell him. But that's where she had me fooled.

"Wow," I laughed. "I see they were right about you. You *are* a bitch." I turned around completely and took a step forward. "Don't worry, you'll get your money and that crappy furniture you want so badly. Hell, you can even keep the house for yourself—do whatever the hell you want with it. Who cares? He won't need it. But," I said, lifting a finger, "when you get your part of the bargain, I never want to see your name pop up on his phone again or even hear that you tried to contact him in any sort of way. If you even attempt, I will *end* you." She seemed taken aback by my sudden change of mood. And maybe I did as well, but love could make you say and do crazy shit. Love could make you bold and fearless. And fearless, I was.

"See, I know lawyers too. Great ones," I went on. "Ones that can ruin your life with the scribble of a pen, *Sheila*. If I were you, I wouldn't test my patience right now. As long as you agree to his nego-tiations and pull your ownership from his shop, you'll get what you want. But don't come back looking for more because it won't happen. You know his shop is his life—his life's work—and you aren't going to take that away from him." I cocked a brow, my hands lifting in the air. "Understood?"

She looked at me as if I had lost my mind. Her face, I think, had even paled a bit. It was funny. In that moment I didn't find her so stunning. She looked lost, like a young girl without her rich parents to defend her.

Funny how the tables had turned.

Trust me, I hadn't lost my mind, but I could tell she'd walked all over Theo for years and he was too damn nice to deny her—too afraid he'd lose everything he worked so hard for if he dared reject her. If I hadn't set her straight, she would have continued trying to walk all over him. That wasn't about to happen on my watch. She wasn't going to make him miserable anymore.

"Wow," she laughed bitterly. "Bold. But you know what? Whatever. I'll let you have your moment." She waved a dismissive hand and opened the mascara. "As long as I get my money from him before the divorce is final, you'll never hear from me again and neither will he. Hell, he wasn't that interesting anyway." She rolled her eyes.

"Oh, no problem," I bit out, turning for the door again and yanking it open. "You'll have your money tomorrow. A checked will be hand-delivered personally by me. That's how soon I want you out of his life." I looked her over, repulsed. "Now stop stalling and sign the fucking divorce papers already. We're ready to go back home."

When I walked out, I heard her laughing, but I knew it wasn't a laugh of victory. It was a *holy-shit-she-isn't-kidding* kind of laugh. I wasn't kidding. I was tired of her and her endless games.

I had the money and I would have given it all if it meant she was out of the picture for good.

I hurried by the conference rooms and when Theo saw me, he lifted a finger and came out. He brought me to a far corner by the window and asked, "What's up?"

"Ran into your bitch of a wife," I said, huffing a laugh. "How did you ever live with her?"

He swiped a hand over his face. "I ask myself the same damn question every day."

"Well, this time she gave *me* an ultimatum. She wants fifty thousand dollars, the furniture from the house, and wants to keep her car. In return, she'll settle with the negotiations and release her ownership of Black Engine."

His eyes expanded, lips parting. "What? You're serious? She said that to you? Fuck, Chloe, I don't have that kind of money to just give to her. I mean—I do, but it'll come out of my savings and I'm not losing out just because she wants to be a spoiled fucking bitch." He scoffed. "Would be like her to run to you just to get what the fuck she wants."

"You won't be broke," I said, grabbing his hand and squeezing it. "My dad left me $350,000. I'll take out fifty for her. You won't have to give a dime. It's no big deal. I *want* to do this, so don't tell me that I shouldn't." I placed a hand on his chest when he started to protest. "I'm sure there's a bank around. I'll find a branch, get a check, and make it out to her and I'll give it to her, just as long as she signs. She'll get her money and other stuff and she'll never bother us again."

He was still shocked, planting his hands on his hips as he looked out of the window. "Goddamn," he mumbled, and then he eyed me, a slow smile spreading across his face. "I fucking love you, you know that?" He grabbed my chin and I focused on his sparkling brown eyes.

"When I say I will do anything for you, I mean it. I haven't touched that money since I bought myself a car and put a down payment on the beach house. It's still there."

"I'm just . . ." He released a heavy laugh, dropping his head. "You're the only person that can make me speechless like this. I'll let Phil know and have him put the new negotiations in writing. In the meantime, you go get a room at the hotel next door. Go and relax. Now. I'll meet you there, just text me the room number." He kissed me hard on the cheek and when Phil popped up around the corner to let him know she was back, he pulled away and started walking backwards. With that sexy, boyish grin, he shouted, "You're too fucking good to me, baby! You always have been! Always my Knight, coming in to save the day!"

I lit up, grinning like a damn fool when he disappeared around the corner.

To my dismay, that smile and the joy I felt as he walked away to finalize his divorce wasn't going to last for long.

CHAPTER 41

Theo

The first thing I did when I arrived at the hotel was scoop Chloe up in my arms and smother her with my affection. Her face, her neck, her entire body. And then I kissed her belly—*my baby.*

"I take it everything went well? She signed?" she asked with a broad, cheesy grin. I placed her down on her feet.

"Yeah, she signed. She gets what she wants and I get to keep my shop and the name."

"Oh, Theo, I'm so happy for you, babe. Seriously! That is great news!"

"It is. I'm honestly surprised it wasn't more difficult than this."

"Yeah, me too." She shrugged. "But that's a good thing too. I found a branch that's only about five miles from here. If you take me tomorrow, I'll get the check. I promised I would hand deliver it to her myself."

"What kind of shit went down in the restroom that I don't know about?" My eyebrows shifted and she laughed.

"Oh, nothing too serious. I just told her that once she gets her money and all the other stuff, to never try and contact you again. I don't think that's too much to ask for. Do you?"

"Hmm . . . I think pregnancy is making you kinda feisty, babe," I teased, pulling my shirt over my head. "I like it."

"Hey, she had no right to be so bitchy. I could read her like a book. She was trying to stomp all over you." She met up to me and wrapped her hands around my waist. "No one messes with my Theo."

I gripped her waist, picked her up, and carried her towards the bed. "No one, huh?" The tip of my nose skimmed her jawline.

Her breath hitched as I lowered my hands, cupping her ass. She kissed my collarbone and I returned the favor, kissing the top of her shoulder.

"Not feeling too sick, are you?"

"Not right now."

"Good." I laid her on the bed and spread her legs apart. Unbuttoning her jeans and wrenching them off, I brought my face back up and crushed her lips with mine. She sighed beneath me, hauling me closer as I unbuttoned my jeans and pushed them down.

When I kicked them off and she wiggled out of hers, she flipped me over, climbing on top of me and dragging my boxers down. I hoisted her up when she was perched atop me again, taking her panties off, and she whimpered when the pad of my thumb skimmed her soft clit.

"You're free?" she breathed, planting her hands on my chest and pushing up on her knees. When I felt her pussy wrap around the tip of my cock, I stiffened, but she kept going, sliding down until every inch of me was inside her.

"Fuck, Chloe," I groaned, head falling back as she lifted her ass and swallowed me whole again. I held her waist as she rode me, staring into my eyes, her fingers running through her hair.

"Are you free, Theo?" she asked again.

"With you, I always will be." She smiled at that, swiveling on my cock. She was so wet, her moans making me hard as hell. She rode in near silence. All I could hear were her sighs and moans of pleasure. She didn't have to speak for me to know she was enjoying this.

The divorce wasn't going to be final until it ran by a judge, but Phil said in six to ten weeks, it would most likely be processed and would pass, so long as the negotiations remained settled.

I would be a single man again. Well, scratch that. I would be *Chloe's* again, and only hers.

Yeah, I would be free. And she knew it too. There would be no fears. No lies. No secrets. There wouldn't be anyone to stop us.

So I let her make sweet, victorious love to me, because after today, she needed it. We both needed it. It felt too incredible to stop, and even when the urge to take control again swept through me, I ignored it and focused on the light in her eyes.

She leaned forward, her hair brushing my cheek, my jawline. She smelled sweet, like vanilla, fresh. Her tits were close to my lips, and I sucked gently on her nipples, cupping her ass as she started a light bounce and claimed what was hers.

She rode me faster, her lips coming down on mine, her body glued to me. Her hand clasped one side of my face and she held on tight, breathing deep, moaning my name in my ear.

"We won," I told her. "And you're mine, baby. Mine for the rest of my life."

She gasped and trembled, coming hard around my cock, sinking her nails into my shoulder with her other hand. I flipped her onto her back as she released, thrusting deep again, not stopping until I felt her legs shaking around me.

Eyes squeezed shut, her teeth sank into her bottom lip, on the verge of climax again.

"Look at me, baby," I rasped, still thrusting. *Shit, I was close.* Feeling her pulsing around me wasn't helping. Not one fucking bit.

She showed me her big, beautiful eyes, hooking an arm around the back of my neck.

And I smiled, bringing my lips down to hers, not kissing, just touching. A feathery light touch, that caused goosebumps to crawl across her soft skin. I was still so deep inside her, still stroking. Still holding on.

And then I said, "I'm free now, baby. I'm yours. Always. *Forever*. I promise."

She brought my face down and started kissing my neck, tracing her tongue around the caresses, building me up even more. I was so hard, so ready to come.

And when she clenched her walls around my cock, it was done. I stilled inside her, cursing beneath my breath, my hand rising up to entwine our fingers. I held on tight as I came—marking my woman.

Owning her.

Never wanting to let go.

"Damn," I groaned as she panted beneath me. We were sticky with sweat now, but neither of us bothered to move.

Pushing up on an elbow, I stared into her hazel eyes and witnessed the bliss—the joy coursing through her.

How she felt so happy with a fucked up person like me, I would never know. But what kind of man would I have been to question it?

I pressed my thumb to her chin, holding it between my fingers, and kissing her full lips. She always tasted so sweet. Everywhere.

"Free," she whispered, and I rolled over, but not without collecting her in my arms.

She sighed a breath of so much relief, and for the first time in years, I did the same.

Damn right, I was free.

After forty-six fucking years, I had finally found myself.

It wouldn't have happened without her.

CHAPTER 42

THEO

Going home, it felt like heavy weights had fallen right off my shoulders, compared to the ride to San Francisco. I'd never felt so unburdened—so glad to finally be able to do what I wanted.

To have Chloe fucking Knight sitting right beside me in my passenger seat, with the windows down and the air billowing past us. To have the woman I loved with every ounce of my heart holding my hand like her life depended on it, smiling at me with the gentlest gaze I'd ever seen on a woman. A delicate one. One that spoke a thousand words.

After she'd handed Sheila the check, we were out of there. Sheila didn't ask any questions. She took it and slammed the door. We didn't want to linger. There was no need. We had a home waiting for us. Yes, *us*.

And . . . also Izzy.

She'd called during the ride to ask about how things went and to let us know she was heading back to Bristle Wave. Chloe was ecstatic, demanding that I stop by the market first to buy food, and also cook dinner for her to welcome her to the new home.

I did just that.

And as I watched my girls eat dinner and laugh, I couldn't ignore the way my heart galloped. This was the peace I had longed for my entire life. This was the kind of life I had wanted, with a woman I truly adored at my side, and my daughter accepting her and me.

There was no trace of anger in Izzy. Nothing negative came out of her mouth about us. My little girl was no longer a little girl. She'd grown—blossomed into the most beautiful woman, one I never thought I'd end up raising.

By me, the man who was once a fuck-up and a loner. Me, the man that had once broken her heart by sweeping her best friend right off her feet and not giving a damn about it.

She'd forgiven us.

She'd accepted, and she was the only approval I needed. Everyone else could kiss my ass.

Chloe noticed my silence as Izzy talked about her next gig, and reached for my hand on the table without looking. I glanced down at it, how bare her fingers were. I had to fix that, and soon.

But for now, I would let her enjoy this. Because she deserved it.

My Little Knight deserved the world and more.

Since I had cooked, Izzy and Chloe offered to clean up after dinner. My phone rang in my back pocket as I shot darts in the garage and downed a few beers, my form of celebrating.

It was Dane, who just so happened to spot some lowlife trying to climb on my boat.

"Shit, I'll be right there," I told him. I hung up and jammed the last two darts in the board. Picking up my helmet, I opened the door and walked into the kitchen, finding Izzy finishing off her wine as Chloe wiped the last of the dishes dry. "There's someone trying to mess with Dirty Black. Dane is out there right now, but he's too old to try and take on anyone alone. I should go help him handle it."

"Oh, crap." Izzy placed her empty glass down on the counter. "Dad, do you need me to go? I know how to swing a wrench. You taught me yourself."

"Nah, I got it, Izzy Bear. Stay here with Chloe. I'm sure you two have something big to discuss anyway. Right, Chlo?"

"Theo! Seriously!" Chloe shouted, shooting her hands out. "It's too soon!"

"Too soon for what?" Izzy questioned.

Chloe glanced at her and then snapped her gaze on me. I shrugged and smirked, walking in her direction and placing a swift kiss on her lips. "I'll be right back. I'm sure you can handle it. You're better at these talks anyway, I'm sure."

Her cheeks flamed red. She tried scowling at me, but it was damn near impossible for her. She was excited to tell Izzy about the baby, too. She'd talked about it during most of the ride back, wondering if it would be a boy or girl. Hoping he or she was healthy. So instead, she broke out in a grin and grabbed Izzy's hand.

"Fine. Go. But be careful!" she called as I started for the door again.

"I will. I love you . . . *both*!" I shouted right before shutting it behind me.

I jumped on Ol' Charlie, clipping my helmet and then opening the garage gate.

Fortunately, the docks weren't too far away from our home. Ten minutes and I could make it. Dane had a nephew who was a security guard of the docks at night and I'd hoped he would take care of it, but Dane only called with emergencies. Apparently whoever this shit was, wasn't letting up, and his nephew hadn't clocked in just yet.

I could see the docks from a few miles away, just over the cliff. I revved the bike and rode faster, chasing asphalt. I should have known something was wrong then, but with the victory of that day, it seemed luck was on my side. I felt invincible, like nothing could stop me now.

I gripped the handlebars even tighter, hearing a car behind me. It came closer and closer, the headlights zeroing in. The car kept coming faster and I glanced over my shoulder, gesturing for him to just drive around. There was no way in hell I was about to speed up on Ol' Charlie on this winding road with jagged edges that led straight to the ocean.

I had a woman to get back to. My daughter.

The car came even closer and then it hit my bike's rear. "What the fuck!" I jerked the handles when I lost control. Before I could pull over, stop the bike, and curse the fucker out, the car rammed me from the back again, but this time it held its place, forcing me forward.

I could hear the car's engine purring, the tires skidding, and then I was being forced to the right. Too close to the edge of the cliff. There were no guardrails on this section.

Nothing to prevent the fall.

"What the fuck are you doing?!" I shouted at the car. My exhaust pipe was caught in the car's grill. I revved my bike, pulling the levers, but it only made the tires skid.

The headlights of the car were damn near blinding me. I stomped one foot on the ground to try and get some balance, but it didn't help. One foot wasn't strong enough.

"Stop!" I had to get off this bike.

But it was too late. One final press of that gas pedal and Ol' Charlie was falling over the edge of the cliff. *I* was falling over the edge of the cliff, yards away from the bottom.

Falling.

Falling.

Jagged rocks pierced my skin as I dropped, feeling bones snapping —my body being flung around and down the cliff like I was a fucking ragdoll. I could hear metal crashing and scraping, smashing into the rock.

My bike.

Before I knew it, my tumbling came to a cease. I couldn't feel a thing. Every single part of my body was numb.

I moved my head to the right and saw shattered light—Ol' Charlie's headlight. I could see the moon. I smelled salt—the ocean—but only for a second.

Because when that next second struck, I couldn't breathe. I felt suffocated by liquid. Hot, burning copper. *Blood.*

And that's when I saw blackness.

It was pitch black.

My heart stopped beating.

And I . . . I couldn't . . . breathe . . .

CHAPTER 43

CHLOE

I should have told him.

Before he left, I should have told him then about Sterling. Because I had a bad, bad feeling. A feeling that sat like a pound of bricks in the pit of my belly. I just didn't think it would be *this* bad.

And now—now my Theo was on an operating table for surgery.

He wasn't breathing on his own.

He looked battered and bruised and . . . and *dead*.

The police had called Izzy over thirty minutes ago, unable to reach Sheila, and I could have sworn this was so familiar. Rushing to the hospital with Izzy during the night because one of her parents had been hurt—on purpose. The cops said it looked like an accident, like Theo had driven off the cliff himself with a car in front of him, but he would have never done that. Ever.

And I knew.

I knew. I had no proof, but deep down in my gut, I knew Sterling had something to do with this. After they'd explained it to us—that a car may have been behind him or in front of him by the tire skid marks—I figured it was Sterling. Theo didn't veer off the road. He wasn't drunk or high or out of his mind. He was *forced* off the edge of that cliff.

There were skid marks. Two different tracks of tires, one of them belonging to this motorcycle. This was no accident. The cops tried to say the car may have come over to try and help.

It was bullshit. Where was that car now? Who gave the anonymous call to the police? Why didn't the person want to say who they were?

Because it was fucking Sterling.

He wanted me to find out.

The doctors were pumping Theo's chest, and my tears thickened. I didn't know what words I was shouting behind that door. I just wanted to be there for him. I wanted to talk to him. Let him hear my voice. Let him know that I was there.

Blood was everywhere, the machines beeping wildly. The nurses were keeping Izzy and me behind the door, trying to get us down the hallway. We didn't want to go anywhere.

"His heart rate is declining. Get them away from the door!" the doctor hollered.

Izzy shouted at one of the nurses that tried to grab her, hissing that it was her father and she needed to be there. After hearing what the surgeon shouted, I could no longer fight as they hauled us away from the door. Of course Izzy put up a fight and I didn't blame her.

But I had something to do.

Something to handle.

He was *not* getting away with this shit. I had no proof. I didn't know what the hell I was going to do, but I would find something— anything to show that he had always hated Theo.

"Izzy! Izzy, come on," I said, taking her from the nurse and bringing her to the waiting area. She was shaking as I sat her down in the far corner and rubbed her arm. "I—I have something to do really quick but I'll be right back."

"What?" she asked, her eyes growing wide and desperate. "No! Where are you going, Chloe? I need you here!"

"It will be quick. I promise."

I stood up and rushed for the exit. She called after me, but I didn't stop or look back. I pulled out my car keys and drove away from the hospital in haste. I didn't slow down until I reached my destination.

Hopping out of the car, I hurried towards the door and barged right in. The unfamiliar faces turned my way, all of them staring like I was carrying a ticking bomb.

And then the woman at the front desk said something, clearing her throat. "Can I help you?" she called out with her nose in the air, suspicious.

"Yes," I breathed, meeting up to the counter and dropping my gaze to her badge. "I—I need to talk to someone about an attempted murder."

I spent that entire night in the police station, biting my nails, calling Izzy every ten minutes for an update. No update. No one had even come to check in with her. She said she saw the nurses rushing in and out, but that it didn't look good.

The detective didn't want to believe me at first. He thought I was making it all up, but then I told him the details—how I'd broken it off with him to be with the man that was in the hospital. How Sterling was sitting in the kitchen in the dark, angry with Theo and me, and claiming that he'd stolen me from him.

He was a jealous, disgusting fuck.

The detective gave me a few eye rolls. His name was Detective Wallace. "I've been told by the investigation team that it looked like an accident, Miss Knight. You don't think that by chance he might have just, I don't know, got impatient, lost control, and ended up riding off that cliff? It is a dangerous road, especially at night."

"No!" I slammed a fist on the desk and he cocked a bushy brow, unfazed. "I'm telling you the truth. Theo has been riding his bike for years. He's never even gotten a scratch on the damn thing. He's ridden that road many times before to get to his boat, sometimes with me on it. I—I know him. And I also know the man that did this. He gets jealous and his anger blinds him. Can you—can you just look him up? Please? I'm sure you'll find his name in the system somewhere. He was apart of a gang once. He has to have some kind of criminal record."

"Once? When?" he asked, mildly interested now.

"It was years ago, but he used to date Theo's dead wife too."

The detective looked at me as if I'd lost my damn mind.

"Look—I know it all sounds crazy now but just look him up. See if you can find something—anything to put him under arrest for so you can question him."

Sighing, the detective grabbed the mouse. "His name?"

"Sterling Martinez."

He grunted as he typed, then shifted in his chair, placing his glasses on the bridge of his nose. He did a few clicks here and there. My knee bounced as he scrolled, and when he found what he was looking for, his eyes grew as wide as discs.

"Holy shit. This man is a felon? Well, why the hell didn't you say he'd been convicted of a felony before?"

I blinked rapidly. "I didn't know. W-what did he do?"

"Says here he was pinned for conspiring. Was almost locked up for second-degree murder. For a woman named . . . Janet Black?"

My jaw dropped. "Oh my God."

"Looks like he had a good lawyer that got the case dropped for him since it was his first offense. He only did two years of probation because it was proved he was a member of the gang. The three men that were caught fingered him for claims of setting up the murder, but they had no proof, which is probably the only reason he was let off the hook. Goddamn it," he grumbled, pushing out of his chair. "Just when I thought this night wouldn't consist of anymore paperwork." He walked to the door and yanked it open, called for someone, and then walked around the desk to pick up his badge and gun.

"If you're right, he's probably still around. Waiting to see if your man lives or dies. Do you know where he might be right now?"

"Um . . . at the house we used to share maybe," I responded. "3618 Merrill Street. If not there, he's going back to Orange County to his mother's apartment." Another detective appeared at the door with a folder in hand, watching as Detective Wallace clipped his gun to his belt.

"All right. Detective Johnson here will keep you company while I make a quick run—ask some questions. I can't assume he's done anything, Miss Knight. But I can check since he has a record of this kind of behavior. Maybe he has the car there. Maybe he doesn't. If he does, he's probably trying to clean it as we speak. I'll send out a few units to search the town just in case he's not there and might be on the run."

I nodded and Detective Wallace took off in a flash. It was the fastest I'd seen him move since he had introduced himself to me.

No matter. I would sit there all night and wait—give them whatever information they needed, just so long as they caught the bastard. He was dead to me.

He wanted to take Theo away from me. His hatred was pure. And knowing that . . . that he could have been apart of Janet's murder—that he may have planned that "gang related" killing—makes me wonder how the hell I lived with a monster like him and didn't realize it.

Did Theo even know? He knew Janet was murdered, but did he know who it was by? They never showed Sterling's face in any files. If his case was dropped, and he was given no sentence, it was meaningless for the media. It was an assumption, but it was most likely true.

I should have seen the signs.

The way he watched me.

The way he spoke to me when he was agitated.

How he grabbed me the last time I saw him and looked at me like he wanted to end me right there for trying to walk away. He would have been a fool to try at that moment, considering he was the only other person to have access to the house. But I was sure that if it came down to it—if I had made him angry enough, then he probably would have tried to kill me too.

CHAPTER 44

CHLOE

24 Hours Later

I never thought I would see him like this.

Lying there. Damaged. I felt hopeless and doomed.

We'd just turned our dreams into reality, and in a flash it felt like it had all been snatched right away from me. He wasn't moving. He was having a hard time breathing. It'd only been twenty-four hours, but I missed his voice.

His touch.

I missed him. Period.

I was so livid last night that I erased every single picture I had of Sterling. Every trace of him was gone, from the photos to his number and even the text messages and voicemails. I hated him. I wanted him dead, but they had no proof.

I saw him when they brought him in for questioning. He wasn't cuffed and somehow his eyes found mine. I grimaced at him, wanting so badly to charge out of my chair and spit in his face. I wanted to even more when he put on the faintest grin and winked at me.

He was a bastard. A cruel, heartless bastard. After that encounter, I had no doubt that he had done this to Theo.

"Theo," I whispered.

No response.

Nothing.

I squeezed his hand, wanting to feel him squeeze back. I only wanted a little reassurance—something to let me know he was there.

"Ol' Charlie shouldn't have gone out like that, huh?" I said, laughing a little. "I'm going to miss him. I know you will, too." My smile faded just as quickly as it appeared, just remembering how long Ol' Charlie had been around. It was a good bike. A durable one that never let us down. Ol' Charlie was a lot like Theo, and I'd lost Ol' Charlie already. That bike couldn't be salvaged.

Damn it. I couldn't lose both.

The door opened before I could shed too many tears. When I looked back, Izzy was walking in with two cups in hand.

"It's hot chocolate," she said, handing one of them to me.

I set it down, sighing. "Thanks."

"You have to get something in your system, Chloe. You're carrying a baby now. I know hot chocolate isn't the best choice, but maybe some orange juice—something? They have muffins, cakes, donuts—lots of stuff." She was pleading now, begging me to eat or drink something. But how could I? Looking at him this way constantly made me lose all sense of appetite.

I felt the tears collecting on my eyelashes as I focused on my lap. "I thought it would get easier for him. Not worse." Here I was thinking Sheila was going to be the biggest threat but I was so, so wrong.

Izzy rubbed my back. "I know. But he'll pull through. He's a fighter. Always has been. It's something I've admired about him since I was a little girl."

It was hard to swallow then. "I feel like he wouldn't even be in this situation if it weren't for me. Like if he were still in San Francisco with Sheila, he would be fine, you know? Safe . . ."

"Oh, please, Chloe. Cut that shit out!" Izzy snapped, placing her coffee down. She grabbed a chair and dragged it beside mine. "Sheila doesn't deserve him. You guys fought for this, right? You won." She gestured towards her father. "I know you can't see the bright side of things right now, but give it a few days. He'll pull through. I know it. He's in there." She gave him a sideways glance and I wasn't so sure if she was trying to convince me or herself. "He's not leaving us," she murmured with a shaky voice. She rubbed his arm, but I caught the way her fingers trembled. "He *can't* leave us. He's all we have left."

The following morning, still nothing from Theo.

But we did have two visitors. The first was Theo's mother.

She couldn't even make it into the room without crying. Her eyes were filled with so much grief. So much pain. I understood how she felt. Izzy was sitting on the sofa when she walked in, and as soon as she saw her grandmother, she hopped out of her seat and rushed for her.

"Oh—Grammy!" Izzy sobbed into her grandmother's chest. Rita. That was her name. I could remember it when she showed me the house. The realtor. A beautiful woman with eyes just as brown as Theo's, but much gentler, eyelashes thickened with mascara.

"Oh, it's okay, sweet girl," Rita cooed to Izzy. "I'm here, baby. I'm here." They held each other, and moments later, Rita picked up her head and caught my eye. "Oh," she sighed. "You come here, too!"

I forced a small smile, pushing slowly out of my seat as she extended her right arm, still holding Izzy with her left. It was nice not to be judged. I figured she knew who I was and why I was here. Theo had told her about me many times. I'd even met her once, before she sold me my home, when I was younger and Izzy and I were still the best of friends.

And though she knew I was the girl—the young girl—sleeping with her only son, she held no judgment. She only provided love. And something about that really made the crack in my chest grow an inch wider.

I hugged both her and Izzy as she whispered to us that it would be okay. It took us a while to get our shit together. When I looked up, Rita was smiling and I honestly couldn't understand how she could during a time like this.

"My Benji is a good man. He always has been. He's had such a hard life," she whispered to us. "But he has always, *always* been a strong guy. He will pull through this. I know he will. He used to fight so many battles for me, but now it's time to see if he'll fight his own. I know you ladies are scared. I know it hurts—trust me, I know. But he's in there and he won't quit. So don't give up on him for a second." She grabbed Izzy's chin to pick her head up. "Do you understand? Not for a second." She rested a warm palm on my cheek and I nodded with a small smile.

"I won't," I murmured and I meant it.

An hour later, Izzy and Rita went to the cafeteria to have lunch that I'm certain they weren't going to eat. I waited in the room, and that's when I heard another knock at the door.

Our second guest, Detective Wallace. I perked up a bit when he stepped in, expecting great news, but by the grim look on his face, I knew it wasn't going to make me happy.

"I stopped by to give a personal update. He was at the house you shared today after being released. Caught packing some things, probably to try and make a run for it—or prepare for it at least. We brought him into custody for questioning again, but I'm afraid we can't arrest him. His car was clean. Not a scratch on it."

"You've got to be fucking kidding me," I muttered, rubbing my forehead with my fingertips. "I bet this makes me look like a complete lunatic, huh?" I scoffed.

"Actually, no." When he said that, I picked up my head and met his eyes. "Miss Knight," he started, rubbing his hands together, "I've seen a lot of innocent people and I've seen a lot of guilty people. The innocent are usually easy to point out. They're afraid for their lives—don't know how to act and think any little thing they say will have them tossed in prison. Those are usually the ones we think twice about. But the ones that act cool, casual, and collected about an *attempted murder* accusation—well, I'm not going to say all, but *most* of them are indeed guilty. Mr. Martinez was way too calm. He said he knew of Mr. Black and even admitted that he knew about your affair with Mr. Black a few years back and even about what you two share now."

I swallowed thickly.

"He was too sure of himself. Too prepared for the questions—like he knew they were coming. We let him go because we had to, but something tells me it won't be my last time seeing him. We have people out looking for evidence now. Around the cliff, on Mr. Black's boat, and a few other places. I also have an unmarked car on him that is off the record. Paying for him personally. Just because his car was as clean as a whistle, doesn't mean another one won't be. Just wanted to let you know that I've got my eye on him. He won't get away with this —not while I'm still standing."

I rubbed my arm, nodding. "Wow. Thank you, Detective Wallace. I appreciate knowing that."

He nodded. "If you hear from him, you let me know. You have my number. Don't hesitate to call." He peered over at Theo and then pushed his lips together, his beard overshadowing his lips. "Take care of yourself in the meantime."

I nodded once and with that he was gone, out of the door and leaving me feeling worse off than I had before.

CHAPTER 45

Twelve Days Later

He still wasn't awake.

Not one shift, groan, or whisper.

The beeping machines had become a tune in my head that I couldn't get out.

I never left the hospital once—not since leaving the police station that night. Izzy had to bring me clothes so I could shower at the hospital, but of course those showers didn't last for longer than five minutes. I didn't want to miss the chance to catch him moving.

He had been in a coma for fourteen days now, and things still weren't looking up. They weren't sure how much damage had been caused, but were glad that he'd worn a helmet.

I was glad too. Theo normally wouldn't have worn one, but he always did at night. They said the helmet prevented major trauma to the head and brain, but that there was still a likely chance he could wake up and not remember much.

I needed him to remember *everything*.

I needed him to remember the first day we met, when I was only twelve years old and developed a raging crush on him. When I turned seventeen and made excuses to come to Izzy's house and spend the night, just to lust over his body. How he walked around without a shirt on, showing off his ink and skin.

How he gave me such trusting smiles whenever I visited.

When I was nineteen, and Janet died, and he was a complete wreck.

When he was in the garage those nights, spiraling, and I helped him up to his bedroom each time, until the one night when he wanted more than just my help. When he took my virginity and turned me into a woman. When I had completely fallen in love with Theodore Black and I hated admitting it, because he was my best friend's father.

And his wife had just passed away.

And he was a wreck.

But I didn't want to let go.

I especially couldn't let go when he took me in the park on the grass—when it'd felt like he'd made the sweetest, most passionate love to me.

When I left for college and didn't hear from him for nearly two years. And they were the two most dreadful years of my life, bearing a secret like ours. But then coming back and seeing him again for the first time.

And doing the same thing with him that I swore I never would.

I squeezed his hand tight, brushing his hair back. He hadn't moved at all. For twelve days, he was stuck. So still—almost lifeless.

His right leg was broken as well as his left arm. A large gash was on the right half of his face. His lip busted. Eye blackened. He was healing, but he looked so bad.

Each day was a sluggish, slow defeat.

Every morning I woke up on that uncomfortable couch, expecting to see his beautiful brown eyes, only to be greeted with sealed eyelids and heavy, rhythmic, machine-assisted breathing.

Heat crept to my eyes, and soon I felt that fire spilling down my cheeks, over my lips. I squeezed his hand tighter, resting my forehead on his arm, listening to the machines beep. Listening to him hardly breathing.

"Theo," I whispered. I wasn't sure how many times I'd called his name. It was all I could do. Cry. *Beg*. "You have to wake up now. Please. I know you're stronger than this. You always have been." Picking my head up, I slid my chair in closer and stroked his hair back again. It'd grown out. He hadn't had a haircut since he came back to Bristle Wave.

"You don't have to wake up for me," I continued, voice soft, "but for Izzy. And for our baby. For *yourself*. I know you can hear me in there. You're free, remember? Free to do whatever you want. All you have to do is wake up. Be free with me, Theo." My voice cracked, the tears much thicker now. "We won. He didn't. They got him. He tried, but he'll never hurt you again. You or me."

When he didn't move, not even a twitch, I shook my head and stood, pressing my lips to his forehead. He was still warm, at least.

And then I rested my ear on his chest. I listened to his heartbeat, the familiar steady beat. I felt his breath flowing through my hair, on my skin, as I looked up at him. I couldn't control my tears. The emotion was eating me alive. I felt the blame for this, like a tangible weight on my chest. It never would have happened if I'd just told him from the start about Sterling.

It was all my fault.

"If you're lost in there, trying to find your way out, search for freedom. If you feel guilty about any of this, don't. If you feel like you should have done something, you couldn't. You didn't know and I blame myself for that. I just . . . I want you here. I want you to share the future with me—the future *we* struggled for."

The machines kept beeping. His breaths were still slow.

Nothing.

Nothing but silence in return.

My heart cracked in my chest and I clutched him tight, sobbing like I had the very first night.

I needed him. I needed him more than words could explain. We'd finally done things right. He couldn't be taken away from me like this.

The pain was already too much, just seeing him lying there, knowing I couldn't do a damn thing, was breaking me to pieces.

But if he was gone for good?

I couldn't bear it. I wouldn't be able to live with it. Because only days ago, our future was so clear. It was so bright and warm and welcoming. It was there for us, all we had to do was catch it.

I brought my fingers down to his, slinking down in my seat.

Minutes went by.

An hour.

Two hours.

As badly as I wanted to give up on the idea that he was coming back, I couldn't. I had faith—even though that faith had dwindled to a small speck of light in the dark.

Three hours now, and at three hours I wept, my cheek rested on his arm, fingers still clasping his.

But then I felt it.

The twitching of his fingers. One by one, they moved.

I gasped, staring down at our hands, and then at his toes. They wiggled.

He squeezed my hand. Lightly, but it was a squeeze I had been waiting on for fourteen long, miserable days.

His eyelids fluttered, struggling to peel open.

He looked right at me, brown eyes glassy.

He looked right at me, as if I was the most beautiful woman in the world. Like he always did when he saw me. Like he knew exactly who I was—like he'd never forgotten.

And his words—his *voice*. The voice I thought I might never hear again filled the empty solitude of this room. Still so deep. Still *his*.

His words filled me to the brim. His small, gentle smile made my heart both ache and heal all at once.

"Oh my God," I sobbed, unable to fight my smile or the monsoon of tears.

"There she is," he rasped. "There's my *Little Knight*."

CHAPTER 46

THEO

FIVE DAYS LATER

"He's lucky he's in jail now." I grunted as I adjusted on the crutches. The nurse helped me steady myself, but I held one hand up. I'd been on crutches too many times to count before. This was nothing new, but this kind of pain was off the charts. "If he was still out there, I'd find him and kill him my damn self."

"Well, it's a good thing you can't now, isn't it?" Chloe laughed, slinging our bags on her shoulder. She came up to me, patting me on the chest. "You look better. Glad you actually listened and stayed the five days they told you to."

"Yeah, I guess," I mumbled. "But I'm ready to go now. I want real food, no more of that bland shit they've been feeding me."

She giggled. "Come on. Iz has the car waiting."

It was hard to settle in after the wreck. The first three weeks were hell. Two of my ribs were broken, my damn leg and arm. I couldn't do much. Couldn't drive, couldn't cook. I couldn't even walk the beach that was right in our backyard, but Chloe made me comfortable until

I healed. Because of him, I had the ugliest scar right above my jawline, but Chloe seemed to find it "sexy."

"You have to relax, Theo," Chloe said, helping me sit on the couch. "I can handle dinner. I know it's not as great as yours, but it's better than ordering a bunch of takeout."

I laughed. "I feel so damn useless. Let me help chop something at the table at least."

"No," she sighed, lifting my broken leg and resting it on the couch. "You relax here and wait until Izzy gets back with the hot compresses. When she does, I'll take you back upstairs and warm those muscles. *All* the muscles." She wiggled her eyebrows.

"That sounds nice." I grabbed her chin and kissed her cheek. "Thank you for looking out for me. Love you."

"Love you more."

Chloe filled me in on everything that happened: about how Sterling showed up the day before we left for San Francisco and her not wanting to add to my burdens when I was heading to face my ex-wife. I really wish she would have told me he was there that day. I would have made a trip over there as soon as she'd filled me in, and pummeled his fucking face in.

It would have been settled then. He would have been the one in the fucking hospital, not me. Threatening her was a threat to my unborn child, and I wouldn't have stood for that shit for a second, no matter what I had going on in my life.

And the shit with Janet? I found it hard to accept, but in retrospect, I should have thought about it. Chloe mentioned he was in a gang—the same gang I used to be in when I was young.

I'd never mentioned to the cops that I had been in the gang. They would have found some way to link the murder to me, and I would have been tossed in jail for it. Accused of something I never, ever would have done to the mother of my daughter.

But all this time, it was that sneaky fuck Sterling. I knew I had a reason not to like him. Hell, I hated him. Not only for taking both my women from me when I had them, but for knowing he was probably the reason Janet was dead, and tried to murder me. He was linked to this. Fucking psycho.

He was watching and waiting for the right moment to strike. Waiting until I was alone in the dark. He wasn't driving his car. No, his car was squeaky clean, so I was told. Probably why it took them several days before they could lock him up.

They had no proof he'd done anything—only allegations from Chloe—which didn't look good because she was his ex-fiancé. But days later, while I was still out cold and had all my loved ones worried, a photographer called the station and reported there was an abandoned car on an empty lot next to their home.

The photographer thought someone was stalking his family. He'd never seen the vehicle parked there before and he was smart to call the cops instead of trying to handle it himself.

They found the front bumper was damaged; a fragment of Ol' Charlie's exhaust pipe was stuck in the grill. And of course Sterling's DNA was found inside, as well as Margie's, but we all knew she wasn't the accuser.

Her DNA was there because it was her damn car. His mother, who was in hospice care. What kind of sick, twisted shit was that? They were certain he was going to get rid of the car for good once he wasn't on Detective Wallace's radar anymore.

I was fucked up, for sure. Every single part of me ached and cried in pain, but I was alive, he was in, and never getting out again, and I couldn't have been more thankful for that.

The best news was that during the trials for Sterling, Sheila had finally answered her phone and heard about it through Phil. She swore she wouldn't tamper with the negotiations after hearing the bad news. She was going to disappear for sure.

Perhaps it was guilt. She admitted that she'd wished something bad would happen to me or Chloe, and it did. Her heart wasn't as icy as she wanted it to be.

Because the negotiations remained unbothered, I was sent the approval for divorce by late fall. It was settled and I was officially free.

I'd been through a lot of shit—shit that I never thought was worth fighting for, but with Chloe it was always worth the battle and always worth the risk.

I'd gone from being a tainted, fucked up mess to falling in love with an untainted and beautiful being.

We were on our way. Creating this future.

It was ours for the taking now. We'd won.

Fuck yes, we'd won.

CHAPTER 47

C HLOE

CHRISTMAS EVE

Things had settled down a lot since Theo's recovery. His divorce was final so he wasn't as stressed as he had been before.

Sterling was charged and rotting away in a prison somewhere—I really didn't care where. Sheila was true to her word, and hadn't bothered Theo since the divorce was finalized. We'd even seen on Facebook that she had a new boyfriend, only two weeks after the divorce was final.

Good for her.

We were good now. Minus my bloating, fatigue, waves of nausea, and the growing belly I had to tote everywhere with me, everything was ten times better. I wouldn't have traded the symptoms for the world, because something amazing was coming out of it. We were going to find out the gender soon, and I couldn't wait.

I think Theo was a little more excited about it than I was. It was going to take a while for my insurance to clear, plus Sterling's trials were catching us up. I was several weeks in and had yet to get an ultrasound, but it was confirmed by blood test that I was indeed pregnant. With helping Theo recover, going to testify, and traveling back and forth to San Francisco, I hadn't had much time to make appointments for myself. Theo's body had to be rehabilitated after his casts were removed. We heard the heartbeat during out first appointment in August. Things had been hectic since, but now that things were calming down we were going to make time.

Izzy took the news about the baby well. She was thrilled for us, but I think more so for herself. She was finally getting a sibling, and was old enough to really enjoy a baby. I was certain she was going to spoil this baby rotten. If not her, then Theo would for sure.

Perhaps that trip to India was good for her—well, both good and bad. She still felt hurt about Cameron. I caught her pulling away a few times—not wanting to be bothered. I'd ask, but all she'd say is that it was *him*. It was a scar on her heart that was going to take some time to heal, and one that left her feeling more guarded than usual, but with her new guy in tow, Noah, we figured she was ready to move on now —to try again.

Noah flew with her to Colorado. She met him on set during one of her gigs. A stunt double. He was very handsome and very goofy.

We all met at the cabin Theo had rented for the week of Christmas. He'd said he needed a vacation after all the shit, and I agreed, so during that week, we spent time in a cabin, surrounded by snow and twinkling nights.

On the day of Christmas Eve, there was a snowball *war*—not fight. Battle after battle of snowballs being lobbed across the yard. It was pretty hilarious.

I wasn't a part of the snowball fights, but it was still just as fun watching Izzy, Noah, and Theo pummel each other with snowballs like ten-year-olds.

By the time they were finished, their fingers like ice, the sun had hit the horizon.

"I have some regular hot cocoa, mint cocoa, and coffee ready in the kitchen! Nice and hot for you guys!" I called when they rushed towards the porch.

Izzy's cheeks were flushed as she laughed with Noah. Theo blew the heat of his breath on his fingers as he followed after them. "Thanks, Chlo," Izzy said, breathless. "It's much needed right now."

"Yeah," Noah chuckled. "I can hardly feel my hands."

"I totally won," Izzy tittered, knuckling his chin.

"Uh, that's a lie," Noah teased, pretending to be offended. "I won all those matches."

Theo rolled his eyes at them when he got closer. "Since you two can't seem to agree on who won, how about we just deem me the Snowball Champion, huh?"

Izzy and I burst out laughing, and Noah smiled a wary smile. He wasn't sure whether to join in or actually agree with Theo. Theo lost fair and square. He knew it, but I was sure Noah was going to let it slide just to stay within his good graces.

I laughed at the thought of that—how unsure of himself he was around Theo.

"Go on inside," Theo said to them. "We'll meet you in the kitchen."

Izzy bobbed her head and grabbed Noah's hand. "Come on. I could use a hot shower too, couldn't you?"

"I hope you mean separately!" Theo shouted after her, his voice booming. When she didn't answer, he yelled, "Isabelle! Separate showers!"

Izzy only laughed when she heard him. Tickled, I stepped up to Theo and wrapped my arm around his waist. "You know you can't hold onto her forever, right?"

"Ehh . . . after hearing that story about that fucker of a doctor in India, I don't trust anyone with her. This Noah kid is too . . . *nice*."

"And being nice to your daughter is a bad thing?" I laughed.

"No." He scratched his chin. "But it makes me even more suspicious about him. Izzy doesn't do *nice* guys."

"Yeah. Well, there's a first for everything, huh?" I grinned. "She needs a nice guy. She's always had a bad habit of picking the wrong ones."

"I guess." He pulled me closer and kissed my forehead. His lips were surprisingly warm. "Come on. Let's get you inside, Little Mama."

I snorted. "Oh my gosh! Please stop it. That sounds so bad!"

"What? It's cute and you know it. You're my Little Mama now." He rubbed my belly and I tipped my chin so my lips could meet his.

He was ridiculous.

Later that night, we all played a few rounds of UNO and charades by the fire while sipping on cocoa and eating Rice Krispie treats. It was fun. I didn't have any complaints at all, other than wishing we could stay longer than a week.

It was peaceful. Theo was smiling more than he had in years. He looked refreshed. Renewed. *Complete*.

And Izzy? Seeing her with Noah gave me hope for her again. It proved she was trying. After Theo's accident, she admitted that she wanted to do better for herself, too. She didn't want to be afraid anymore. She wanted to take risks and live. I agreed it was the best thing to do—not to hold back.

Theo, of course, didn't want anyone dating his daughter, but he wasn't against Noah. He was tough on him, yes, but only for good reasons. He loved Izzy. She was his baby girl, and always would be. But he knew he couldn't be the only man in her life for long. Soon, he'd have to hand her over, and I knew he was going to lose his mind when that day finally happened.

But until then, he was fine. As long as she was happy, he was happy. That's all that mattered to him.

On Christmas Day, after unwrapping gifts and devouring an amazing breakfast and lunch whipped up by Theo the Incredible, Theo and I decided to go out for more firewood for the fireplace before it got dark.

It was so serene outdoors. All we heard was the wind, chiming of the jingle bells, and our boots crunching in the snow.

We were quiet for the most part, taking it all in—the snow-covered pine trees and frosted shrubs. The cool, crisp air. It was beautiful, a trip I would never forget. And not just for this one reason, but one much greater.

Theo came through the trees after searching for wood. When he returned, his face was flushed and his eyes were wide. His axe was gone. "Chloe, there's something you should see over here," he said, eyes going hard. "But I don't know if you'll like it."

I frowned when he pointed towards the area he'd just come back from. I was sitting on a large boulder with a tumbler of hot chocolate in hand, scrolling through my phone and waiting for him to return.

"What is it?" I asked when he helped me off the rock.

"Just come. See for yourself." He released my hand, giving me a wary glance. I was nervous now. What was it? A dead animal? Something worse? Was someone hurt?

I pushed through the thick brush of trees, glancing back every so often at Theo, who wore a solemn mask.

"I'm a little freaked out here, Theo," I laughed nervously. "Shouldn't you be in front of me?"

I looked back and he shrugged. Just a shrug. What the hell?

I was about to stop, but then I saw twinkling lights through my peripheral. They were flashing. Christmas lights. Brows furrowed, I continued ahead, pushing the pine needles out of my way and following the trail.

An opening finally appeared and I realized I was standing in the middle of it. There was a picnic table set up with desserts. Cakes, cookies, and some coffee and milk. The table was dusted with snowflakes, candles recently lit.

My heart nearly failed me when I realized what this was.

My own winter wonderland.

I walked closer, studying the twinkling lights, and that's when something in the distance caught my eye. It was hanging from a tree branch on a red ribbon, a few steps away from the decorated picnic table. Slowly, I walked towards it, and when I got close enough, I gasped.

"Oh my goodness," I breathed, lifting it up. There was a diamond ring tied to the end of the ribbon. It had a large, square diamond with a gold band. It was so damn beautiful. "Theo," I called, taking the ring down.

I turned, searching for him, but he was no longer standing.

He was right in front of me on one knee, looking right up with soft, whiskey eyes.

"I can't tell if you like it or not," he said, teasing.

I was frozen, not by the weather, but by this—*all of this.*

"This is—wow. *Wow.*" I had no words.

He reached up and took the ribbon from me. When he untied the ring, he held it up and smiled.

"You ready for this?" he asked, fighting a grin.

I sank my teeth into my bottom lip, nodding like a schoolgirl and clasping my fingers.

"Chloe Knight, I want you," he started. "I want you for the rest of my life. I want you to be my bride, and soon my wife. After all we've been through—all we've done . . . well, I can't see myself without you again. I figure if I don't officially claim you as mine now, I may lose you again. I mean, I wouldn't let it happen—not even over my dead body—but you know what I'm saying." I couldn't help the laugh that bubbled out of me, or the tears that were building up at the rim of my eyes. "I want you in mind, body, and spirit, baby. I want us to live this life together. I want us to cherish it and have no regrets. Through the ups and downs, the good and the bad, I want you at my side." He sighed. "So, what do you say? Will you marry me? I've never been the type of man to beg, but if I have to crawl around on my knees in this snow just to make you my wife, I will, and you know it."

He flashed a pearly, crooked smile, and I didn't bother hesitating on my answer. There was only one word on my tongue—only one word I could say.

"YES!" I squealed. "Yes, Theo, I will marry you, baby!"

I'd never seen him smile so big. So wide. He hopped to his feet and slid the ring onto my finger. And after he did, he clasped my face in his large, warm hands and kissed me.

He kissed me so deep.

So whole.

So passionately.

He kissed me like I meant the world to him, and perhaps I did. He meant the world to me too. He always had, since I was twelve years old.

The man of my dreams was mine now.

All mine.

Holy shit.

I couldn't believe it.

Forever. Always.

That's what we promised each other that night while kissing beneath the snow and twinkling lights, slow dancing, and laughing, and not knowing what the hell we were doing.

It was a promise that would remain.

One that would never, ever be broken.

EPILOGUE

CHLOE

SEVEN MONTHS LATER

Bells sounded and I sighed, sitting on the built-in window bench and staring out through the windowpane.

It was a beautiful day.

Sunny. Warm.

It was the end of summer.

I rubbed my flat belly, dropping my gaze, studying the ivory silk of my dress.

Today was the day . . . and I was a nervous jumble of mess.

There was a banging on the door and then Izzy barged in. "I found it!" she chimed, nearly out of breath. I stood as she rushed my way with a box in hand. She opened it when she met up to me and revealed a decorative hair comb. It was made of pearls and diamonds.

My eyes stretched. "Oh my God, Izzy." I gaped. "Where did you get this?"

She smiled like she was proud. "I bought it with the money I got from my last gig." I started to speak but she took the comb out of the box and held up a hand. "And before you say anything, I still have money left over from it. It didn't cost me too much. Noah helped pitch in." She winked. "Consider it your wedding gift. Now turn around. Let me put it in."

Smiling, I turned and she reached up, sliding the comb of it above the knot in my styled hair. "Gah, Izzy, I'm so freaking nervous. I'll probably start shaking and trip over my own two feet when I walk down the aisle. I mean, my *mom* is here," I huffed as she spun me back around and fixed a few of my stray tendrils. It was an elegant up-do. Really pretty. A woman named Elle (someone Izzy met during one of her gigs) did my hair and makeup for a cheap price. I could admit that I looked stunning. I'd never seen myself so dolled up, like some sort of goddess.

My dress, a halter-top that flowed like silky petals at my feet, was beautiful and oddly, very comfortable. Izzy helped me shop for it. It took us three months to find the right dress.

It was hard finding the *one*, but this dress was perfect. I refused to let Theo see it until our wedding day. I hadn't seen him all last night or this morning. Bachelor and bachelorette parties.

"Oh, forget your mom's even here," Izzy scoffed. "She's already acting like a cocky bitch. She probably only showed up to show off that hideous green dress."

I laughed. "And . . . where are they?" I asked.

"With Kim. I saw her making her way to her seat before I came back here. It's almost time to start." She gripped my shoulders. "Everything is okay, Chloe. I swear. We have it all under control. The only thing you have to worry about is walking down that aisle and making my dad the happiest man on earth. That's not too much to ask for, is it?"

I shook my head and breathed a laugh. "No. Not at all."

"Good." She kissed my cheek and then started blinking her tears away. "God, see what you did? I'm so glad this is happening, Chlo. I really am. I love you, baby love."

Aww. My nickname. I hadn't heard it in years.

I giggled, reeling her in for a hug. "Don't cry. I can't have my maid of honor going out with running mascara." I rubbed her back. "But I love you too, boo."

"Waterproof," she chimed over my shoulder.

I released her and then exhaled, trying to gather my nerves again. There was a knock at the door. It was time. "All right. Gotta go. Just remember," she murmured, "this is your dream. *Your* day. Don't let anyone take that away from you."

I nodded and she took off, picking up the gold heels to match her dress. She was out of the door in no time, but left it wide open for me to come out.

A woman named Nadia came into the room, smiling at me as she picked up the train of my dress. She was a part of the wedding dress package. Help me find the perfect dress at the bridal store and also show up on wedding day to make sure it fit okay and didn't get dirty.

"You ready?" she asked over my shoulder, Russian accent heavy.

I nodded, picking up my bouquet of flowers. "Definitely."

The walk felt like it was miles away. We were in a mansion on the beach. An outdoor wedding, just like I had always dreamed.

I walked down the hallway, my heart beating a mile a minute. I took in deep, full breaths as I heard the whispering and murmuring growing louder.

And then I saw the room. The white and gold color scheme. The flowers embellishing the walls, running along them like vines.

Only a few more steps and I would be outside.

Eager now, I kept walking. I kept my steps measured for Nadia, even when I felt the sun kiss my skin. I was outside now, and when I met at the door, everyone stood, staring at me in awe. I saw so many familiar faces. Some of the teachers at the school. Some of Theo's old friends, and a few guys that worked for him.

Our wedding was small, so small that all we needed was a maid of honor and a best man, no extras. It wasn't traditional, but it worked for us. Of course, Theo's best man was good ol' Dane, who looked really good in a suit, by the way. My maid of honor was Izzy, who looked absolutely stunning in her gold gown.

There were a few men I'd seen at the bar. All of them clean, to my surprise. But then I picked up my gaze. And I found the priest. And beside him, My Theo.

"You ready for this?" Mr. Lint asked from the door. Mr. Lint—the principal and a great man who reminded me a lot of my father—hooked arms with me and escorted me up the aisle.

I could feel my heart pounding now, like a drum, with each step I took closer and closer to my Theodore. He wore the widest smile I'd ever seen, and a tear had already lined his cheek when he caught sight of me. I smiled back, so ready to be by his side. Ready for my role as his wife.

As *Mrs. Black.*

His tuxedo was crisp and clean, his tie ivory, like the pearls in the hair comb Izzy had just put in my hair. His hair was trimmed neat around his ears, still long enough to push my fingers through at the top.

Here For You by Laura Welsh was playing, the music surrounding us. I felt the eyes on me, but I kept going, ignoring all but one pair. *His.*

When we were up front, Mr. Lint kindly handed me over and Theo gave him a gracious nod.

Nadia adjusted my dress and then took her seat up front, next to Kim.

I grinned at them, and Kim did a small wave with Joanna's hand. In her other arm was Sophia, who was soundlessly sleeping. My girls. *My babies.* Gorgeous twins. Joanna was the vibrant one. Always active. Always giggling, and she did just that when Kim waved her tiny little hand, while Sophia's little head bobbed in her sleep.

I loved those girls more than I ever imagined was possible. They were my life. I never thought I could love someone so much—so hard. They meant everything to me, and looked just like their father, with bright brown eyes.

I scanned the crowd again. There were so many faces.

And hell yes, we invited Theo's mom, and made sure she had a front row seat as well.

"Hey," Theo called, and I looked over at him. He was smiling, but his eyes were still glassy. It was adorable, seeing him like this. "Just focus on me, angel," he murmured, and he took my hands.

I nodded, feeling the tears sliding down my face now.

When he looked at the priest and bobbed his head, it had begun.

My vows were just okay, but his? Oh my goodness. His were filled with words I never thought I'd hear the real Mr. Black say.

This wasn't the rugged, hardcore Theo Black that grew up on the wrong side of the tracks. This wasn't the damaged and lonely man I found in the garage.

This was someone who had grown into something greater than I could have ever imagined.

I was never going to forget his vows.

"Chloe," he'd said, no cards in hand. He'd memorized it. He still had my hand in his and was stroking it with his thumb. "I could go on and on about how much I love you. Seriously, I could. I could repeat those words every single day, for the rest of my life, and I wouldn't get tired of doing so because they are the truth. And it's not that I just love you. I am *in love* with you, even after all these years. You've given me so much hope—so much to look forward to in this lifetime. When I was at the very bottom, you grabbed my hand and picked me right up. When I was at my loneliest, you were there for me. When I felt like I had lost it all, you held my hand and you showed me what it meant to be loved. You showed me that I would never be alone as long as I had you." He was smiling hard now, still misty-eyed. "I know we've had some rough patches and spent way too much time apart. I know sometimes you questioned whether or not I would stay, but I can guarantee you right now that I am here, Chloe. And I am not going anywhere. Not ever again. You are my Little Knight—the young, beautiful knight that saved me, and brought so much light into my world. And this time, I want to be yours. Even if I'm not your knight in shining white armor, I will take the black. Because in the dark, pitch-blackness was where I found you. With all the darkness I had inside me, you transformed that and filled me with gold. Bright, blazing gold." He squeezed my hand, his tears falling now. "You gave me two beautiful babies. You gave me something worth living for. For that, I will never be able to repay you. With you, I am free, and with you, I will die a free man, too. I don't care about our differences or what people say. All I care about is you, Chloe Knight. The love of my life. The sun in my sky. The heaven I've always sought. You are my family now. *My life.* And I will never be able to repay you for giving this old man another shot at life and love."

There was no way in hell I could control my tears. I was a blubbing mess. Seriously. It took me several seconds to calm down. After having Joanna and Sophia, I'd become more emotional. Every little thing made me want to cry.

But when we said "I do" and the priest declared us man and wife—when I became Mrs. Chloe Black—I kissed him with all I had in me. I felt the fire burning through my veins—a blaze I knew would never go away.

Because he was mine.

My tainted, beautiful, perfect man.

We'd gone through it all. We'd seen the ups and the downs.

And on this day, we were here. And we couldn't have been luckier.

So, this was joy, huh? This was what all those romantic movies and novels I read were all about. Well, they were right. There was no way to explain this feeling.

The bliss.

The power.

The love.

We had two beautiful girls. I still had my best friend, Izzy, and he had his daughter. We were a family. One big, happy family.

Finally.

Our reception was a true celebration. Everyone had a good time. I sat side-by-side with him, danced with him. I was whole-heartedly *in love with him.*

During our slow dance, he was beaming like the sun.

"What?" I murmured, feeling the eyes on us, completely ignoring them.

"Just can't believe you're officially mine now," he said, his forehead dropping on mine.

"I always have been," I whispered back.

"Always will be?"

"Always," I answered.

He kissed me and the crowd hooted and hollered, mostly the men that worked for him that, I'm certain, were drunk by now.

I grinned behind the kiss. Embarrassed as hell? Yes. But I didn't pull away.

This was life. This was *perfection*. I never, ever wanted this moment to end.

"I love you, Chloe," he told me as he held my waist and tugged me closer. "Forever and always, baby. I am *free* with you."

The End

SWEET NOTIFICATIONS

Thank you SO MUCH for reading!

To get notified about new release alerts, free books, and exclusive updates, join my newsletter by visiting www.shanorawilliams.com/mailing-list

CONTACT SHANORA

Feel free to follow me on Instagram! I am always active and always eager to speak with my readers there!

Instagram: @reallyshanora
Twitter: @shanorawilliams
Facebook: Facebook.com/ShanoraWilliamsAuthor

ALSO BY SHANORA WILLIAMS

NORA HEAT COLLECTION

CRAVE

CARESS

DIRTY LITTLE SECRET

STANDALONES

TEMPORARY BOYFRIEND

100 PROOF

DOOMSDAY LOVE

DEAR MR. BLACK

FOREVER, MR. BLACK

INFINITY

SERIES

FIRENINE SERIES

THE BEWARE DUET

VENOM TRILOGY

Please visit www.shanorawilliams.com to check out these titles.

77436394R00168

Made in the USA
Middletown, DE
21 June 2018